BRILLIANT

BRILLIANT

SHORT STORIES

DENISE ROIG

Signature
EDITIONS

Cover design by Doowah Design.
Cover photos by Ariel Tarr.
Photo of Denise Roig by Ariel Tarr.

Acknowledgements
This book was printed on Ancient Forest Friendly paper.
Printed and bound in Canada by Hignell Book Printing Inc.

We acknowledge the support of the Canada Council for the Arts and the Manitoba Arts Council for our publishing program.

Library and Archives Canada Cataloguing in Publication

Roig, Denise, author
        Brilliant / Denise Roig.

Short stories.
Issued in print and electronic formats.
ISBN 978-1-927426-42-5 (pbk.).
--ISBN 978-1-927426-43-2 (epub)

        I. Title.

PS8585.O3955B75 2014   C813'.54   C2014-905379-7
                                         C2014-905380-0

Signature Editions
P.O. Box 206, RPO Corydon, Winnipeg, Manitoba, R3M 3S7
www.signature-editions.com

for Beauch,
who took me there

&

in memory of my father,
Raphael Roig

"Those who come to the Arab world today can scarcely know what stood there or what was true when that world was intact and whole."

—Fouad Ajami, *The Dream Palace of the Arabs*

"A man is what? His genitals? His wives? His mind? His money? A man is what? The city pulsates under the din of cranes, drills and motor cars. The wayside is a shock of sand, white, merciless, unpretty. There is no romance here, how could there be? The air murmurs with money. A bright glaze hovers and shimmers across the city. A bird of passage, I wait, I wait."

— Edna O'Brien, *Arabian Days*

CONTENTS

RICE DREAMS

"Of your Highness everybody on this universe feels proud.
Wherever you go you'll find your supporters and lovely crowd."
— Inscription in Heritage Village, Abu Dhabi, 1987

The palace called at midnight. They'd run out of both *maamoul* and *aish el bol bel*, the little nests stuffed with whole pistachios, and, of course, *baklawa*. Twenty kilos, Bashir wrote down next to *maamoul*, thirty beside *baklawa*. The sheikh couldn't live without his *baklawa*, especially the tiny logs layered with crushed hazelnuts. That every one of his palaces around the city employed a staff of pastry chefs who could be woken at any hour never seemed to occur to Sheikh Mohammed bin Zayed Al Nahyan, crown prince of Abu Dhabi and Deputy Supreme Commander of the UAE Armed Forces. No, Bashir had come to realize, Sheikh Mohammed wanted *his* sweets.

Hard to believe the sheikh was no longer the slick-haired, boyish leader whose faded twenty-year-old photo looked down from every wall of every shop in the Emirate. He was still a slim man. Not that you could tell with a *khandoura*. A man could gain five, ten, twenty pounds and there would be no waistband to betray him. A *khandoura* hid a man's shape, it hid…and Bashir made his mind go someplace clean and safe. He should not be thinking about what was under a man's *khandoura*.

He indulged a yawn as he slid his mobile phone closed and hauled himself from the depths of the 100-kilo bag of flour where he'd been napping. Though the sheikh himself hadn't made the call, though they had, in fact, never met, Sheikh Mo seemed to know it was him, Bashir el-Masri from Alexandria, who answered these eleventh-hour emergencies. How they ran out of sweets at midnight wasn't his business. Why they needed them by 4:00 a.m. wasn't his business either.

"Karim! *Yallah!*" A head poked up from another flour bag. Karim was on tryout this week, a kid from Jordan who'd worked in the pastry kitchen at Mövenpick in Petra. He had some things to learn, like how to keep his mouth shut, but he was quick and eager and knew his way with mixers and ovens.

"Another order?" Karim's dark, poorly cut hair was standing up in front, making Bashir want to laugh. But he kept it in check, not wanting to get too familiar.

"Of course, another order. When Sheikh Mohammed calls, it is always with an order. You think he calls to chitchat?"

The boy—though he was taller than a boy, taller than Bashir—got to his feet, came to stand next to him at the metal counter, where Bashir thumbed through the recipe binder. The pages had ripped long ago where the punched holes were; none looped through the rings. A few greasy sheets flew to the floor and Karim scrambled to catch them. They looked at the recipe for *baklawa* together, Bashir nodding to himself. The order of ghee was due in by 8:00 a.m.; they'd have enough for tonight. The boy was fidgeting with the front of his loose pants, eyes down. Why could he not stand still? And then Bashir saw. He used to wake like that when he was that age. An embarrassment, but also a pleasure. *Haram* to think about this now, though, with the boy so close.

They got started on the dough. Flour, water, more flour. What else was phyllo? Karim had worked under a French chef in Jordan. "I like the *millefeuilles*," he'd said in his interview.

"You won't be making *millefeuilles* here," Big Ali, the supervisor, had told him. "Strictly Arabic sweets at Al Zaabi Finest Bakery."

That first day—no pay—Bashir had paired him up with Little Ali, Big Ali's nephew from Aleppo. At the end of an hour Bashir could see that Karim was faster and smarter than Little Ali, who ducked out every half hour for a smoke and to text his "cousin" back home. (Bashir suspected it was really a girlfriend.) There was no getting rid of Little Ali because of Big Ali, but Bashir had pushed to take on Karim. They needed another body in the kitchen, what with Sheikh Mohammed and his *maamoul* and National Day coming and Little Ali doing less and less. Big Ali relented, but no pay for the first two weeks, just room—even if this was a bag of flour—and board: a share of the food Annabelle cooked for them every noon.

The bosses still sometimes questioned the propriety of a woman in the kitchen. But then Big Ali would invite them down from the offices upstairs for a plate or send lunch up in a nice takeaway container. And that would be it for complaints until the next time someone would get a bee in his *ghutra* about "a girl down there" and remind them they were getting away with something not quite *halal*. Annabelle's lunch specials silenced them.

"Annabelle? She come in today?" From his second day, Karim had asked this every morning.

"Of course, she comes in. How many times do I have to tell you?" Bashir said. He was too tired for stupid questions. God love Sheikh Mohammed, *masha'allah*, but it was late and he'd been standing all day, all night, with just an hour on the flour bag. "Get me the scale. Go!"

Even after three years, Bashir knew only a little about Annabelle, and nothing about how she'd landed the unlikely job of cooking Filipino food every day for a bunch of Arab pastry guys. Annabelle was tiny with a long braid and a smile even Big Ali couldn't fight. She wore one outfit at all times: a pink T-shirt with rhinestones spelling "Crown Jewels" and tight jeans. It took six months for Big Ali to convince her she had to wear a chef's jacket and one of the white, elasticized caps if she wanted to work in the kitchen.

"You want me to look like a dork, Big Al?" Annabelle talked like an American teenager who spent her days reading fan magazines. How old she was, no one knew or dared ask, though it was discussed endlessly among the guys. Big Ali thought she must be around thirty; Bashir put her closer to forty. Karim, when they asked him—a rite of initiation on his first day—said, "Oh, no, Miss Annabelle is young! She is…twenty-two!"

By now they knew what she made every day of the week: Sundays, tofu and black beans; Mondays, chicken pie; Tuesdays, *mechado*; Wednesday, chop suey; Thursdays, *pansit* Canton with shrimp; and Saturdays, "surprise meal," as Annabelle called everyone's favourite: a stew with small, perfect squares of supremely tender meat in a smoky barbecue sauce. Lamb, some thought. Veal, Little Ali once volunteered and everyone had laughed. Veal? Their tight bosses would spring for veal? Big Ali knew it was beef. "I see the packages!" he insisted. But Annabelle would never confirm what the meat was. "That's why it's called surprise," she said with her blazing smile, though every now and then she'd say it was pork and watch their faces. "Such good Muslim boys," she'd say with a sigh. "I'd never do that to you."

It happened sometimes. Bashir would sift and dust and roll and then he'd be pulling trays out of the oven. It was like waking up in the morning from a sound sleep with images—his mother, a goat, a naked man—floating up from the night. How did he get here? Where had all the in-between steps gone? He had no memory of fitting the discs of phyllo inside the giant round trays, patting down kilos of crushed walnuts, scoring the layers into diamonds, pouring the ghee. Who had done all that? But here were the trays of golden *baklawa* to prove he hadn't been curled on a bag of flour all night.

He sent Karim back to the other side of the room, nudging him toward a larger bag this time. "Rest," he said, the closest he could come to saying "good job." Karim went to sleep at once. Bashir stood at the work table—if he took his weight off his feet, he'd sleep too—and waited for the driver from the palace. It could have been ten minutes or half the night—time was elastic at this hour—but the knock came, the driver swept in with two helpers, and the trays of *maamoul* and *baklawa* were loaded onto special pastry racks in the refrigerated van.

The sheikhs thought of everything, marvelled Bashir, as he lowered himself onto a bag close to Karim. Such vision. And his sheikh, his Sheikh Mohammed, was the smartest, the best, the most supreme. Bashir liked looking at the old black and white photos of Sheikh Zayed, the father of all this prosperity, dead now five years. People whispered that his sons, the current rulers, didn't come close, that they were mercenary where he'd been generous, calculating where he'd been spontaneous. But they didn't know Sheikh Mohammed, Bashir figured, not the way he knew him, even if the currency of their relationship was a platter of *maamoul*. Food spoke worlds. And nothing spoke with greater love than sweets.

For months now, he'd been trying to translate this love into something tangible. Not more *maamoul*. Sheikh Mohammed could have *maamoul* whenever he wanted. He, Chef Bashir el-Masri from Alexandria, needed to reach into his soul, use his Allah-blessed gift. He must make him something no one else ever had or ever could. Watching Little Ali shovelling vegetable biryani into his mouth one afternoon—grains of basmati in saffron shades of yellow, orange and red—it came to him. Rice was porous; it could take on any hue of the rainbow. It was as much an artist's medium as clay or paint or butter cream.

He wouldn't cook the rice; that would make it far too fragile, perishable too. But raw, uncooked rice—plump, white Egyptian grains—would last years. It would endure, like his devotion. Working from the head-and-shoulders portrait hanging on the pastry kitchen wall, Bashir spent a week drawing—and erasing—the design on a piece of baking parchment, then another week mixing the colours to perfectly match the photo. The sheikh's hair was easy—black as an oil spill—as was his *khandoura*, which nicely soaked up white acrylic. The ruler's skin tones were trickier. Flesh contained so many shades. It was only in the last week that he'd finished the face, grain after grain placed first for effect, then glued onto the wood backing.

He could only work after the kitchen shut down for the night, after Big and Little Ali had gone to their flat the next building over, after Annabelle was back in the rented room she shared with three other Filipinas. Everyone knew he was working on something— it was hard to keep secrets entirely secret in the kitchen—but every morning Bashir slipped the board and the bowls of dyed rice back in a cabinet behind the dough sheeter. As with the *maamoul* tonight, there was a deadline: National Day, December 2. Red, white, black and green flags would be flown and waved and stuck into *ghutras*, painted on cheeks, decaled on cars drag-racing down the Corniche. You had to be amazed. From a scattering of tribes on a wedge of oil-sodden desert to this, a real country. All in thirty-eight years.

Bashir planned to deliver the portrait himself, hitching a ride in the palace van, squeezed between the extra trays of sweets the royal family always ordered for the holiday. He'd imagined it so many times: his humble, but beautiful gift extended and accepted. There was still the *ghutra*, the sheikh's head scarf, to finish, then the spraying of the fixative, then a light varnish…

He woke to Big Ali nudging him with a foot. "Bashir."
He nudged harder, more like a kick. "The bosses are here."
In two seconds, Bashir was on his feet, smoothing hair
and apron. "The bosses" could mean two things: the three
Indian managers upstairs, Aziz, Armand and Ajmal (The
Three As, Annabelle called them. "You number four,"
joked Big Ali. "You our boss, Annabelle.") Big Ali really
did love her. Not that kind of love: the good kind, Bashir
had tried to explain to Karim his first day, and Karim had
nodded solemnly.

But "the bosses" could also mean the Emirati owners,
the Al Zaabi brothers who'd taken over the bakery when
their father died in an SUV dune-bashing crash three
years before. They'd been fourteen and sixteen when
the accident happened, too young to be involved in the
business, though the younger one liked to drop in, snap
his fingers and order a platter of a dozen different sweets
to keep the counter staff on their toes. No one downstairs
had given much thought to the boys until this year. Nizar,
the oldest, was going to university to earn a degree in
business. The youngest, Rashid, rumour went, was raising
race horses and wanted to sell off the half-dozen bakeries
his father had built.

By the look on Big Ali's face it was not the bosses
upstairs who were gracing them with a visit. The Three
As were official and officious and approached their jobs
as sacred contract—especially keeping costs down and
keeping the Brothers Al Zaabi happy, or at least not
unhappy. But staff knew how to shimmy around the
managers' useless, ever-more-complicated procedures,
their edicts ("No more real butter? Are they nuts?" said
Big Ali.). The more seriously the men upstairs took

themselves, the less seriously they were taken by the pastry cooks at Al Zaabi Finest Bakery.

"Both boys," Big Ali whispered. Big Ali whispering was enough to fully wake Bashir. Big Ali did not whisper.

The brothers had changed since they'd visited the pastry kitchen a year ago. Nizar was now shorter than his younger brother, though he was obviously the older, with a man's build and a neat goatee. Rashid wore a backward baseball cap. They both nodded at Bashir, then turned their attention back to Big Ali.

"I can get you anything you like," said Big Ali, looking around for a place to seat the brothers. "Cappuccinos? Lattes? *Maamoul? Baklawa?*"

"We've eaten," said Nizar.

Still, Big Ali cleared a space at the table where Annabelle served lunch every day. Little Ali went running to find a wet cloth to wipe it down. If Big Ali didn't whisper, Little Ali didn't run. Coffee was brought and small plates of *maamoul* and *baklawa*. Little Ali found a vase with a plastic rose that he placed next to the sugar bowl.

"Please, please," said Big Ali, nearly bowing. The brothers looked at each other. Nizar cocked his head and the two sat.

"How is business?" asked Nizar, taking out his BlackBerry. "In your estimation, that is."

"Good, good!" said Big Ali. "Orders, big orders every day. Crown Prince is our most devoted customer. If we keep him happy, we must be doing something right, yes?" And Big Ali grinned so hard, the space where he'd lost a tooth showed.

"How much more did we sell this quarter than last?" asked Nizar, eyes on his keypad.

"This quarter?" asked Big Ali, and already he looked smaller. "I will check, sir. It's in the computer, sir."

"You don't know the numbers off the top of your head?" asked Nizar, still not looking at him. Rashid was also studying his BlackBerry, though some sort of game seemed to be on the screen. "You should know the numbers like that." And Nizar snapped his fingers like that.

"I will check, sir. I know we did good, sir."

"Good is a useless word unless it is attached to a number," said Nizar, and Big Ali, who'd continued to smile, finally stopped.

"What's wrong with you guys?"Annabelle asked when she came in at ten. "You get food poisoning or something? You look sick."

Big Ali took her aside. "They want to cut staff," he told her.

"So I go, right?" said Annabelle, picking up her denim shoulder bag from where she'd dropped it on the floor, pulling the strap over her head and crossing it over her sequined T-shirt so the els in "Jewels" was covered.

Big Ali would never tell her the reasons. Someone — one of The Three As? A rival bakery? — had texted Nizar Al Zaabi that he'd better check things out at the Hamdan Street outlet. Annabelle was cooking pork in the pastry kitchen, they said. Annabelle was "giving sex" to Big Ali. She was also "lazy," "taking cash," and crossing herself when the call to prayer sounded. Any of these could lead to deportation, Nizar told Big Ali. "But we are good locals, not like some. You fire her today. Understood?"

There was more: Karim would not be hired. Bashir had to work seven days, not six, at the same salary. Big Ali had to email a daily earnings and output report, and from now on Little Ali would be in charge. "You're old," Rashid told Big Ali, the only thing he actually said during the ten-minute meeting.

It made no sense. Of course, it made no sense. "He's my daughter's son and so I love him, but he work like shit!" Big Ali said to Bashir after the brothers left. Little Ali, when told of his promotion, put on the tallest paper toque and went outside to text the glad news to his cousin. Annabelle hugged each of them, Karim weeping when she put her arms around him. But, of course, he was leaving too.

The kitchen was deadly quiet by eleven. Kitchens should never, ever be quiet, Bashir thought as he prepped. He gave all the doughs — phyllo, croissant, *khnafeh* — a rough time, thinking of Nizar and Rashid as he pounded, rolled and cut. He couldn't imagine this place without Annabelle, her flirty warmth, her funny heart. But it was when his thoughts slid over Karim that the pain came. He was an unholy man, a man who needed to keep his eyes down where they belonged. But what if Karim had stayed? All those nights together in the kitchen with no one else about and Bashir in charge? He could have asked for any shameful, wondrous thing. And Allah would have forgiven. Allah always forgave bad humans. That's why He was Allah, and Bashir only a pastry chef who, peace be upon him, liked boys.

It was a terrible week. Overnight Big Ali seemed to drop a stone. "Eat!" Bashir said after a few days. "You need your strength." Big Ali hardly seemed to hear him. He now spent most of his days in the windowless, flour-coated office, doubled over a calculator. "I don't know computers," he confessed to Bashir. Little Ali had never taken off his toque from the first day, and now swanned around the kitchen, tasting things and shaking his head. He left early every day. An idiot, Big Ali and Bashir agreed, but now the boss. Even The Three As actually looked at Little Ali when they spoke to him now. "Maybe they're next," said Big Ali.

But it was a bad time to have a bad attitude because National Day was coming at them and orders were flying in from hotels, restaurants and smaller bakeries that passed Al Zaabi's pastries off as their own. The palaces were quadrupling their orders for everything. The Three As looked grim, smelling disaster a week away. "We tried to get Karim to come back for a few days. We even offered to pay him," Bashir overheard Aziz tell Little Ali. But Karim had already landed a job with Mister Cake making 100 dirhams a day. "No thank you very much," he'd said.

"Who does he think he is?" said Little Ali.

Time blurred into a migraine of flour and ghee. Nights fell on top of days. Bashir slept standing up; he rolled lying down. Still, he preserved a few hours each night for the portrait. It was truly becoming—Bashir blushed to admit it—a Work of Art. As he glued the last rice grains in place, he let himself imagine Sheikh Mohammed's face on opening it. In that moment when the wrapping fell away, when the sheikh beheld his image in a hundred shades of rice, he would know how deeply his people loved him, none more than Bashir el-Masri of Alexandria.

The layer of varnish was tricky, at first lifting some of the paint from Sheikh Mohammed's cheek. When Bashir saw the pinky-brown coming off on the small brush, his heart nearly failed. It took until the next day to figure out how much to dilute the coating so it would protect and shine, not destroy. He was a pastry chef, a man to solve problems. If he could figure out how to nearly double their production for the week — simple: no sleep — he could solve this too.

When he applied the last coat of varnish at 4:00 a.m., the dawn of National Day, Bashir knew he had captured something none of the photos had. It was the way the supreme commander held his head. All the photos — from Abu Dhabi to Ras al Khaimah — showed the Crown Prince looking straight on. Bashir had tilted his head just slightly to the right; amazing, the softening effect of a centimetre or two. Sheikh Mohammed radiated, if not outright compassion, receptivity. Come to me.

It was crowded in the back of the refrigerated van and the Pakistani driver hadn't completely understood why Bashir had to accompany the six dozen trays of pastries to the palace. He looked as sleepless as Bashir, shrugging irritably in the end. "No ride back," he said.

A light rain was falling as they went out into what was not quite day. Bashir had wrapped the rice portrait — smaller in his arms than a tray of *maamoul* — in layers and layers of bubble wrap, sealing off every joint with tape so it was safe as a baby.

They wouldn't let him past the gate.

"National Day," one of the dozen Indian guards told him.

"I know it is National Day," said Bashir. "That is why I am here." He smiled largely, gestured to the package. "For Sheikh Mohammed."

Now three other guards joined the first. One poked the package with his stick. Some of the plastic bubbles popped, he jabbed it so hard.

Bashir pulled the package to his chest, tried to protect it with his arms. "Call the kitchen," he said. "They know me."

"They know me," one of the guards mimicked. "And why would His Highness know you?"

"I make his pastries," said Bashir.

This made several of the guards laugh. "Doughnut man," said one. "Big doughnut man."

Annabelle was gone and Karim, too, and Little Ali was in charge now and he was so very, very tired. "Fucking Paki," said Bashir and then all twelve were around him. One yanked the package so hard, Bashir fell back, nearly losing his grip.

"Let me see it," said the one who'd called him doughnut man. He tore at the plastic, the bubble wrap falling in wads to the ground as it began to rain more heavily. It never rained on National Day. The other guards ran back to the kiosk, shouting in Hindi.

When the last layer was ripped away, the guard looked up at Bashir, then back at the portrait. "What is this?" he said. "Who is this?"

Bashir watched as the guard poked at the portrait with a fingernail, dislodging a few rice grains, then a few more, and the rice — black, white, flesh — fell like rain on the pavement.

FRIDAYS BY THE POOL IN KHALIDIYAH

See, there's this guy, Mathieu says. "Are you listening? *Voyons*, Angie, don't fall asleep yet."

They're in his villa this time, Maribeth, her maid, having asked for Saturday, not her usual Friday, off. Maribeth's cousin, Daisy, is taking the bus down from Dubai. They'll go to mass Saturday morning at St. Mary's, then to supper at Chow King. Maribeth smiled when she told Angie of her weekend plans, as if looking into the horizon of a beautiful future.

"Okay, Madame?" she said.

"Okay," Angie agreed, only later thinking: Damn. She won't be able to have Mathieu at her place with Maribeth there. She much prefers meeting him in her flat.

She wants to sleep. She always wants to sleep after coming, and coming in the heat is so intense. It was 46 degrees Celsius when she pushed open the iron gate of Mathieu's Al Raha villa an hour ago. They never waste time, shedding clothes in the entryway, Mathieu already hard, Angie already sweating, even with the AC pumping.

"Maybe it's an urban legend," says Mathieu, pressing closer. He's forty-two, French, educated in the UK (city planning) and good-looking in a Gérard Depardieu, large-man sort of way. His wife and twin daughters have gone to the family's château in Languedoc for the summer. He and Angie have been taking advantage of this for the past week, silly with their new freedom. They're four months into what Mathieu calls their *petite aventure*. A long time for him, she senses.

"So there's a guy," he says.

"There's always a guy," says Angie. In their haste, they've forgotten to roll down the Roman blind. The sun beats at the master-bedroom window.

"True," says Mathieu. "And this story I'm trying to tell you, *c'est vrai aussi*." He likes slipping into French with her, though she's told him many times that her French is of the most rudimentary, high-school kind. *Moi, je suis américaine*.

"Kabir swears it's true," he continues, and gives her exposed nipple a slow lick. Kabir is Mathieu's driver. He's from Peshawar, like most of the cab drivers in the city. Maribeth doesn't like him. She claims he tried to goose her once, though that wasn't the word she'd used. "He *pince* me," she said. "*Pincer?*" said Mathieu, when Angie reported the incident. "Very French."

"This guy, he's a local," Mathieu continues.

A sheikh? she wants to know. So many of these stories, the ones batted from one expat party to another, are about royals. Or near-royals. In this frypan of a city, you're a royal, a near-royal, or a cab driver. Or colonials like us, Mathieu would add.

"Stop interrupting," he says, slapping her thigh. "So he has this house, see? Well, it's more of a palace. It's as large as — *écoute ça* — the Abu Dhabi Mall." Mathieu reaches for a cigarette from the glass nightstand. He's held off for nearly ten minutes since their grand bilateral climax, but can't wait longer.

Angie was drifting, but now she struggles to sit up. She's trying to picture a house as big as the Abu Dhabi Mall. The mall — her least favourite in the city — is three city blocks long at least. She conjures a man in a starched, white *khandoura* strolling down the vaulted halls, the hem of his robe gliding over dark marble. It would all be halls, she imagines. Maybe he uses Rollerblades or a golf cart.

Where did Mathieu say he'd heard this story? She *had* been falling asleep. Of course: Kabir, compulsive gossip, who drops his prayer rug whenever, wherever the call to prayer sounds and who likes her maid's ass. "I don't believe it," she says.

"But this is the good part, *mon ange*," says Mathieu, exhaling. Mathieu's way with a cigarette — the continental cool of it — is nearly enough to make her say, *I will love you forever.*

"Light?" he'd asked four months before, as both waited for their cars to be brought outside the Emirates Palace Hotel. It was the night of the first Abu Dhabi Classics concert. If you cared about the arts or just wanted to be seen, you were there. "Light?" He'd turned to her and in his eyes, amused, certain, she saw how things could play out. For a while, anyway.

"I'm listening," says Angie.

The guy jets all over, every week somewhere new, says Mathieu. Moscow, Mosul, Bangkok, Kuala Lumpur. The whole world is his playground. And wherever he flies, his falcon is there in first class with him.

"Drugs? Arms? Mercenary?" she asks, and Mathieu looks at her like she might be on drugs herself.

"What do any of these guys do?" he says. "What do any of these guys *have* to do?"

Angie has just met a lovely Emirati man over lunch at the Noodle House, a chance meeting at one of the restaurant's long wood tables, where it takes more effort not to speak to the stranger next to you than to ask and answer the usual "where are you from how long have you been here what do you do?" He was twenty-seven, he told her, and must have seen her as an attractive "auntie," a woman old enough to be safe to chat with. He had just returned from the States where he'd studied naturopathic medicine. "I have been privileged to go abroad and learn," he said. "We have far to go in the UAE. We do not know yet how to unify all parts of our being, our bodies and souls and minds." He'd been so earnest, so diffident, this young man with his manicured goatee and perfectly pressed *khandoura*, that she felt inclined to believe him. This was more than the usual my-country-needs-me speech. "I think you mean that," she said to him. And he'd given her a quizzical, slightly bruised smile.

"Go on, *mon beau*," she says.

Wherever the man with the mansion travels each week, he finds a woman and brings her back to Abu Dhabi. "He does whatever he wants with her all weekend and then"—Mathieu shifts her from his chest as he rights himself against the pillow—"on Sunday morning he sends her back to wherever she came from."

"A playboy," she says. "UAE style."

"But here's the UAE twist. The car that takes her back to the airport? The Hummer or limo or whatever it is? The man orders the woman to fill it with money. However much cash she can stuff into that car she takes with her." Mathieu looks flushed, almost triumphant. "*Incroyable, non?*" he says, and stubs out his smoke.

She imagines a late-model silver Mercedes, then a black Maserati, which becomes a massive, white Land Rover. A leg, like one belonging to a Vegas showgirl, spike heel dangling from high-arched foot, dangles out the half-open back window. The girl of the week has been toppled backward from the weight of the money, only her perfect nose and perfect mouth visible between layers of 100-dollar bills, bushels of bills that remind Angie of the leaves she and her brother used to rake every fall in Massachusetts. It would be American money, she supposes. As the car drives off, a few loose hundreds fly from the window.

"Does he see her off?" she asks. And Mathieu looks at her again with something like annoyance, and gets out of bed. "What would that mean?" he asks. "That he cares? Don't be romantic."

"It would show there are manners behind his money." She hasn't planned to say this, didn't know what she would say. But the man, the one who takes lonely walks through his home, would want to be seen as a gentleman by the women. She feels absolutely certain of this.

"But don't you find it so Abu Dhabi?" he asks. "Isn't it outrageous? Why aren't you reacting?" Mathieu faces her as he pushes his arms into a robe. He's trimmed down since he started biking again this summer. She likes to think it has something to do with her.

"I thought I *was* reacting," she says.

In its fiscal and sexual excess, the story resembles others she's heard. But this one brings a downward pull. She imagines the man again, pacing his endless halls, trying to figure out where to fly off to next, the woman being escorted away, bills stuffed into her cleavage and too-tight heels. There is so much paper she can barely breathe.

"So what do you want for lunch?" he asks, tying the belt of his white terry robe. "I've got cold chicken. Leftover mutton biryani. Your choice."

Maribeth is in the kitchen when she gets home, busily hunched at the far counter, as if chopping vegetables. But when Angie comes closer, she sees that her maid is fixing herself a cup of tea. "Madame!" she says, turning quickly. "I did not."

Most of Maribeth's sentences are missing something, a verb, a noun, sometimes any context at all. But after five years together—longer than Angie's been with anyone since Firaj left four years ago—she doesn't often need clarification. Besides, Maribeth is as certain of her command of English as she is in the existence of the Blessed Virgin Mother and All the Angels and Saints. When corrected, she closes her eyes, breathes in a prayer for patience with these picky people and their picky language and blunders gamely on. Lately Angie finds herself sounding scarily like her maid.

"Madame!" Maribeth raises both hands to her cheeks and Angie feels herself already weary. It will be bad news about one of the Filipinas in Maribeth's vast circle. Angie has tried to help a few, going over their work contracts, pointing them in the direction of the labour board. The law is actually on your side, she tells them, and they look at her doubtfully.

"One of your friends is in trouble," says Angie.

"No friend, cousin," says Maribeth. "Daisy."

"Before you get into the story, MB, can you fix me a cup of tea too?" says Angie. It's Maribeth's theory that on the hottest days you don't drink iced tea or lemonade or cold mango juice. You drink hot tea. Putting something hot inside when it's hot outside, "cool you out," says Maribeth. When Angie told Mathieu this last week, he laughed. "*Elle a raison*," he said and rolled her on her side.

Maribeth turns back to the stove, places the kettle on a burner. She does this so slowly Angie knows she's annoyed at having her story interrupted. Maribeth relishes a good soap opera, especially when it's happening to real people.

"I take it Daisy won't be coming down from Dubai tomorrow," says Angie. "Her boss is being a pain again, right?" She hopes this is all the drama in store.

"Worse," says Maribeth. "Boss fire Daisy."

Daisy is the opposite of Maribeth. She's tall for a Filipina, easily five-seven or five-eight, with a long ponytail and bushy bangs. She's terribly thin. Maribeth is short and thick with a wash-and-wear haircut. Angie has never seen her in a skirt, even for church. Daisy exudes sweetness and compliance. Maribeth, a bristling, watchful efficiency.

"But I thought she was with a new family," says Angie. Daisy's last employer, a Syrian, kept her locked inside the family's villa, not allowing her out to wire her salary home to an extended family of six. A network of Filipinas took turns passing at arranged times to intercept an envelope stuffed with creased dirhams, which the locked-up Daisy would drop from a third-floor window when the family was out. Several times neighbourhood kids got there first. The employer before that, a French couple with triplets, docked half of Daisy's monthly salary when she came home half an hour late from Friday mass.

"Bad man," says Maribeth, pouring Angie's hot water, splashing some on the counter. "Man bad."

"Which man?" asks Angie. The only good man in Maribeth's book is her husband, the long-suffering Eduardo, back home in the Philippines. Privately, Angie thinks he's a wimp, a mooch and possibly an alcoholic. When Maribeth goes home every July for two weeks, Eduardo seems to resent the time she spends with their three children. "Sex, all time sex," Maribeth once confessed, shrugging.

"New boss!" says Maribeth, looking peeved. "Who you think, Madame?"

"Cut me some slack, MB. I can't remember the horrors of all your friends' work lives. I have my own, remember?" And Maribeth shoots Angie a look that lands where she knows it will, right in Angie's uneasy Western sense of justice and entitlement: I have nothing to complain about/I have everything to complain about. Since the global financial downturn, or GFD as Angie calls it (great fucking debacle), Berlitz has cut her teaching load by half. Every month she worries the school will lay her off. She's not Arab, after all. Firaj, now doing a tour of duty in Islamabad, sends money when he thinks of it.

"Okay, I know it's different," says Angie.

"You bet," says Maribeth, taking Angie's cup and steering her out of the kitchen into the dining room. She puts Angie's cup on the long, polished table, sits in the adjacent chair.

The long and the short of it—though none of these sagas are ever short, thinks Angie, trying not to look at her watch—is that Daisy's difficult Egyptian family has turned into two difficult Egyptian families.

"Sixteen person," says Maribeth. "Poor Daisy. She sleep three hour."

"But that's illegal," says Angie, feeling, in spite of herself, the quick fury these stories still churns up. "Jesus, Maribeth."

"I tell her no good people. I tell her back when," says Maribeth.

"But now they've fired her?"

"They say," says Maribeth, shrugging. "But still make her work. Maybe just…" and she struggles with a word.

"Threaten," supplies Angie.

Her mobile is ringing from somewhere in the apartment. Angie feels Maribeth willing her not to answer it. "Sorry, MB," she says, dashing first into the kitchen, then into the entryway, trying to remember where she dropped her purse. Mathieu has programmed her phone to play an old Donna Summer song, *Hot Stuff.* It's cheesy, but she loves it.

"*Mon ange*," he says, when she finally locates the phone on the powder room counter. "*Ça va?*"

"Maribeth's telling me another horror story. Daisy again. What am I supposed to say to her at this point?"

"Just listen," says Mathieu. "Be, you know, *sympathique, mais pas trop.*" Mathieu keeps telling her she is a bit too involved. Boundaries, he says. He barely speaks to his family's live-in nanny. She's from Indonesia, a devout Muslim. Contact with a man, any man, makes her feel uncomfortable, he insists. Angie can tell by his breathing that he's taking a cigarette break. What with the GFD, he's going into the office even on Friday afternoons. "I must make myself *indispensable*," he says. It's lucky so many French words are the same in English, otherwise Mathieu would be translating all the time and that would get to be a drag for him. "*Ennuyant*," a word he says with a sigh when he talks about his old life in a suburb of Lyon or having to explain things ten times to his Emirati boss, or domestic conversations (and sex) with his wife. Angie takes this as a warning.

The plan has been that he will take her to dinner tonight at the Shangri-La, a hotel out by the Grand Mosque. A canal runs through the grounds, like Venice. But the real selling point is that the hotel is out of the city so they're not likely to run into any of his co-workers, though Mathieu has told her that some are also seeing *des autres*. "Maybe it's an Arab thing," he says. "One man, several women? *Qui sait?*"

He'll send Kabir around at seven to pick her up. It's only three now, which leaves time for a quick wrap-up to Maribeth's story, a nice long nap and a nice long bath. But when Angie goes back to the dining room, Maribeth isn't there. She's even forgotten the teacups. Angie reluctantly carries them into the kitchen, surprised not to find Maribeth at the stove starting to make sticky rice or plantains, comfort food from home. Maribeth loves when Angie eats out and she doesn't have to cook lentils or quinoa or whatever healthy regime Angie's on that week. "You too thin," Maribeth says. "Better before." After Firaj left, Angie lost thirty housewifely pounds and she doesn't intend to gain an ounce back. Mathieu says she looks like Audrey Tautou, with her bobbed, dark hair and small frame. *Gamine*, he says, which makes her feel young and cute and not forty-seven. No breakfast, a few bites of chicken at Mathieu's. She'll be able to eat well tonight.

Moving down the cool tiles of the hallway she makes out the sound of Tagalog from Maribeth's tiny bedroom. She's on the phone, probably telling the latest Daisy news to a friend, so maybe they can skip the rest of the story for today. Angie unrolls the fabric blind in her own bedroom—too small, she thinks for the thousandth time since moving in last year—and falls onto her bed. After lunch, they'd made love again, this time on one of the daughters' beds, which seemed to excite Mathieu. Fridays take it out of her.

Angie wakes to the sound of Maribeth calling through the door. "Madame!" When Maribeth first came to work for them, Angie, fresh from five years with Firaj in Washington, protested over the "Madame." It was too formal, made her feel matronly. I'm American, you know, she tried to explain to her husband, who'd grown up with servants in Amman. But Maribeth was not to be budged. She was Maribeth—she tolerated MB, Angie's nickname for her—and Angie was Madame. Those were their names.

Angie tries to get up. There'd been a tiny glass of Chardonnay at lunch. Maybe Mathieu refilled it. She can't remember. Maribeth is still calling. She will stand there calling all afternoon if Angie doesn't get herself to the door.

Angie begins to say something not gentle, not patient, but Maribeth's face is streaming with tears. In all their time together, with all the dramas and traumas, all the friends and relations, Angie has never seen a tear on that face. Her heart tips.

"The children?" she asks, and feels her knees actually knock against each other. She's never met the children, of course, doesn't have any special feeling for children in general, but she's always liked seeing their photos, seeing how they change each year: attitudinal, smart-cookie Alicia, now sixteen; tall, sweet Eduardo Junior. And the baby, Ernesto, eight, who has some sort of problem, but is clearly Maribeth's favourite. She, Angie, is *helping* these kids. Yes, Maribeth does her ironing, washes her car, cooks her meals, but some larger good is being done too.

Maribeth shakes her head.

"So what is it?" Angie feels relief and a tinge of annoyance. If it's not about the children, why did Maribeth wake her up? Why is she bothering her with something or someone else? Priorities, she thinks. Not everyone has to matter that much.

Still, the tears are new, and she takes Maribeth by the arm, brings her into the room, sits her on the bed. "Okay, what's going on, MB? Is this still about Daisy?"

In English stretched to its outer limits, Maribeth tells Angie that the fifteen- and sixteen-year-old sons of one of the families have been raping Daisy for months.

"One hold down, other do. Fat boy," says Maribeth. "Too strong. Maribeth little skinny. Family…" and she struggles to find that word again…"threaten. Say she whore. Send back in Philippines. Daisy want to jump."

Angie tries to remember the apartment. Once, on the way to a party in Dubai, she drove Daisy home, Daisy thanking her over and over, until Angie had asked her to please stop. The apartment was way up. Twelfth floor?

"She cry, cry," says Maribeth. "I think do it."

"So what did you tell her?" Angie is on her feet, but Maribeth can't seem to get up; she's stuck to the bed.

"MB! What did you tell her?" Angie finds her purse, phone, sandals.

"I say, 'God love you. God forgive you.'"

"God has not one single thing to forgive Daisy for, Maribeth. Of all the misguided… Come on, get your bag."

They don't speak until they got to Jebel Ali, half an hour still from Dubai proper. In the hour of silence, Angie has had time to wonder what she is doing, but more to the point, what she will be able to do.

She's wanted to pursue this impulse before, to show up at the door of an offender and demand the immediate release of the underpaid nanny, harassed driver, abused maid.

Once, in the first year after she and Firaj moved to Abu Dhabi, to a compound in Al Mushrif, she'd heard screams coming from the villa next door, then an hour later an ambulance pulling into the shared drive. They had only a passing acquaintance with the neighbours, a couple from Belgium (a bit stuffy, but pleasant enough) and the two Filipinas who worked for them.

"I don't understand," she'd told Firaj. "What could they possibly need two maids for? They don't even have kids." And Firaj had explained that most likely one did the shopping and cooking, the other took care of the house. "Polishing the silver, who knows?" he'd said. "You'll never get this, will you? When money is no object, people don't have to do anything they don't feel inclined to do." His own mother in a suburb of Amman still employed a live-in maid, though she was a widow with no grandchildren.

Angie didn't know the maids' names, just raised her hand in greeting when she saw them. One had a sweet smile; the other only bobbed her head. The smiley maid seemed to be gone, Angie noticed about a week after the ambulance. She'd been the one who usually went out with the Belgian woman to help with the shopping. Now it was the other one who unloaded the plastic bags from the back of the SUV.

One afternoon when Angie was leaving to pick up their mail at the post office, she found the maid standing next to her car. "Please," she said, looking around. "Please." The woman looked so desperate, Angie coaxed her into the car.

"I need phone," said the woman. She wasn't especially young, Angie saw now. "I am Inez." The other maid was in the hospital, she said. The man had thrown her against a wall, then knocked her to the kitchen floor when she'd refused to give him a massage. There was blood. The man had finally called an ambulance. But now there were other problems, said Inez. The couple had taken away her mobile phone, afraid she might tell someone what had happened. Madame was yelling all the time and the man was now looking at her. "You know?" She kept turning around to look down the street as she spoke. Madame was due home any minute from a luncheon, she told Angie. "Today I wait for you. You always wave."

If the phone got traced back to Angie, she'd have to deal with the couple. There could be legalities, complications. She might get Firaj into trouble. Then she noticed Inez's hands, chapped, scabbed, scarlet. It hurt to look at them. She opened her purse, rummaged for her phone, handed it over. But the charger. She'd have to run inside for the charger. A bronze Land Rover appeared in the rearview mirror.

When the Belgian woman climbed down from her SUV a minute later, head bent into her mobile, she waved to Angie, who watched as Inez, standing on the curb as if she'd been waiting all this time for Madame to return, took the Paris Gallery bag she was handed. Inez did not look back, but Angie had seen her slip the phone into her uniform pocket as she sprang from the car.

For the next few days, Angie called her mobile. No one answered, no one returned the calls. She told Firaj, in minimal detail, what had happened. He wasn't impressed. "You've got to be more discreet. Who knows who these people are connected to? Remember that we are guests in this country. And even though we are the majority and Emiratis amount to…what? barely 15 percent of the population…it's *their* party." Coming here had meant a promotion from vice-consul to consul. "The higher I go, the more scrutiny," he said.

At the end of that month, they'd moved into their permanent accommodations, a new villa in Khalidiyah, just a block from the Corniche. It was an elegant duplex, with a winding staircase to the second floor, and a private pool. They hired Maribeth a week after moving in. Firaj stayed a year, before getting posted to Jakarta. By the time Angie was ready to join him six weeks later — she'd stayed behind for the movers — Firaj had fallen in love with an Indonesian woman half her age.

She wondered sometimes about Inez, if she'd ever been able to use the phone, how long it had stayed

charged, if it had been discovered. She wondered what
had happened next.

It's impossible to get into Dubai any more. The traffic,
the pile-ups, the detours around detours, signs pointing
nowhere, massive construction sites of half-finished
high-rises.

"MB," says Angie, turning finally onto the road
running along Jumeirah Beach, "you're going to have to
help here."

"What you plan, Madame?"

"MB, you know as much as I do."

"Don't know, Madame."

And for the second time this afternoon, Angie wants
to shake her. "What's going on with you? You're usually
so feisty." Maribeth looks straight ahead. "I don't know
what to say to these people," says Angie. "They might
kick us out. They might call the police."

They will, of course, be seriously outnumbered
— sixteen put-out Egyptians against one small American
woman and one suddenly chastened Filipina. It's so
insane it's nearly comical, nearly noble.

Maribeth is murmuring. "What, MB?" Angie asks,
and Maribeth lifts her rosary.

Nothing is looking familiar on this stretch of
Jumeirah Beach Road. Maybe she's turned the wrong
way. When they first came to the UAE six years ago, it
had been so much easier to navigate this wild-times city.
She and Firaj would come up for a weekend of clubs,
restaurants, shopping, drinking. Dubai brought a sense
of, not home exactly, but short glimpses of the familiar,
something you could get your hands on quick. Abu

Dhabi was saner, but she hadn't necessarily wanted saner in those days.

Angie comes into another snag of late-model cars, most of them honking, and now nothing looks familiar. "Where are we, Maribeth?" asks Angie and her phone rings. She'd hoped to leave Mathieu out of this, at least for now. Perhaps at dinner, overlooking a concrete-lined canal, she will tell him about their mission. He might even be moved.

"Where are you, *chérie*? I hear cars. Are you driving? I thought you were going for *un petit dodo*. You need energy for tonight."

She could lie, tell him she's forgone the nap for a small shopping splurge. A lingerie run to La Senza for an after-dinner treat, like a pair of black lace thongs he can tear off with his teeth. Mathieu likes that sort of thing, likes her little plots as The Mistress. But she needs information or she will waste the afternoon into evening, driving, or trying to drive, through the parking lot that is Jumeirah Beach.

"Where's the Dubai Marina?"

"*Quoi*?" he asks. And she's forced to give him the short version of Daisy and the boys.

"I keep telling you stay out," Mathieu says. "It is not your affair, *comprenez*?" And Angie remembers the way he looked at her a few hours ago, as he was tying his robe. "So no dinner," he says.

"Of course, dinner. It's not even four. This won't take that long. We get Daisy, we're back in the car." But the swell of earlier conviction shrinks as she tries to imagine the scene. All those people standing in the foyer of the apartment. Voices rising, Daisy crying. Who does she think she is?

"Well, don't get yourself killed or deported," says Mathieu, and tells her how to reach the cluster of thirty high-rise apartments on the beach.

"Do you have friends who live there?" Angie asks, grateful as she makes a U-turn. "You seem to know this place like the back of your hand."

"You could say that," says Mathieu, and Angie feels a catch of anxiety as she tucks the phone back in her bag. Not that she can let her mind go anywhere near that right now. There's something completely pathetic about the girlfriend of a married man suspecting there's *another* girlfriend. Almost as pathetic as being the girlfriend. But she can't think about that either.

"Okay, MB, I really do need you," says Angie, and Maribeth sighs and slips her rosary into her purse. Only now does Angie notice what Maribeth is wearing: her tightest jeans and the yellow T-shirt she and Firaj brought back from Disneyland Paris. Donald on the front; Mickey on the back. "That's us, MB," says Angie, pointing to the shirt and for the first time all day, Maribeth smiles.

Angie drives slowly between the towers until Maribeth tells her to stop. "There," she says, leaning forward, pointing up. Angie starts to count the floors, then stops: something else not to contemplate. At least there's no police, a good sign. There's also no parking, this being a Friday. What might have been a space right in back is taken up by a Volvo parked diagonally across two spots. She finds a space in front of the next tower, sits for a moment. Maribeth has slipped her rosary out again, the tiny beads clicking.

"I pray do right," says Maribeth.

They ring the doorbell of apartment 1201. They knock. No one comes. Maribeth points to a few pairs of shoes on the shoe rack. "They out," she pronounces, and begins to pound on the door. Since they've gotten out of the car, she's back to her old self. "Daisy!" she calls into the door. "Daisy!" And then something in Tagalog.

They hear someone behind the door. Slowly, slowly it opens. And there, standing unsteadily, is a very old man. He's barefoot, dressed in a long, off-white *jelabiya*, a crocheted white skull cap on his head. A stricken-looking Daisy stands behind him. Maribeth goes in, stepping around the man, grabs Daisy's arm, says something sharp to her.

"She don't want to leave," says Maribeth, turning back to Angie, still outside, suddenly uncertain of what to do. She was armed for a throng of hysterical people, not a feeble old man.

"Daisy, you have to come with us," says Angie.

"But the old man. I can't leave him. I have to stay." Thank God Daisy's English is as good as it is. It will make convincing her easier.

"You have to, Daisy. This is a very bad place for you."

"Yes," says Daisy. She's not going to argue about that. But she won't leave the old man by himself. "It's my job," she says pleadingly. "Maybe he die and I be responsible."

"Daisy, what these people are doing is not only morally…" Angie can't find a word strong enough or clear enough. "It's illegal. You have to come with us."

With the door open, they hear the elevator being called down. And then Maribeth is racing into Daisy's room to retrieve her purse, her phone, anything of hers they can take, Daisy running after her, protesting. Angie keeps watch at the door. The old man stands guard, too, though he seems to have forgotten what he's guarding. Maribeth reappears, dragging a sobbing Daisy across the length of the living room, through the front door, and together they push her past the elevator, into the stairwell. As they descend, Daisy keeps stopping to argue: "They will punish me!"

"Shut up!" says Maribeth.

Angie only realizes when they reach the ground floor how badly her legs are shaking.

They walk quickly, not looking anywhere but down, to the car. Maribeth gets in back with Daisy, who continues to cry softly, and Angie eases onto Jumeirah Beach Road. She can only ease. The road is completely blocked now. It's Friday late afternoon, time to party, to Do-Buy, as Firaj used to say.

And so it is over. And so it isn't. The Egyptians still have Daisy's passport and her work visa. Daisy will need a new sponsor, a place to live, a way to keep her three sons and sick mother and gay brother in Cebu alive. She will not forget the shame of the sweaty boys. She will not forget the old man standing in his prayer clothes at the open door.

Angie used to love Fridays. They would sit by the pool in Khalidiyah, getting so hot they were nearly unconscious, then slip into the water, coming instantly alive. Firaj would make couscous with chickpeas and feta, mix up a pitcher of sangria. They would talk about sheikh so-and-so who ordered the mangroves dredged so his yacht could squeeze through, about the Pakistani cab drivers who propositioned her when her skirts were too short, about Rapunzel, the Filipina waitress at their favourite restaurant, who had the most beautiful smile in the world and made $2 an hour. People were so kind and so cruel.

OASIS, 1962

She shakes her head, the black cotton of her *shayla* whipping back and forth as if caught in a windstorm. The long coil of her braid swings with the fabric. Lord, give me words that will help. My Arabic, still new, feels small next to her need. Her boy, the size of a scrawny baby, lies on the sand between us. He's not moving.

She grabs my hand, clutches it to her chest. Her face is covered, but I can read everything in that grip. She wants me to change the world, nothing less. I do what I've been taught, place my hands on the child's bony chest, compress once, then again, again, put my mouth over his blistered lips. His eyes flutter and the young woman — a girl, not more than fifteen — lets out a cry that carries as much grief as relief. "Doctora, Doctora!" I can't correct her, not when life and death have just collided, but I feel like a sham. I am no doctor.

Later, Dr. Kennedy has to hold me, I'm shaking so badly. "Happens," he says. "And don't worry about being called doctor. Doesn't bother me," and he laughs. Pat laughs like he talks: short, quick, no time to waste. He and Marian, doctors from the States, look like desert rats already, sun-bleached hair, wind-tough skin, although

they've only been here at Oasis Hospital for two years.
Still, they're old-timers compared to yours truly, fresh
off the plane from Dunelm, Saskatchewan. "Must have
sand in our veins," says Pat, by way of explaining their
adaptability. The Bedu call them Kenned and Mariam.
What will they call me? Gertrude? Nurse Dyck?

Later, as we set up our cots under the moon, Marian
takes me aside. "How are you?" She has the softest voice,
even when issuing orders to Aslam, their Pakistani
houseboy and our all-around helper. Marian's a true
Christian and a mother herself with four children. "I
don't know if Pat told you about our first night here, how
we hadn't even unpacked, didn't have our supplies, and in
comes a woman, fully dilated, ready to go. I delivered her
nearly on the spot—an uncomplicated birth, thank you,
Lord—and two hours later we had her and her brand
new baby boy in the Land Rover on their way home.
They named him Mubarak."

"The blessed," I say. It's one of the first Arabic words
I learned.

"He was our little blessing too, because the women
in the villages began coming in after that. They began to
trust us."

Trust. This is what I need, I tell myself, pulling the
sheet over my head. Trust in God, trust that this is where
I should be.

It's much cooler out on the sand than in the mud-
brick buildings of the hospital or our pre-fab residences.
And quiet. I am still getting used to the quiet of the
desert, so different than the quiet of the prairies. Soon,
though, the silence will be broken by Bedu on the move.
Dressed in clothing that has barely changed since the

time of Abraham, they will walk past our cots and bedrolls, pulling their camels, the women chattering away as *salukis* yap at their heels. A joyous, clamorous dawn.

You practically need a magnifying glass to find the Trucial Oman States on a map of the world. Dad had never heard of the place. "Saudi Arabia? You're not going to Saudi Arabia, Gert!" I tried to explain that it wasn't Saudi, but an area on the Persian Gulf between Oman and Saudi, a protectorate of Britain. "It's becoming something, Dad. After a thousand years of poverty, they've discovered oil." They needed hospitals, doctors, nurses. I needed a place to put the gifts God had given me. How could it not feel providential?

I read Wilfred Thesiger's book, *Arabian Sands*, and felt the desert pull me. The Bedu were people I wanted to meet: brave, friendly and sturdy. I fashioned my version of a veil, cutting out holes for the eyes, to see what it was like to be a woman in that world. I felt anonymous, but free, too.

With my family's cautious blessing, I accepted a nursing job at Oasis Hospital in Al Ain, an oasis equidistant from Dubai and Abu Dhabi, about two days by camel caravan. Bundled in two sweaters, a heavy winter coat and snow boots — it was, after all, minus 30 in Swift Current — I flew to Bahrain last December. From there it was a twin-propeller flight to Dubai via Doha, then an eight-hour Land Rover ride to Al Ain. Our driver, a local, forded the sand dunes in the four-wheel drive. Or tried to. Clouds of fine sand billowed up as our tires churned, the grains sticking to my face, blowing into my eyes and nostrils and mouth, finding every crevice. We stopped to push the car and I took off my new sandals. They say once you get sand between your toes, you can never get it out.

A man came in with a snake bite this morning. Snake bites, scorpion stings, these are common, the downside of sleeping under the stars. Pat was in Dubai ordering medical supplies and Marian was in the middle of a delivery, so it was just me. The man, who'd parked his camel behind the hospital, was in obvious pain, though he kept smiling, placing his hand over his heart and bowing his head. I gave him the antidote, though he didn't seem to understand that he had to swallow the pill, not rub it on the bite itself. Finally, I held a glass of water to his mouth and he understood. Pill down, he pointed to himself:

"Mohammed," he said.

"Gertrude," I said, pointing to myself.

"Grapefruit," he said.

"Gertrude," I repeated, trying not to laugh.

"Latifa," he said.

"Gertrude," I said.

"Doctora," he said, nodding as if this was the final word on my name.

When I told Marian later, she nodded too. "Latifa means kind and merciful in Arabic. That man must know something, Gertie. And Doctora...well, take that as the sign of deepest respect."

From Gertrude Dyck to Doctora Latifa. Quite the leap.

I'd always imagined an oasis as a single palm tree perched by a pond. Perhaps the image came from a Bible story Mother read to me as a child. Clearly that illustrator never saw Al Ain. The whole area is an oasis: vast palm groves, sweeping fields irrigated by the most ingenious water system I've ever seen. (And I *am* a prairie girl.) They call them *falaj*, aqueducts that are both underground and above ground, and which bring water from the Omani Hajar Mountains to the plains. Our lifeline.

And our lifesaver. How hot does it get? family and friends keep asking in their letters. The hottest day here—easily 120 degrees—is more intense than the coldest January night in Saskatchewan. What to wear in this heat, especially for a Western woman, is a challenge. I've settled on cotton dresses, with light *shalwar* trousers underneath. Modesty is like a religion here, so I'm vigilant, especially as a newcomer. After all, we're the first uncovered women many of our patients have ever seen. And probably the first Westerners to use our *falaj* as a swimming hole. With dimensions of four feet by six feet and a depth of eighteen inches, none of us are exactly doing the back stroke. We sit, blessedly cool at last, under a palm roof, little fish nibbling at our legs.

Sheikh Zayed, who rules Al Ain under his brother Sheikh Shakhbut, ruler of Abu Dhabi, is our hospital's patron saint. *Mafi fayd mal bedon al seha*, he says. Wealth without health is useless. He is so dedicated to his people, so concerned about their welfare. He's the brains and will behind the construction of the *falaj* irrigation system. He's the vision behind the construction of three schools here, a leap ahead of Abu Dhabi, which still has no formal education system. Many members of Sheikh Zayed's family live in Al Ain, and Marian tells me some have already come here to have their babies. Future sheikhs, part of the royal lineage, are being born in our little hospital. Imagine.

Until recently, only 50 percent of babies survived and only two in three mothers came through childbirth alive. While we were folding sheets a few nights ago, Marian told me about a fourteen-year-old bride who came to the hospital last summer. "She knew nothing about conception or the birthing process. All she knew was that she had a swollen belly and there was a baby in there." The girl, terrified when her water broke, walked for kilometres over the dunes. She'd heard that on the outskirts of Al Ain a concrete building housed kind strangers who helped the sick. "She was afraid the baby would come out of her mouth," Marian said, trying not to smile.

"Lord, what did you tell her?"

Marian hesitated, as if this was perhaps too personal to share. "How could I explain to this innocent what actually happens? 'Consider me your mother,' I told her. Two hours later she gave birth to a beautiful baby girl."

How do our patients pay for medical care when so many have so little? The sheikhs have thought of this too, issuing nationals a *burwa*, something like our new national health insurance in Saskatchewan. But instead of a plastic card, *burwas* are just small slips of paper. Sometimes they're rolled into a ball and tied into a corner of a *shayla* or stuck in a man's *sufra*, his turban. Of course, sometimes the *shayla* gets washed in the *falaj* or the *burwa* gets eaten by a goat. We laugh ourselves silly over the tales we're told.

There is nothing charming, though, about the serious disease still rampant here: advanced cases of TB, children with pernicious, life-threatening diarrhea. There's a stoicism in these people. As Pat said to me the other day, "In the desert there isn't much you can do but submit."

Everywhere we are greeted with open arms. Families who've had babies with us issue pressing invitations. "You must come to see your baby." Marian says that whoever cuts the cord is honoured forever as The Mother, sweet compensation for the children God has chosen not to bless me with. When we arrive, our patients run out to meet us at the car, then walk with us to their homes. Sometimes these are beside a dune or inside a date garden. There is always food to share, and, of course, coffee.

At first I found the coffee impossibly strong — thank goodness for such small cups — but the longer I am here, the more I love the smell and the ritual. It can go on for ages — the roasting of the beans over an open fire, the crushing with mortar and pestle, the boiling and foaming up of the liquid two, three times, then the pouring over pounded cardamom seeds. My new friends tell me that when they travel by camel, the coffee pot is the last thing packed and the first thing unpacked.

It's difficult for me to write anything about Sheikh Zayed that doesn't sound like overstatement. But if anyone can carry his people into the twentieth century, it is this man with the long stride, children always running by his side to keep up. He is a man as large as the desert. But I was surprised to discover he's also a practical joker. Once when Marian and I had gone to visit Sheikh Zayed's mother, he was there, standing by the car. As we said our goodbyes, he played with his camel stick in the sand. "*Haneesh*!" he called out suddenly, the Arabic word for snake, meanwhile scribbling a wavy line in the sand. We jumped back and he roared with laughter.

Whenever Sheikh Zayed sees me now, he calls out, "*Marhaba*, Latifa!" Hello, Latifa!

My identity, it seems, is sealed.

THE KNOWLEDGE

Mohsin thinks this is nothing. You drive in the desert, he says. Abu Dhabi is not a real city. Not like London or Paris or Rome. Mohsin has not been to Paris or Rome, but he pronounces this with authority. Sami can see his brother Mohsin's mouth: turned down at the corners, disdainful but humouring. Sami talks to Mohsin often in his head, especially when driving, which means all the time. Perhaps he even speaks to him in dreams.

Sami's back at Al Zaabi Finest Bakery, already the third pick-up of the day. Shhhh, he tells Mohsin. You are wrong. Abu Dhabi is a real city. You come see. For thirty-four years Mohsin has been driving cabs in London, six more than Sami has been head driver for the Al Qubaisis, a family one rung down from the Al Nahyans, one remove from royalty. My life, Sami tells Mohsin silently as he gets out of the SUV, has been touched by luxury.

It's already so hot his khaki shirt is stuck to his back, his whole back, not just the small of it. He will change at the next stop. Saeed Al Qubaisi likes staff to look military-sharp, no sweaty men in damp *shalwar kameez* in *his* employ. Sami appreciates this. My life, he thinks, passing through the bakery's air-conditioned entry, has been touched by excellence.

Dania, the Palestinian counter girl, looks up, smiles slightly, drops her gaze. They have known each other for more than ten years, but both watch over-friendliness. "This place has eyes," she told him once when he inquired after her young son, living in Jordan with extended family. He'd willed himself not to look up at the security monitor in the ceiling, and nodded, complicit. The camera is always on, training itself on who comes and who goes, though who would steal *maamoul* and *baklawa*? True, Al Zaabi's Arabic sweets are delicious, the best in the Emirates, some say. But really...*maamoul*? Working for the Al Qubaisis, he can have all the *maamoul* he wants. Platters of *maamoul*, the really big ones Saeed Al Qubaisi prefers, are kept in the kitchen's cold storage, the pastries stacked in steep, perfect pyramids. You have to slip them carefully from the top, then fill back in with fresh ones, otherwise it looks suspicious. But there is always another tray waiting for this small, artful deception. He is here to pick up half a dozen more trays. My life has been touched by...and he searches out the right word for Mohsin, always listening, always ready to jump in with an objection...by abundance.

Dania orders the two Bangladeshi helpers to load the trays into the back of the Land Rover. Last year, Sami asked Saeed Al Qubaisi about installing bakers' racks in one of the Land Rovers. "The trays, Sir, they slip around," Sami explained. His boss has yet to commit. Sometimes he takes months to make a decision, often not making any at all, unlike Sultan, his father, who hired Sami twenty-eight years before. There was a man who said yes, no, in, out, stop, go. You jumped when you saw him coming. His son isn't a bad man, just mixed up. It's on account of the poems he writes. Poetry excites a woman, kindles her body and mind, Saeed told Sami once when they were driving to one of the family farms. Years before, Sultan had hired a down-on-his-luck cousin to manage it; a generation later, the manager still needs managing.

Perhaps Sir is right about pretty words being the way to a woman's heart, but poetry softens a man, makes him moody, full of questions not answers. If Sir was writing traditional *nabuti* poetry, praising the heroes of the desert, that would be different. But Sir writes about women, their supple skin, their honeyed voices. It's not quite decent. This is what Sami thinks. No, this is what Sami *knows*. Even Mohsin would agree. But then Mohsin doesn't think much of Sami's bosses. What do you expect? says Mohsin. These people were nothing, a bunch of tribes fishing for pearls and growing dates until the Brits found oil. It's a country built on black stuff gushing from a hole in the ground. What kind of achievement is that? In London, Mohsin drives lords and ladies, members of Parliament, rock stars, once David Beckham himself. People of substance, he says.

Sami's mobile vibrates in his pocket as he double-checks the trays. In the absence of real bakers' racks, he's fashioned something from Ikea shelving that he's paid for himself, no need to trouble the boss for something so trivial. Fine, fine, Sir might say if he took the time to look back there. Brilliant, Madame might say, though her eyes wouldn't move from her iPad. It's Madame on the mobile now. She doesn't wait for him to say *marhaba*. "Go pick up Rashid from school. He's been bad again."

Rashid, Rashid. What will they do about Rashid? Already there's talk in the household about sending the youngest Al Qubaisi to boarding school in England. "Not London," Madame says. "Somewhere with no distractions." Distraction is only part of Rashid's problem.

Sami swings onto 15th Street, careers through the roundabout, a Hummer riding his bumper, then flows out the other side. Rashid texts him: "Sami, way r u?" Rashid loves to text. "I'm good, aren't I, Sami?" Rashid asks nearly every day. "You are," Sami answers.

Rashid is waiting outside the British School Al Kubairat, a tubby boy in a *khandoura* who already looks like a little man. Rashid opens the car door and lunges across the back seat. Three boys in blazers and ties watch from the curb, smirking, as the Land Rover pulls away.

"Faggots," hisses Rashid from the back seat.

"Seat belt," says Sami.

"Where?" says Rashid.

"Home," says Sami.

"No fun," says Rashid.

He's right. With Madame studying for her university classes, with Sir writing poetry in his own villa across town—"Poets need complete peace and quiet, Sami"—with Sultan, named after his grandfather and the oldest, doing military duty in Ras al Khaimah, Eiman graduating from university in Al Ain and about to get married, Hassan training his camels in Madinat Zayed, it's often just the two youngest rattling around the compound: Asma, sixteen and Sami's least favourite—the girl's too smart for her own good—and Rashid, ten going on four. It doesn't help that the two hate each other. The once-strong Qubaisat clan isn't what it was, Sami admits, turning at the evangelical church. What is? says Mohsin. Except, of course, *our* royal family. (Mohsin loves the Queen.)

They've argued this before—both in phone calls and in his head. Sheikha Salama, a Qubaisat, gave birth to Sheikh Zayed, the father of the country, Sami tells Mohsin. She is *our* Queen Mum. But he can hear the amused snort.

She married a murderer, Sami. His own brother yet. What's to be proud of?

Yes, brother, I know, brother, sighs Sami, easing onto 26th Street and then through the Delma roundabout. Arabian sands cover a lot of history.

You mean blood, says Mohsin.

"Sami," whines Rashid from the back seat.

"Seat belt," says Sami.

"Happy?" says Rashid, and Sami hears the click.

He should drive the boy home. He should. But what's there? More nannies, cooks, gardeners, drivers and maids than there are parents or siblings or friends. Homework that will not get done despite threats and punishments. Five TVs that will be on with no one watching. Three *salukis* growling for food and attention, their nails skittering and scratching on the marble steps outdoors. Sami pulls onto Khaleej al Arabi.

"Hey," says Rashid.

"You asked," says Sami.

But already Rashid is bent over his iPhone, gone, lost. They could drive all the way up the E11, all the way to Jebel Ali, the Emirates' vast port, a place Rashid was fascinated by once—"Boats! Boats!" he would cry when little. They could take the ring road around

Dubai, passing Sharjah, Ajman, Umm al Qawain, Ras al Khaimah, swinging across to Fujairah on the return, a private, grand tour of all seven Emirates. From sea to desert to sea. Rashid's world, birthplace and birthright. But the boy, lost in battles with mythical beasts and spear-wielding women, their bosoms filling the tiny screen, would barely notice.

"Yes!" he crows from the back seat.

See, says Mohsin. See what your job is.

Sami tried London for a year when he was nineteen, in the early 1980s. He'd needed to go somewhere, anywhere, after the girl he'd loved since age six fell in love with the American exchange student at her private high school. Love was supposed to be simple, mutual. It wasn't supposed to make you want to die. Forget her, little brother, said Mohsin. Come to London.

Mohsin worked for a taxi company started a decade earlier by a man, like them from Peshawar, now a millionaire. Maybe a billionaire, Mohsin said. But Sami couldn't get The Knowledge down, though he took the London cabbies' test three times. ("Three times? That's nothing. I did ten appearances before I passed," said Mohsin.) But Sami hated the drizzle, the smell of Wimpy burgers, the grotty damp of the flat he and Mohsin shared with four other young men from home. He found the British unsettling. Chirpy, distant, friendly, aloof, push, pull. They chatted and smiled, but didn't register anything other than what was in front of them, what they already knew. Dear, darling England! They could not imagine the life of a young man far from home, heartsick and homesick. And those were the *good* ones.

"How do you take it?" he'd asked Mohsin, when his brother would tell stories after his shift. Some customers, if they'd spent too long in a pub, called him "Paki" or "Pac-man." Mohsin shrugged. "I go heavy on the brakes. Bounce them around. They can call me whatever they like. I'm the one behind the wheel."

Sami had tried once more to face down The Knowledge, borrowing a scooter from one of his flatmates so he could memorize the 25,000 London streets that might come up on the exam. There were 320 standard runs—how could that many *anything* be standardized?—through central London alone. Still, some of it was finally getting into his head and staying there when they got the news that their mother was ill.

"You go," said Mohsin. Grateful for the chance to leave all those streets with their funny names—Amen Corner, Finsbury Pavement, Mincing Lane…damp streets, too many streets—Sami packed a small bag and boarded a plane for Abu Dhabi. The plan was to spend a day in the new-oil, upstart city where their mother's older brother—also a cab driver—lived. The two would make their way to Lahore, then on to Peshawar. By the time Sami landed in Abu Dhabi, their mother was dead.

The rest, says Mohsin, is history.

A good history, retorts Sami. A happy history.

Whatever you say, Mohsin says.

"Sami," says Rashid.

"Yes," says Sami.

"I'm hungry."

The traffic is slowing. Only an accident, a bloody one, slows traffic on the E11. Sami has heard stories about the M1 in Britain, that you're as likely to end up in an ambulance as at your destination. But Britain can't match this. Driving is blood sport in the UAE. Sami has seen things that make him toss at night—an arm on the side of the road; an entire body's worth of blood smeared on the pavement; bodies rolled in muslin and stacked like building material in the back of a pickup.

Be careful out there. Check your mirrors, Mohsin says, when they talk once a week, though Sami hears it more as further reproof than brotherly concern. They're both middle-aged men now. It's too late to play protector and protected.

Bad traffic, awful traffic. Though he has no real idea where they're going next, Sami chafes at the standstill. It's claustrophobic to be surrounded by SUVs, many even bigger than theirs. Two finally let him in; he navigates the lane changes, moving right again and again across six lanes, until he can creep off the exit ramp. Others have the same idea: he's rooted again. But there on the right is a sign giving them a destination.

"Sami?" It's a question now, not so much a demand. "Am I good?"

"You are good, Rashid," says Sami, turning onto a smaller highway. "You go to Akhdar City, Rashid?"

"No I don't know maybe yes," says Rashid, and Sami can tell by the way his voice muffles that the boy's head is down, his attention scattered again.

"You know Akhdar?" Sami asks.

"Yes!" crows Rashid, an answer that has nothing to do with the question.

The boy's a loser, says Mohsin. Like his father, like all those people.

Give him a chance, says Sami.

Maybe he has too many chances, says Mohsin. He has too much, *period*.

Sami drove Rashid to a birthday party a few Fridays back. Rashid doesn't have any friends, not really. But this boy, a new Canadian kid in the class, was keen to make a good impression and invited the entire class. Only half turned up at the ballroom in the Beach Rotana Hotel. "What kind of a place is that for a kid's birthday?" Mohsin asked on the phone the next weekend. "Why don't they go to the beach like normal kids? Don't you have nice beaches there?" And Sami had tried to explain that this is what children did here, especially if they were locals. "Throw money at the youngsters, right?" Mohsin said. "Teach them what's important."

"It was too hot for the beach," Sami added. No parent would let their kid attend a beach party in May. But Sami never complains about the impossible, burn-through-the-sandals heat to Mohsin, who already has too much ammunition.

At first Rashid hadn't wanted to go to the party. "I want to stay home," he said. "I want to play at home." But Madame had insisted, and Rashid's nanny, Lilibeth, had promised to order a cake from Al Zaabi Finest Bakery just for him for afterward, even though he wasn't the birthday boy, and Sami had offered to take him to buy a special toy for his friend. "And maybe one for you too."

"I want the same toy," Rashid finally agreed.

Madame had pressed 2,000 dirhams into Sami's hand as they were leaving. "Make sure it's something nice, nothing that looks cheap."

The kid-size electric cars at Toys "R" Us — the most expensive thing in the store — cost a little more than this, so Sami had to throw in 120 dirhams of his own. He couldn't interest Rashid in anything other than the car for himself, not even the latest version of X-Box.

Rashid had stood at the counter shaking his head over and over, even after Sami explained that he didn't have the money to buy a second car. "We'll come back next week, even maybe tomorrow, and get you the car, okay?" Sami promised.

"Tonight," Rashid said.

"How late are you open?" Sami asked the checker.

"Ten," she said, and Rashid had given her the thumbs up.

But at the entrance to the hotel ballroom half an hour later, the boy's better mood evaporated. "I don't want to go," he told Sami, who'd planned to duck into his favourite shawarma shop across the street, visit with an old friend who often went there after prayers on Friday afternoons. Sami had ferried the toy car in on a hotel dolly, no one offering to help. He was tired and sweaty. Oh, for a cup of Lipton's Yellow Label.

"But your friends are here," said Sami, knowing this wasn't true.

"I go in if you stay," said Rashid. "You are my friend, Sami."

"Poor boy," Sami said to Lilibeth the next day. They sometimes talk about Rashid, shrugging, shaking their heads. What are they to do? What *can* they do? "I tell Madame that boy is good boy, but needs special help," says Lilibeth. "She doesn't want to hear." Lilibeth is a tiny, plain woman, older than she first appears, and better educated than some of the other children's nannies. She has a good heart, Sami tells Mohsin often. But Sami didn't tell even Lilibeth that before the games and cake and gift-giving, before most of the other guests had arrived, Rashid had ripped the gift paper from the huge box and insisted on riding the car round and round the ballroom while the birthday boy and his parents watched.

"I was showing him," Rashid protested when Sami told him on the way home that this was not polite, good-guest behaviour. He also didn't tell Lilibeth that Saeed Al Qubaisi, dropping in for coffee and a chat with his wife later that night, slipped him 3,000 dirhams to buy another electric car and that he had done just that, hurrying into Toys "R" Us minutes before they closed. (Lilibeth would see the car soon enough.) He didn't tell Mohsin about it. Any of it. Nor that the car had held Rashid's undivided attention for one day.

"Akhdar City," Sami says to the back seat as he tries to follow the signs, "is an amazing place. No country has anything like Akhdar." Sami doesn't know if this is exactly true. There must be other projects like Abu Dhabi's experimental green city. People were so worried about the environment nowadays. High-class problem, according to Mohsin. People starving, that's a problem, he says. People not believing in God, that's a problem. But if we run out of energy, Sami argues back—imagining Mohsin's emphatic head-shaking—then what? None of the rest will matter. Since when did you get so fatalistic, little brother? Mohsin says. You're not going to the mosque enough, are you?

Their faith, their practice, their bedrock. It had been the one place they could find each other in the past. But then Mohsin had made some new friends, younger fellows coming from home to the UK. They've got something, these guys. Clear as a bell, says Mohsin. Know where they're going. Mohsin is planning on making the *hajj* next year. What about you, Sami? Mohsin has begun to ask this in every phone conversation. Don't you think it's time to make the *hajj*? None of us knows how long we have, he says. *Now* who's the fatalist? Sami retorts, but only in his head.

"I need food!" Rashid has come alive again and kicks the back of the front seat.

"Patience, Rashid, patience," says Sami, knowing that the word means nothing to Rashid. It doesn't mean much to any of the Al Qubaisi children. Eiman, who turns twenty-one this year, still stamps and screams when she doesn't get what she wants in the very next minute. Patience, Sami and Mohsin's mother used to tell them, is the highest virtue. It is golden.

The mobile again: "Sami, where are you?" Asma, who has only contempt for her mother, would be mortified to know how much she sounds like her on the phone. "I need you to pick me up. Now." Sami hears a crowded room behind her. Lately she's been summoning him at all hours. "Friends," she always says. But the night before she had him come to a run-down villa in the industrial part of Musaffah. "Friends, who do you think?" Asma glared at him in the rear-view mirror when he asked.

"I need to be picked up," she says again.

"Where are you?" Sami asks, dreading rejoining the gridlock.

The girl's usual bravura seems to fail her. "I'm not sure."

"I've got Rashid," Sami starts to say.

"Never mind," says Asma, composed and imperious again, and hangs up.

Alhamdulillah! There's an Adnoc station right on the service road. Sami turns in, manoeuvring carefully past the long line-up for petrol, but calls Madame before parking. "Fine," is all she says and hangs up before Sami can even tell her where they are or that Asma has just called, that she's out there somewhere.

Rashid orders three Big Macs, grabbing a dozen packets of ketchup for his three cartons of fries.

"Are you sure you can eat all that?" Sami asks and Rashid looks at him scornfully. But food, especially in large quantities, always perks Rashid up. In between open-mouth chewing, he quizzes Sami on soccer. Sami's up on the British teams, via Mohsin, but falls down on the Brazilians, Rashid's current obsession. "See, I'm smarter than you," says Rashid.

Sami looks at his watch. He hopes Akhdar City is still open. He hopes Asma finds a cab.

"Right?" presses Rashid.

"Right," says Sami.

And then, as if he's wearing ear buds and singing along to a pop song, Rashid suddenly chants, "Baba loves a lady, Baba loves a lady."

"Your mother is a good woman," says Sami. He doesn't really believe this after all these years of working for Madame, but it's sweet that Rashid appreciates his father's devotion.

"No," says Rashid, shaking his whole body so adamantly that the wrappers from the Big Macs flutter to the ground. A Filipina is there in an instant, picking them up. She smiles nervously at Rashid.

"Your mother is a lady," says Sami, starting to feel anxious.

"Different lady, Sami. Russian lady. Don't you understand? Are you stupid?"

Watch out, whispers Mohsin.

"Baba loves a different lady. Different." Rashid shouts the word as it's written, all three syllables.

"We go," says Sami, gathering up the sticky packets and used napkins. He hates leaving a mess behind for the workers. They are not as lucky as he's been. My life has been touched by…but he can't at that moment think what it's been touched by.

"She's a nudie," says Rashid, slurping the last of his Coke. "I saw her. Big ones."

"Where?" Sami asks, even as he hears Mohsin hiss: Back off.

Rashid looks at him as if he's an idiot. "On her head. Where do you think?"

"At Baba's villa?" Sami needs to leave this alone. He absolutely has to.

"Of course at Baba's villa. Where do you think?"

Sami gets up, takes Rashid's elbow and leads him out of McDonald's, back to the Land Rover. Rashid is many things — a troubled boy, a spoiled boy — but he is not a liar. The other children in the family are better at this. Sultan, Sami knows, cheated his way through university. He will never reveal how he knows this, but he does. Now he can't look at the eldest son, once his favourite, without feeling a cloud pass over his heart. Sometimes it's better not to know people too well.

So why does he have to know *this*? How is knowing this going to help anything? Because now the pieces are flying into places where they should have landed months, even years ago if he'd had half a brain and half the trust: the separate villa, the weeks away from home, the smell of perfume in Sir's bedroom, the trips to Hong Kong and New York without Madame. The poetry. And now Mohsin will never shut up. Those people, he says. Godless.

The Adnoc station is jumping as they leave, long lines for petrol, longer lines inside for fast food, for coffee and candy and cash from the bank machine. Cigarettes and DVDs and Tampax and condoms. You can buy anything over there, can't you? says Mohsin. Sami once saw bottles of special lubricant for exciting a woman, right next to the Panadol and mouthwash. He'd looked away fast, but he'd seen it.

From the back seat, Rashid sets up the chant: "Akhdar! Akhdar! Akhdar!" Once out of the station with its fever of bright lights and big cars, it's dim and silent. Sami follows the signs through long stretches of sand and scruff. The sky is darkening quickly, the road narrowing from four lanes to two. They pass no other cars, not a good sign. The endless landscape can still take Sami by surprise, still makes him vaguely uneasy, even after all these years. Of course, Abu Dhabi is dense and developed compared to thirty years before, when this highway didn't even exist, when there were only a few petrol stations in the entire city. But he finds the desert distances somehow more unsettling now, as if all the new high-rises — the giant, tilted sausage of the Gateway building, the massive obelisk of the Mubadala headquarters — make the spaces in between yawn wider. The city is spreading wildly out here: Khalifa City A, Khalifa City B. But each isolated development looks lonelier than the next, pretty sand-coloured villas surrounded by nothing. Sami prays they reach something soon.

And then, as if he's been supplicating himself before ever-present Allah, the lanes widen to four and they're curving around a grand, circular driveway. Akhdar City, the sign reads: Welcome to the Future. Not many other people seem interested in that future this evening: Three cars sit in the parking lot. Sami gets out of the SUV, opens the back door, leans over to undo Rashid's seat belt.

Rashid looks up from his mobile. "Home?"

"Akhdar," says Sami. "They have interesting little cars here."

"I like *big* cars," says Rashid.

"I know," says Sami. "I do too. But these cars drive *themselves*."

"No!" says Rashid.

Sami nods, waits.

With a sigh, Rashid heaves himself from the back seat. He seems to have grown wider and taller since Sami picked him up two hours ago. They walk to what could be an entrance. Now that they're inside Akhdar City, now that they're past the impressive driveway, it all looks smaller, rougher. Sami sees that they're actually in a building site, one that hasn't seen a lot of recent action, judging by the dirt-encrusted Caterpillars standing abandoned like hulking sandcastles. A laminated plaque hangs near what he hopes is a garage for the tiny cars. PRTs, Sami remembers from a newspaper story. Personal Rapid Transport. In the photos they looked like white pods on invisible wheels and barely tall enough for a boy.

"Akhdar City is a modern Arabian city that, like its forerunners, is in tune with its surroundings," Sami reads aloud from the plaque. "As such, it is a model for sustainable urban development regionally and globally, seeking to be a commercially viable development that delivers the highest quality living and working environment with the lowest possible ecological footprint." Who do they think they are? scoffs Mohsin.

But Rashid is looking up at Sami with questions all over his face. "What is forerunners? People who run for something? And footprint? Is that like what the *salukis* leave in the gardens and what makes Baba so mad? And what is eco…you know."

Sami doesn't know. It's all high talk and big ideas. You're right there, says Mohsin.

"Let's go see the cars," Sami says. He needs to keep them moving, not just because of Rashid's flickering attention, but because he needs to rub out the thing he now knows. How is he going to look Sir in the eye again?

A man in a uniform steps out of the shadows. He speaks in rapid Arabic with a heavy Jordanian accent. Rashid grunts. "What?" says Sami, who missed the last bit. "Can we ride in the cars?"

"No," says Rashid. "Broke." And he kicks a stone out of his way with such force Sami winces.

"Sir, sir," Sami calls to the man, who's walking away. "Could we just look at one of the cars?"

The man shrugs and points to something off in the distance.

PRTs, a dozen of them, sit in a row in a glass station. The glass is also covered with sand, though Sami — after three decades as a driver here — knows it could have been washed off only that morning. Sand moves fast. It beats you every time.

Before Sami can stop him, Rashid makes for the cars. Miraculously, both the door to the station and the door to the first car in line open for him. "Sami!" he waves, and Sami, looking around for the guard, runs over and climbs in. Compact isn't the word for these things. His knees are in his chest. Rashid, mesmerized, presses a button and the door closes. Without any warning, without any reason, the car beeps and begins to glide out of the station. Gaining speed, it zips across the empty lot, across sand and tumbleweeds, across the land that someday will be home to a city the world has not yet seen. A global hub for renewable energy. A model of sustainable technologies for all nations. That place you live, says Mohsin. It's not a model for anything.

Sami is nervous, swivelling back to front. What if the guard realizes they've taken the car? What if they hit something, a rock, a tree, a person out here? The sky is starry, but with no streetlights, no real road, they're rushing into blackness. Madame, he suddenly thinks. My job.

But Rashid is lit up, his whole body quivering with excitement. "Look, Sami, no hands!" he crows.

"What do you need hands for? There's no steering wheel!" Sami shouts back. The car, which runs on electricity, whines as it careers down what might or might not be a road. Rashid loves it, but Sami can't imagine most Emiratis putting up with the noise or the cramped space. The PRT will likely go the way of so many other fine ideas here. The flash of a bright new thing followed by the drudgery of having to make it actually work.

"No hands!" Rashid cries again. And looking over at Rashid, a little man, a big baby, *ghutra* slipping off his head, Sami sees that he is happy.

Sami, Sami, sighs Mohsin. What are you doing with your life?

Shhhh, says Sami.

FOLLY

They were living in their third villa by then. Tucked behind the American school in Khalidiyah, this one had French doors in the living room that opened onto a sunken pool lined with blue and gold Iranian tiles. Each of the eight adjoining villas faced the same aqueous view. The Canadian neighbours to the left had seemed promising. Harris worked in administration at Al Nahyan University; Deborah was a teacher at the Horizon School, that sad place where Emiratis sent their disabled children. "But it's not sad at all," the wife had insisted, her face pained and well-meaning.

By now, though, even Molly had begun to distrust first bursts of friendliness. "We must have you over for dinner!" did not, in most cases, ever result in dinner. Promises, promises, said Talbot, who had come to hate pretty much all of it.

Then the Cassels moved in next door. The villa had been vacant for nearly four months, the financial downturn having finally reached their sandy shores. The wife, Carla, was Brazilian, but had bounced between Canada and New Zealand growing up; Gomez was Argentinian on his mother's side, French on his father's, and schooled in Hong Kong. They'd just come from two years in Singapore; before that, three years in New York. This was one of the things Talbot could still feel dazzled by: how wide the net was, how large the world. He'd never met anyone from Brazil before, never given much thought to Singapore. And here, this international life.

He'd tried to describe it to his mother back in Oban. "But these people you keep meeting, they have no real home to speak of, do they?" she said. When they'd first moved to Abu Dhabi, Talbot had encouraged her to visit. But every time he or Molly brought it up — Molly genuinely loved his mother — she'd laugh her tinkling little laugh. He began to realize the prospect of a trip here, leaving her seaside Scottish town, terrified her. Now that he'd come to live in a state of terror himself, he was relieved his mother had so little courage and curiosity.

Gomez Cassel knocked on their door the night they moved in. He didn't have the right adaptor for their baby monitor. "You'd think after all our moves, I'd have it figured out." He shrugged, smiling through obvious exhaustion. "You never really get used to it." It was late, a little after nine. Talbot ducked into the fridge after yanking at cords, chargers, converters in their still poorly organized kitchen drawers. "Here," he said, also handing over a cold bottle of Leffe. "You probably need this more than an adaptor."

Gomez looked as if he'd been told the sheikhs had decided to deal him in. "I was going to run out and buy a six-pack, and then…" he laughed, "Carla reminded me where we are. 'You're not in NYC, chump.'" He was a spectacularly tall man with greying curls. Close to fifty, Talbot thought, though it could just be the hair.

"How many kids?" Talbot asked.

"Two at college in the States. Two with us here: Britannia, she's six, and Jesse, our baby."

"College," said Talbot, "wow." Wondering how it all computed.

"Second wife," said Gomez and gave Talbot a wink that threw him. Challenge, collusion, what? But then Molly came into the room with Manda in her arms and they'd talked nannies, going rates and the whole visa business.

"Better get back," Gomez said. "One of the two is probably having a meltdown by now. Or one of the three."

They said they hoped to see each other again soon. "Get the kids together," said Gomez.

"We'll never see them again," said Talbot after he left.

"The pool," said Molly.

"Doesn't count," said Talbot and took Manda from her. Their daughter was nearly asleep, her three-year-old weight and warmth settling him as it always did.

When the first wave of redundancies hit the real estate sector, Talbot hadn't been too worried. He certainly wasn't staying up nights like some of his colleagues at Amaal Properties. Bruce, a fellow Scot, had gotten so freaked, he'd landed in emergency at Sheikh Khalifa Medical City with shingles and heart palpitations. He was back at work the next week, looking like someone who'd fallen from a great height and somehow survived. Bruce had been a showboat when he'd arrived two years before, buying a white Mercedes SL convertible with his first-year bonus, dropping the names of ruling family members. "Gotta love this place," he said a lot. He was one of the few unmarried ones, spent most of his weekends in Dubai. Word back then was that he was shacking up with a Malaysian flight attendant from Etihad *and* her roommate.

"How do you get away with shit like that in a place like this?" Talbot had asked Molly.

"You really think it's so different here?" she'd answered. Sometimes Talbot's naïveté was charming. But the longer they were together—twelve years now—the more she seemed irritated by it, like it was a kind of obstinacy, a failure to get with the program.

"Yeah, I do actually. Can't have a beer on the front step, can't hug or kiss in public. You're my wife and if I hold your hand in the blinking mall, I get funny looks, but if you're two guys you can?"

"I've got used to it," Molly said. And she'd gone back to sewing sequins on a leotard for Zoë, their seven-year-old, who'd been invited to a ballerina birthday party. Zoë had wanted a custom-made tutu like some of her friends, but Molly had said, no, they could make something themselves. "There's got to be a limit," she said. Talbot had watched as she secured each tiny sequin with silver thread. Even if he knew what to do with a needle and thread, a job like this would drive him round the bend. Molly made it look easy. He secretly took her in—she didn't often welcome admiration—the red-blond hair that curled up in humidity, the small, high-arched feet. Unlike some British women who came here and got broad in the beam, Molly had kept her compact swimmer's body. She didn't look that different from their days as young lawyers in Glasgow, a long, long time ago.

They did see the Cassels again. Two days later, as he and Molly unloaded the pile of Spinney's bags from the SUV, the family pulled into the canopied spot next to theirs. Gomez looked delighted to see them. Spotting Talbot's racing bike leaning against the carport wall, he gave a thumbs up: "You ride?"

Gomez's wife — tall, tawny, so stunning Talbot nearly had to look away — was considerably younger. What had he done to win such a prize? Talbot wondered. It must have to do with money, though he didn't know what Gomez did for a living. Probably something in oil and gas — people here said it as one word, oilngas — the ubiquitous job description that came with luxury housing, paid tuitions and swollen salaries.

The wife walked quickly to them, put out both hands. "I'm Carla. You've no idea how you saved our lives the other night." Women this gorgeous were often short on warmth and charm in Talbot's experience, but Carla held nothing back in her handclasp, chatted animatedly with Molly, ducked to talk to Manda. Britannia and Zoë, close in age, eyed each other for ten seconds before deciding they'd be friends for life, or at least for the afternoon. Even Manda and Jesse caught each other's eye before turning away shyly.

And so it was decided: dinner that night at "The Cassel," a line Gomez must have used before. "We have a table, three folding chairs and an air mattress. Party central."

Gomez's accent was hard to identify. Spanish perhaps, but with a British inflection. Carla sounded British too, until she hit some vowels that sounded like some of the Kiwis he worked with. Both spoke colloquial, idiomatic

American. They could be from anywhere, thought Talbot. Or nowhere, his mother would say.

The Cassels' furniture, Gomez explained that evening, had been stuck in Jebel Ali port for the past week. "Welcome to the UAE," said Talbot.

"Welcome to most of the world, really," said Gomez. "Getting our stuff to Singapore was a complete disaster. Right, Car?"

Carla, sitting across the table, breaking up chicken biryani with a plastic fork for Jesse — they'd called in a massive order to India Palace — shuddered. "We finally had to buy all new stuff. Well, Ikea; so we didn't go completely broke. When our furniture arrived eight months later, we had to put it in storage. That's what's sitting at the port right now. We haven't seen the stuff in four years. Maybe we won't even like it any more. Maybe we'll go, 'God, who bought this crap?' " She laughed, taking Molly with her. It was nice to see his wife laughing. She'd grown quiet in the past few months. As things had turned to dust at work, she'd retreated.

"Hey, somebody help me out with these *dosas*. Talbot, you're eating like a bird." Gomez was coming around with two takeaway containers and a ladle Molly had lent them. The two older girls had long left the table, having eaten like birds themselves. What was food compared to watching *High School Musical* on the portable DVD player with someone who also thought Troy Bolton was the coolest boy in the world?

The Cassels, it seemed, had always lived next door.

Talbot arrived at work the following Sunday — a bit hung over; they'd been up late watching *Lawrence of Arabia* with Gomez and Carla — to the news that his boss and his boss's boss had been let go. "Bloodletting," said Bruce, who came into Talbot's corner office and closed the door behind him. Bruce looked scarily calm. Maybe it was the effect of the excellent South African wine — they'd blithely made their way through two bottles of red the night before — but Talbot's left leg began shaking, something that happened only after a long bike ride. "Better not look like we're plotting," said Talbot, getting up to reopen the door. "Heads down."

"We wish Mr Don Beaton and Mr Chuck Gardner the best in new indevors and there trial and cror," read the official memo. Did they make mistakes like this in Arabic? Talbot wondered. Without Don to proofread every word that went out of Amaal Special Projects, they were going to sound like illiterates.

All week they waited for their bosses' boss to show up, or at least send a memo. Najib Mubarak was an Emirati who made few personal appearances. If you spotted him in the hall, you knew to duck into your office or the washroom. He shouted, he stomped, he carried on. "Sounds like a hoedown," Chuck, who came from Oklahoma, would say. Mubarak was thirty-five, a short, fit man in the starchiest *khandoura* Talbot had ever seen parade through the office. Stanford, London School of Economics, Harvard Law. BS, MBA, LLD, brilliant son of a bitch.

So far Talbot had managed to stay out of the line of fire, but this couldn't last long with his superiors now gone. Talbot, Bruce and the three other team members kept their eyes glued to their screens, their BlackBerrys, their watches. By the end of the week, Bruce was starting to look off-kilter again, his meds, Talbot assumed, not able to keep pace with the strain.

He talked to Gomez about the situation over beers by the pool. End of April and it was already too hot to sit outside until after dark. The girls were splashing themselves silly in the shallow end, the babies were in bed, and Molly and Carla were inside making a seafood salad. "I don't want to spoil it for you," Talbot said. "You guys just got here." Gomez shook his head. "Hey, man, it could be me. We've been chasing this crisis all over. You're not safe anywhere." He looked Talbot straight in the face. "You're not alone, my friend."

"Why did they leave Singapore?" Molly asked in bed that night. They'd just made love — fast, not enough time for much to happen for her. They'd picked up speed over the years. There were reasons — kids crying out in the night, fatigue, the preoccupations of life abroad, and in the past year, days and days going by, so that when their bodies finally met it was like an emergency.

"You've heard Gomez: architectural projects drying up left and right. At least here they're still building. As for what *really* brought him here" — Talbot reached out to stroke her stomach, wanting to draw out what had been so brief — "probably the usual. The allure of the East…" Molly gave a small snort in the dark… "belly dancers, yachts, cash. Lesser men have fallen."

"I don't think he's one of those," said Molly, rolling away, leaving Talbot to another restless, twitchy night. When he finally fell asleep around 3:00 a.m., he dreamed of Oban by the sea. Something about walking up to McCaig's Tower, the replica of the Coliseum that stood on the town's highest hill. A banker named Fisher

McCaig had lobbied for its construction back in the 1890s, another equally depressed era. More than 300 men had been hired to build the huge, roofless, useless thing. Talbot's great-grandfather had sanded some of the columns. Hardly anyone visited it any more, but it still stood as one man's hope to turn his little town around.

Or one man's folly, Molly said. She didn't much care for Oban, often wondered at his attachment. "It's like a poor, tacky, Scottish version of Miami."

"Miami is already tacky," he laughed.

"My point," she said.

Molly had grown up in Edinburgh, the only surviving child of well-off parents. Two brothers had died in their mid-twenties of cystic fibrosis, the youngest only months before she met Talbot in law school. Molly was at the time madly, hopelessly in love with another man. Hopeless because the man was married and older and one of their law professors and in no way willing to overturn his life for her.

The weight of those times and his young man's conviction that they were meant to be together, that he could diminish the pain of her life to date, that she really did love him and would come to love him even more, had only begun to hit Talbot lately. What crazy hope! Dumb hope, really. This must be middle age, he sometimes thought. Gomez was good to bounce things off of, the madness at work, but also these other random, not always welcome, sightings.

Biking helped. He'd been a serious cyclist when he was younger, biking straight up to McQuaig's Tower, then hitting the thirty-kilometre stretch to Loch Lomond and back four or five times a week. Jobs, marriage, kids had compromised the old discipline. But when Talbot first arrived in Abu Dhabi—Molly and the girls had stayed in Glasgow for nine months while he sorted their new life—he bought a racing bike from someone leaving the company.

"It's keeping me sane," he told Molly over the phone, not telling her about the traffic, the speeds at which drivers took even alleys, the accidents.

Talbot had met Mathieu and Victor on the Corniche that first summer. Victor was stretching, Mathieu jogging in place, their bikes leaning against the railing. The sheikhs—father and sons—looked out benevolently, proprietarily, across the water from LuLu Island. (The twenty-storey-high portraits still gave him a start sometimes: Who *are* those guys?) Talbot was jogging that morning because he'd discovered a flat on his Italian racer. The job was too big for his repair kit and this being a Friday morning, even the Adnoc station down the street had been closed. He'd taken off at a sprint, no destination in mind.

None of the three could remember later who approached whom, but within a minute the important fact was established: they were expats on bikes. Talbot was the most experienced cyclist, so he'd be their coach. They'd meet Fridays as early as they could haul their asses out of bed and hit the empty streets.

When Gomez's furniture and belongings were finally delivered the following week, he wheeled his Japanese racer to Talbot's front door. "A beauty," Talbot said, feeling sheepish relief that his new friend's bike wasn't one of those stratospheric racers; if anything, it was a notch below his. Since things had gone pear-shaped at work, he'd watched himself channeling more ambition into the morning rides, into the care and keeping of his bike. He was thinking of buying a second one on the next trip home.

"Come out with us Friday," Talbot said.

Later, he would try to remember the look on Gomez's face: relief, worry, gratitude. "Hey, I'm just an amateur," said Gomez. "Sunday rider. Well, Friday rider here."

"We're no Olympians. Just sweaty guys on bikes," Talbot said.

This wasn't in any way true. Since meeting nearly two years earlier, the three men had each upped their personal best. And best, especially for Victor, meant ever-diminishing times. For a relentlessly relaxed Aussie, he was a demon competitor. Talbot hadn't minded stepping back a bit and letting Victor surge ahead. Mathieu was solid and steady, keeping them anchored and laughing with his filthy French jokes. They'd become fast boys, bad boys, on bikes. Gomez, if he was any good at all, might make a natural fourth.

But Carla wasn't happy about it when the subject came up over drinks by the pool that weekend. "These streets are a bloody nightmare! Every day there's a story in the paper about someone getting mowed down. You're not riding out there." She was normally so easy, so accommodating.

"We take off early," Talbot reassured her. "No one's out at that hour."

"You are," said Carla, who was balancing Jesse on one leg while trying to drink a beer.

"We're just blokes on bikes," said Talbot. "Blokes with helmets, I might add."

"Yeah, yeah, I know what happens when a man mounts a bike," she said, clearly trying to lighten things up. But she gave Gomez a warning look.

"More later," said Gomez and everyone dropped the subject.

Molly had said not a word, not unusual for Molly these days, but Talbot realized that she had never objected to his riding here, never voiced concerns over the hell-bent drivers, the fearsome possibilities. She just let him be. He should be grateful for that. He should.

Mubarak appeared unannounced at Talbot's office door the next week. There was no time to clear away the muffin and coffee, no time to quickly text the other team members: *guess who's cming 4 brkfst?* Mubarak, tall from this angle, gestured for Talbot to stay seated. "May I?" he asked as Talbot struggled to his feet anyway. He hoped last night's Beaujolais wasn't coming through the perspiration pumping now from pits and forehead.

"Sir?" (Talbot had never known what to call Mubarak, Don and Chuck having conveniently made direct conversation with him unnecessary.) Talbot offered the chair that didn't have anything on it.

"Call me Najib," Mubarak said, seating himself and turning a beneficent smile on Talbot that only made more heat surge through his trunk.

Sinking back into his desk chair—should he get up and move the pile of papers and sit next to Mubarak, man to man?—Talbot felt his leg begin to jump. Better to stay where he was.

"I'll cut to the chase, as you Americans say," Mubarak said. "You stay, everybody else goes. You decide when and how to tell them, but by the end of the month I want their exit visas. You…" and Mubarak breathed in and stretched out one sandalled foot — "sissy sandals," Zoë called the white patent-leather slip-ons worn by local men — "will assume the positions of Don and Chuck. You will be compensated, though of course you won't be making *both* their salaries" — Mubarak chuckled at this — "since the whole point of this exercise, painful for everyone, I assure you, is to cut costs." He said the last two words as if they might actually cut through something resistant, like metal. "But make no mistake, you will be compensated. After all, you will be doing the job of two. And, I must add, hopefully a better job than those two did."

They shook hands — "Congratulations! We'll talk after the redundancies are put through," Mubarak said — and then he was gone, leaving a trail of questions Talbot had been too stunned to even think of. It was one thing to be doing the project managing of Don and Chuck. But what about the work the others were responsible for? What kind of a team would it be now? And better *how* than his predecessors? Don and Chuck were excellent attorneys, consummate professionals. Both legs began to bounce.

For a few days Talbot said nothing to anyone — not to Molly, not even to the other team members. Every time he glanced at their strained, expectant faces, he'd resolve to put everyone out of their misery. He couldn't even make eye contact with Bruce, who'd taken to extreme hours, coming in before Talbot and leaving after him, as if this might stave off employment disaster. This couldn't go on indefinitely, or even one day longer, but still Talbot held off.

Gomez was sitting by the pool when he came home Thursday afternoon. It was three days after Mubarak's edict, the beginning of what they called a weekend here and Talbot couldn't take another hour in the fearful quiet that now reigned in Amaal Special Projects. "Migraine," he'd told Bruce, packing up at four. Gomez kept hours like Talbot's most days—out the door by seven, home at eight or nine, blood-pressure hours. Something about the way Gomez was sitting on the pool chair—he didn't jump up, expression glad and open, his trademark greeting—and the fact he was still wearing his suit trumpeted bad news.

"Gomez?"

Gomez glanced up, smiled, almost, then turned back to face the pool. Some kid had left a Barney blow-up raft out there. It listed slightly in the warm water, very purple.

"They got me first, old man," he said. "Didn't even unpack all the boxes."

"What?" Talbot said stupidly.

"She'll leave now. 'If this job doesn't pan out,' she said, 'I'm gone.'"

Talbot moved to sit next to him, but Gomez got up. "I'm not good company," he said and walked to his villa, closing the French doors behind him.

Talbot didn't say anything to Molly that evening—now there were two pieces of information withheld—waiting for her to acknowledge something. She and Carla seemed to be getting closer. Women talked, didn't they? But Molly was her busy, efficient self, focusing all her attention on supper. Alicel, the nanny, was off for her usual day and a half, staying with her sister downtown, so it took longer to get the kids settled. Zoë was grumpy, itchy from a sunburn, and arguing with Molly about what pajamas to wear. Listening to them from downstairs, he hoped it wasn't early-onset hormones. He hoped they weren't spoiling the kids by having a nanny. He hoped Gomez was okay, that Carla would stay, that Bruce wouldn't have a complete breakdown, that he could keep this thing together.

He kept waiting to say something. But with the kids in bed, he and Molly settled into the sectional and the silliness of a *Coronation Street* episode, part of the boxed set his mother had given them the Christmas before. Molly seemed relaxed, almost chatty. She was looking forward, she told him, to coffee with some new Irish friends the next week. "I'm dragging Carla with me. She normally hates these ladies' things, but she needs to start meeting people." Still, in bed later, she would let him only stroke her breasts while he stroked himself, the diminishing returns of their love life.

Talbot was pulling on his biking shorts the next morning when he heard a subdued knocking at the front door. Gomez—bloodshot eyes the only sign of yesterday's crisis—stood on one leg, the other tucked up high behind his buttocks. His racer gleamed behind him on the walkway.

"Let's go," he said.

It was especially misty that morning, the humidity almost visible as they streamed down Khaleej al Arabi.

Talbot was relieved to see that Gomez wasn't half bad, using his long legs to advantage. With a few more weeks, he could almost be at par with Mathieu. When they stopped for a water break, Gomez was nearly purple with exertion, but his eyes were bright. "Hey, man, you're going to best me," Mathieu said, pouring water over his head. "You're wicked good," said Victor. This would be good for Gomez, thought Talbot. He'd be able to negotiate another job here, no question. Architects with his credentials were still in demand. Just the week before, Talbot had brokered a contract with an architect-engineer for a five-lane bridge from one of the ruling family's palaces to one of their private islands. They'd laughed over the impossibly complex design — three engineers had already been fired from the project, started five years before. It would be a bridge used by few, perhaps only one, though that one was adamant it be built no matter how many engineers crashed and burned in its execution.

Gomez fell as they made the turn onto 19th. Talbot had meant to warn him about the speed bump, but had forgotten, then remembered, then thought it was too mother hennish to say anything. Of course, Gomez would see it. At least they weren't up to speed at that point, the bump slowing him down, but Gomez hit the pavement hard, careening right, onto his shoulder.

"Fine, fine, I'm fine," Gomez kept telling them. He'd stood right away to show them how fine he was, but by the way he was holding his right arm, Talbot knew he wasn't. A lone cab, probably coming back from an early airport run, spotted them and took Talbot and Gomez to a clinic back on Khaleej, which then sent them by ambulance to Al Noor Hospital. "Dislocated shoulder.

Big deal. It could have been worse," Gomez kept saying to Carla, who had turned into Molly. Silent.

By the end of the next week, they were gone. "No point in staying," Gomez told Talbot. "She doesn't want to and it's easier just to pack up at this point." They were going back to Singapore where they still had friends and work contacts "and a good physio," Gomez laughed. "See where greed got me?"

By the end of the week after that, Talbot's team was gone too. It had been easy, too easy, to hand out the bad news. No one had freaked. "We knew anyway," said Bruce, who was going back to Aberdeen. He actually looked better than he had in a long while. Every time in those last days when Talbot's BlackBerry would signal an incoming text—Mubarak had taken to texting twenty to thirty times a day: Had he found any Emirati replacements yet? Bruce would throw Talbot a look of pity.

But Molly's months of silence were over. The day of Gomez's bike accident she talked half the night. The morning Talbot told her what had gone down at work, he'd had to stay home until noon. "You leave for work now, I'll be on a plane tonight," she said. He was stunned by the magnitude of her misery.

"Are you happy with anything?" he asked at some point. "Does anything about me please you?"

It took too long for her to say: "You're a good father."

She held him responsible for the accident and for the family's departure. "The one bright spot," she said tearfully.

"I didn't fire Gomez," he said. "You can't put that on me."

In the middle of one of their grievance sessions, the doorbell rang. It was Deborah, their Canadian neighbour. "I know we kept talking about it," she said to Talbot, who'd been stunned by the sudden sunlight, the rush of heat. There was a world out there. "But we really would like to have you over for dinner. Would Saturday work?"

"Tell her no," said Molly, when he went back upstairs.

As the next week inched by, her honesty ramped up. "We were thinking of having an affair, you know. We talked about it. I wanted to."

And when Talbot, too hurt to answer, just looked at her, she repeated: "Gomez. I wanted Gomez."

Later, when Molly was in the shower, he surprised her, taking her standing up, something he'd never done before. And in that fury, she was almost his.

COFFEE

"If I never hear another British accent in my life, it'll be too soon," Cherry says, and our table ripples with laughter. "I mean it. One more 'brilliant,' one more 'forward planning'—like there's any other kind of planning?—one more 'crikey' and I'll crack. You don't count, Annie March, honestly you don't."

Annie raises her skinny latte. "I *am* a Brighton girl," she says cheekily and tugs a white gauze blouse over her massive chest. "Shelf tits," we called them back home. "And I hate to break it to you, luv, but *crikey's* Aussie lingo."

"Well, I'm tired of them too," says Cherry. "We're the only ones who've got the accent right."

"That is debatable," says Annie in her plummiest voice. "And don't forget: We arrived on these forsaken shores way before y'all."

"Twenty years in Pittsburgh," drawls Dorothy. "Come on, Annie, you're a Yank like the rest of us." She leans into the table. "Okay, just tell me what we're going to do about those damn Democrats and their stupid health bill."

"Say, Obama, who's yo' mama?" Cherry wags her head, sounding every bit like Queen Latifa. Everybody laughs again, but no one really wants to talk boring old health care, stalled bills and congressional committees. We've left that long behind. And probably, if we're honest, we were never all *that* interested.

"Marisol got into the gin while we were in Dubai this weekend," says Dorothy, looking around the table. "Bottle was down an inch."

"Why don't you just fire her?" says Maureen from the far end, waving to Rosie, our usual waitress. Maureen always arrives late for our coffee mornings. After ten years, the Filipino wait staff at La Brioche makes sure there's a chair for her.

"Hi, Mum," says Rosie. She always has a big smile for us. We make sure to leave her an extra dirham or two. Spread the wealth, right?

"Really, Dorothy, you've been more than patient," says Annie.

"Hand Marisol off to another family. Let them deal with her," says Cherry. "I know, I know. I'm bitch incarnate. But I don't have problems like those. Let them know there are consequences, honey. Like jail."

But we don't really like talking about jail ever since Ronni's husband, Steve, spent a week in the prison out near Al Ain. Some gossip cuts too close to home. Ronni doesn't come to our little gatherings anymore. Cherry, who lives in the villa next door, says Ronni's family is thinking about going back to New Jersey. "Kind of had it with the UAE. Steve's looking into other opportunities," says Cherry.

Maureen snorts. The rest of us look deep into our lattes.

When we first came to Abu Dhabi — Cherry and Dorothy fourteen years ago, Maureen a year later, Annie and me the next…point being we're long-timers—it was all different. The glory years, Cherry calls them. "We reigned. We rocked. Of course, the Brits were always trying to rock faster and harder."

Still, there was plenty for all. Plenty of spacious, two-storey apartments facing the Corniche, plenty of parking for the Mercedes and BMWs. Nannies weren't so mouthy, just grateful to have a job. You were considered crazy if you paid them more than $200 a month. "You're not running a charity!" we used to tell some noble newcomer who wanted to pay at-home rates. ("The girls don't expect it. Don't go starting a revolution!") You could drive into Spinney's for frozen pizza and peanut butter or to pick up your dry cleaning, and you didn't drive round and round looking for a parking spot. They didn't have that eyesore of a recycling bin out back either, the brainchild of some granola-type from Vermont who hadn't considered it would be overflowing with wine bottles come Sunday morning. Weekends we'd golf, brunch at the Sheraton or the Royal Meridien. And not for 300 dirhams per either. *Yallah*, it was great.

Ronni was a newcomer compared to the rest of us. She still had that my-what-an-interesting-place naïveté. She was a soft person, a nice person, the first to offer help. Naturally we talked about her when she wasn't there. Worse, we laughed at her. Did you see that hippie get-up she wore at Brice's birthday party? Did you hear what she said about Sarah Palin? (We agreed: closet Dem.) Did you know they're paying their Filipina 3,000 dirhams a month?

This last we saw as a major infraction. A thousand dollars versus 250? We laughed but we were pissed. Ronni said it was only fair, that Steve made enough money and that Jenny made her life possible. "I have a me again," she said. With three kids who even she admitted were a handful (Brice, the youngest, had behaviour issues) and a husband who didn't do much around the house, Ronni called Jenny The Gift. The Gift got more days off per week (two) than any of our maids, a higher salary and an excess of verbal appreciation that made Cherry and Maureen shriek. "Stop saying 'thank you' so much!" Cherry said once after Ronni hosted a coffee morning. "It's her job, for chrissake!" Leave it to Cherry to say what we all thought.

But now it had all changed again. Everything changed: one year radically different than the one before; one month full of people and parties, the next so empty you could see clear to the bottom. One day everything bright and right, the next everything so wrong you could hardly lift your head from the sweaty pillow. Steve got on the bad side of management at the newspaper by trumpeting his journalistic principles. And then there was the incident in the roundabout: "Who would be crazy enough to give anyone the finger here?" he told anyone who'd listen. But no one did and Steve spent that week out in Al Ain and now they were looking to leave.

Steve and I had a thing once. Not a huge thing compared to some of our friends. Maureen had a mini-breakdown when their golf pro went back to his wife in New Zealand and Annie ate her way to a size 16 while her husband went ape shit over his Lebanese secretary a few years back. Yet here we are — calmer, wiser, menopausal — still friends downing lattes every Sunday morning.

Steve and I do talk sometimes, so I knew he and Ronni were thinking of going home. He'd called a few days before from the golf course as I was cruising Al Wahda Mall, no specific purchase in mind.

"You always were a good listener," he said after we'd chatted a bit. I was standing outside Victoria's Secret. Inside I could see a local woman and two younger women, daughters probably. A trio of *abayas*. The mother held up something lacy and skimpy and the younger girl, *shayla* slipping, doubled over laughing.

Steve told me about Ronni's crying jags, Brice's mood jumps. Everything that wasn't quite right before his incarceration got amped up after, he said. "Hey, what'd you think of Obama's latest caper? Universal health care, what a crock. We're going to end up like Canada. That's one thing I dread about going back. Those guys are in the White House now."

"But, hey, no more Brits," I offered.

"Brilliant," he said and we laughed.

> <

The ladies, they go home now, taking needles and puzzles. They try so hard, smile so big. Sometimes I want to say, Relax! We fine.

They come: Sondra and Beth and Ronni—funny name for girl!—every Tuesday in morning time. The embassy give us hot room upstairs from bedrooms and we see ladies turn pink and sweat. Poor them. "How do you stand it?" Ronni ask me today. She tie her hair up in elastic. I hate to say, but she look better with it regular. She has pretty hair, pretty eyes. But mostly her heart.

"Okay, Loissa, what shall we do today?" She always say that, her teeth white shiny. I think she is maybe forty, no grey. Sometime I will ask her. I like her, she like me. I think other girls little jealous, but she is nice to every single Filipina (maybe in the world?) so no one fuss.

She teach me crochet. I already know, but I want Ronni be proud, so I act like I know not even one thing, how hook goes, how you hold little baseball of yarn. "Like this!" she say, and she show and I do. "Quick study!" she say and looks like maybe cry. I joke, I laugh. I tell her, we okay really and we thank you so much. Maybe Ronni already sad and we make her more sadder.

Lunch they go. While crochet, my stomach hurt from empty. Fish and rice, all time fish and rice. We like pork, tofu, plantains, melon, too, but only fish and rice. We have fish sometimes on tip of bad. Smelly. "No money!" Embassy men say and shrug, fat Filipinos with passports. They can come and go, go and come. In shelter we are 300 Filipinas. All run from bad employer. But now no place to run. Now no passport, no visa, no money, no home.

I go back to bed after lunch. Only place that is mine. I be here so long, I graduate to bottom bunk! Honour, says Carmela. But she giggle. Sure, honour live in room with eight bunkbed. New girls sleep on roof on blanket. Head to head, toe to toe. Too many blanket. Too many crying Filipina. Embassy say nothing. Our country need this country. No fuss, just quiet, quiet. Embassy keep us Filipina. We are safe, but we are lost.

I nap, dream of my house. Fish in dream too, pretty funny. No escape the fish! Me and little Manny, and Rodriguez and Mom, everyone at table. I try cook fish, but nothing happen. Big fish, gold colour, but stay raw.

Then Rodriguez laugh and laugh and take me into bed and love me like he use to.

"You cry." Paulina shake me.

"Rodriguez," I say. Bed on top blocks ceiling, can see nothing.

"Sex good?" say Paulina and laugh big.

I hurt for that man, that boy. And then Carmela come and Emeline and new quiet one, Daisy. They smile and smile and come close so we all under top bed like tent.

"I make coffee," say Carmela and slap my cheek.

> <

Eiman likes the ones with rubies on the heel. They go all the way down, a dozen on each four-inch spike. "I want those," she says, pointing. I say, no, too much bling, and she gives me her sour Victoria Beckham face. We're not looking at the same magazine. I have *Seventeen*; she has *Vogue*. Because she is five years older, she gets the serious fashion magazine. Now that she's getting married to our cousin, Salman, she is the only female in the household anyone cares about. My nanny listens to her more than me.

"It's going to her head," I say to Mother. "She's acting like a sheikha." What I mean is bitch, but Mother won't tolerate that language from us, though she uses the word plenty with the maids.

Mother has come down earlier than usual to the breakfast room. Now that she's decided to get her degree ("Art history, what is art history?" my father said. "Why do you need to know this?"), her hours are more like ours, school hours. Her *abaya* is open over the size zero jeans she bought in London, her hair up in a sequin clip, face already perfectly made up. No one believes she is almost forty.

She claps her hands. "Fatima, why are you standing around looking like an idiot?" Fatima, tiny in her pink headscarf and blue uniform, slippers quickly out of the room. Mother turns back to the table, sizing us up. I slump lower over my magazine. "Sit up straight!" she thumps Eiman on the back.

"Hey!" growls Eiman. "I'm the good daughter, remember? I'm the one you love." And she gives me a get-even look.

"I love all my children, you know that," says Mother.

"Even Rashid?" I ask.

"Even Rashid." She sighs, thinking maybe how our little brother still wets his bed though he is ten, how he's made four nannies quit. She snaps her fingers and Sami, one of the drivers, comes into the breakfast room.

"Madame?" he says.

Mother looks at her watch. "Al Zaabi Bakery at 10:00 a.m. Pick up the *maamoul*. Tell them we pay next week." She waves him away. "I wish these people spoke better Arabic. You'd think after twenty years, thirty years, they would learn."

She's been saying this for as long as I can remember, even about Sami, who speaks fine Arabic. And it's only gotten worse, with all of us — me, Eiman, Rashid, Hassan and Sultan — speaking English not just to our nannies, but to each other. "Our language is dying!" Mother likes to say, looking tragic.

But the preservation of Arabic is not at the top of her agenda this morning. Ellen, her professor at the university, is coming over for a tutoring session.

"I didn't know professors made house calls," says Eiman, flipping through pages of *Vogue* ads. She's preparing her exams for a degree in business at Al Ain University. She can't wait to move out. Of course, marriage will take care of that too.

"Your father talked to the president of the university," Mother says, picking up a small corner of unbuttered toast and frowning at it.

"So you don't even have to show up for class?" I ask. I've already caused a few disturbances among my friends. "A degree is useless if we don't earn it," I keep telling them. "For sure it's useless out *there*." But most of them don't care. They'll get the degree, marry and never, ever work here or out there.

Fatima's back with a pot of coffee, a platter of sliced *halloumi* and cut-up cucumbers and tomatoes.

"Where's the bread?" I ask.

But Mother shoos her off and Fatima goes back to her station near the kitchen door, where she will wait if we need her. Her face is usually a smooth blank, but this morning her eyebrows are tensed, like something hurts.

"You need to eat a lot less bread, Asma. I mean it." And Mother fixes me with the look that used to intimidate me. I look away, out the window where the gardening staff is trimming a date palm. Our head gardener stands below one of the ladders, waving his arms and shaking his head. Eiman gets up, her magazine sliding to the floor. She doesn't pick it up. "I told Salman I'd call him between classes. You know how he gets if I don't call," and she rolls her eyes at Mother.

I will go to university. I will work. I will eat what I want.

> <

After coffee with the girls at La Brioche, I take a cab to Marina Mall, drift into a couple of shops, buy another purse, a birthday card for Russ (fifty-six next week), then wait outside in the usual line-up for a cab. The sun feels dangerous. A small plane with a long streamer makes obscenely loud loops over the Corniche, plunging and climbing. Just watching makes me queasy.

Two local women and their Indonesian maid, her arms full of shopping bags, nab the next cab, my cab. "Well, that was rude!" I say and they glare at me. The Indian couple behind eye me uneasily and gesture elaborately when the next cab pulls up. "Yours! Please!" I can still hear the plane as we pull away. Practice for an air show probably. Either that or we're being attacked by the Iranians. "Crystal Tower," I tell the driver. "Now." He keeps a nervous eye on me in the rear-view mirror.

But home, I can't settle. Russ is in Oman on business until Thursday. It's too late in the morning for golf, too hot even for me who's learned to play a reasonable game in 100-degree heat. I think about Skyping Chris in New York, but even my workaholic-hedge-fund-analyst son won't be up at this hour. And I can't call Annie or Cherry and say, "Hey, let's meet at Dome for lunch." We've just had coffee.

I download shots of our last trip—Russ surprised me for our thirtieth with a long weekend in Casablanca. I go online to see what my darling Tea Party's up to this week, then log twenty minutes on the treadmill. Dora's left her signature rice and chicken dish on the counter as she always does on Sundays. But all I want is bread and cheese, a nectarine. I eat standing up. And then, nothing. There is nothing to do. No one is waiting for me anywhere.

> <

This no place for free-loaders. When I hear that word, I laugh. English has good words. People free of loads sound like my employers. Not royals like family of Carmela, thank you, my God. But people with so much money they could pay all Philippines' debt. Whole country, serious! But not enough to pay me.

My old boss, she never nice one minute. Agency think good match because we same age, thirty-one. She very beautiful, very rich, very bad. Hard to believe someone be like this.

One morning I am up at five like every day, washing cars. Mercedes, two. Land Rover, two. Plus Sir's Maserati. Hot already, sun beating headache into me. Employer, she come out, inspect. She find tiny wrapper, maybe from driver, on back seat of Land Rover. March over, stick paper in my face, then slap two sides. When I cry, she call me name. She call me hundred name in two years, but worse is Stupid. I am many things, not all good. But not stupid. One piece paper! This happens!

Carmela much more worse. She happy now. Okay, more happy. None of us happy. (I lie little bit to Ronni.) Carmela work in Crown Prince palace. He not bad man, well, she never, ever meet Prince. But Carmela is nanny to nephew of Prince. Little boy who is monster. He kick her, he poke her. One time he set her clothes on fire while she sleep. Devil boy. But nobody believe her, even when see burn uniform. Blame her. Then much worse, no pay for five month. Her family in Philippines get no food, no rent. Middle of night she catch bakery truck at palace. Please, she beg driver. Otherwise boy kill me. He very scared, but good Muslim. He drive here.

Carmela, my friend. Strong lady. Make good coffee too.

> <

Ellen is small and pretty in a plain sort of way. You could never imagine her naked. She wears a beige Ann Taylor suit, nothing haute, and arrives carrying two bags, a dark leather laptop case and a gift bag from Patchi, the good guest, someone who thinks she's clued into our ways: *Always bring chocolates if an Emirati invites you to their home.*

Fatima shows her in, but doesn't have enough English, and Mother must be upstairs changing again, so I introduce myself.

"Oh, yes," she says. "You must be so excited about university. And your upcoming wedding too."

"I'm Asma, the other daughter," I say. "Sit down please."

"I'm so sorry," says Ellen, and I can tell Mother never mentioned she had two daughters. "What are you studying?" She looks around for the appropriate couch to sit on.

"English, geography, history, business studies, French, maths, physical education, information technology, UAE social studies, Koran…" I'm growing breathless, but she did ask.

"Of course," she says, sinking finally into a couch. She looks even smaller now and her face is tight with trying to say the next correct thing. "High school. I remember those subjects. Not UAE social studies, of course. Though it sounds more interesting than learning about the Pilgrims."

"Pilgrims?" I say. "I didn't know you had pilgrims."

"Our original settlers in America. Back in the 1500s. Or maybe it was the 1600s. I kind of forget…" and she trails off. "They were like our Bedouin." Now she looks really doubtful. "Well, maybe not. History really isn't my field of expertise."

"I thought you taught history." I know exactly how this sounds.

"Art history," says Ellen. "Ancient art history. Greek. Roman." I watch her try to regain her authority. "Is your mother here?"

"Upstairs. She's late. Get used to it." I know I've now crossed into obvious rudeness. Ellen opens her case and sets up her laptop on the coffee table. She avoids my eyes, but keeps stealing looks at her watch, a hot-pink Swatch that says: I may be in a business suit, but I'm fun. Fatima pads in with trays of sweets—we keep them in cold storage perfectly arranged in pyramids for guests. "Oh, my goodness!" Ellen says. Her eyes are jumping out of her face. Fatima smiles slightly. Mother has told her not to smile too much because that draws attention. Ellen takes a bite of *maamoul*, swallows, then tucks the rest, when she thinks I'm not looking, into her napkin. She doesn't like our pastries. They're really big *maamoul*, Baba's favourite.

Mother sweeps in, hands stretched out to her teacher. One holds her new iPhone. Her *abaya* is open.

Underneath she's wearing skinny black jeans with zippers halfway up her shins and a clingy white cashmere sweater. In her ears, dangles of freshwater pearls. On her feet, the same heels Eiman pointed to in the magazine. Where did she get those?

"Sit! Sit!" she says, waving because Ellen has stood. "I'm a bit late, aren't I? Please forgive a naughty student. But I am here now, ready to work!"

Ellen glances at me, but when I don't move, she angles the laptop toward Mother. "I thought we'd start with a lesson on aesthetics. It's a good place to begin."

"I'm sure you're right," says Mother, switching off her mobile, but not before giving a quick check for messages.

Fatima glides in. Her hands shake slightly as she holds a platter of savoury pastries in front of Ellen. "Oh, my goodness!" Ellen says again, but seems unable to choose. Fatima hovers.

"Try this." Mother points to a mountain of meat pies. "*Sfiha*. Very good meat. The best."

"I actually don't eat meat," says Ellen. "But I will have some coffee. I love Arabic coffee. Oh, I almost forgot," and she reaches down to the Patchi bag. "I brought a little something."

"*Habibti*! How kind! You Americans are so generous." Mother hands the box of chocolates—large, Ellen's spent a lot—to Fatima, who now has to place the pastry tray on the coffee table. Mother cocks her head slightly toward the kitchen. These will be added to the offerings in cold storage. Chocolates make the rounds from family to family, guest to guest. A giant circuit, a grand tour of recycled sweets, especially during *iftars* and Eid. But Ellen will never know this. She thinks we'll share them tonight as a family, have them for dessert with our coffee, comment on her excellent choice: "She has a real sense of Arabian hospitality, that one!"

> <

"Stars & Stripes Forever" plays from my purse. A bit of home, Russ said, when he programmed it as my ring tone. I've been waiting for something to happen all day, all week. And here's Cherry, incoherent.

"I'm so glad you're there!" she cries. "No one else is home. No one is ever home in this awful place."

Her husband on that killer stretch of the E11? Bad news from her son in Dallas? A scary mammogram? What?

"They've gone. They've fucking gone."

Steve just called her from the airport. "'It's the only way out, my love. Got in too deep,' that's what he told me. They pulled a runner. They pulled a fucking runner," and Cherry begins to wail. I'm thinking: my love? *My love?*

"But we'd heard they might be leaving." I could say many things right now; this seems the safest.

"Not like this. This isn't a proper goodbye. We were going away this weekend. To that new resort out near Liwa, facing the Empty Quarter. Just the two of us."

"You and Steve. And he was going to pay? With what? Qasr Al Sarab rooms go for $1,000 a night." It's the nastiest thing I can think to say.

"Don't get all moral on me," says Cherry. She isn't crying any more. "Steve told me about you. And you were so chummy with Ronni."

"Come over," I say.

"I'll never, ever see him again," Cherry sobs.

"Just get a cab, okay?"

> <

Ellen is still on the first slide of her PowerPoint when Sami arrives with the boxes of *maamoul*. Mother waves him toward the kitchen storage room and turns her eyes back to the laptop, but I can see Ellen is bothered. She keeps looking at me. Maybe she thinks I am in the way, that I am intruding on her lesson. But I have nothing else to do this morning and this is not as boring as most things.

"Plato had a great influence on the field of aesthetics," Ellen is saying, when there is a scuffle behind the swinging door to the kitchen. She stops and waits but when there is nothing else, Ellen clicks to her next slide. "The four elements, Madame Qubaisi, these are the cornerstones of modern aesthetics."

Sami hurries in. "Madame, it is Fatima." Mother looks more annoyed than concerned, but follows him. There's loud conversation behind the door, during which Ellen goes onto the next slide, checks her watch again.

"What happened?" I ask Mother when she comes back, but she ignores me.

"Please excuse the interruption," she says to Ellen. "You know housemaids: always a drama! They should be paying us!"

Ellen murmurs something, but I can see she's a bit put off. She skips to the next slide. And then comes the sound I've heard all my life, familiar as the *muezzin* calling everyone to prayer: the sound of two hands clapping.

"You'll have to excuse me," Mother says, standing. "My husband." And she's gone.

"She won't be back," I tell Ellen, who looks like she's just seen a camel trot through the breakfast room.

"Why didn't he just come in?" She's so stunned, she's not watching what she's saying, is forgetting the delicate footwork around our cultural differences. "If he needed her, why didn't he just...?" But now she's heard herself. Her whole body shrinks. She closes her laptop without turning it off.

"The measure of a man is what he does with power," I recite. It's the only quote I know from Plato. I like it. It feels subversive.

Ellen sits back against the pillows, though she doesn't reopen her laptop. "How do you live here?" she asks and I see that she really, really wants to know.

If she really, really listens I will tell her about my friends and the things we do, how sometimes we dress up in our brothers' *khandouras* and *ghutras* and sneak out, pretending to be boys. How sometimes we even kiss each other. How we will do almost anything to feel alive.

> <

Back home they do not know. They keep coming. Why? Money. Say goodbye kids and husband. Mother, father, everyone.

I go Hong Kong first. Crazy Americans who got four boys. Go UAE, cousin tell me. Big money. I pray Blessed Virgin Mary and get message: Go!

First, think: Bad, but not *so* bad. Then Madame begin breaking me. Hands shake, can't sleep. So tired cannot carry baby without feel very scared. If I drop her—she big baby, so heavy—I be dead. Madame make me write every thing I do: iron shirt, stove on, baby nap. Every thing in book: start time, stop time. I say, Madame, instead of write, let me do. Take too much time! She hit me. Only bad nannies say no, she say.

Every day more tired. Cars, kids, but keep go. Then the Baba touch me in my private place. No, I say. No money, he say. We go like that. Three month. One morning cannot get out of my bed. "I am breaking," I say to Mother Mary. I pray and pray. Go! she say.

Night I jump from window. Not far, but ankle crack, so I crawl to street. Cab come. No money, so he want sex. I wait another cab. He bring me to embassy. Some good people.

Carmela know my story.

"Hey," she say, when she think I am sad.

"Hey," I say back.

"Crochet," she say and bring out yarn Ronni give. "I make you hat," she say.

"Hat?" I laugh. "Maybe snow here!"

"Yeah." She laugh. "Maybe snow."

> <

We don't end up talking about Steve at all.

"Remember that crazy couple from, I can't remember where, Manchester? No, Liverpool. They used to throw these huge bashes on their yacht, hire half the waiters in Abu Dhabi," says Cherry. "I saw Elton John there once."

"I think it was Tom Jones," I say.

"Were you there too?" Cherry's eyes are swollen, but she's got her legs tucked under her on my loveseat and her hand wrapped around a glass of wine. I've refilled it twice, will need to put on a pot of coffee to sober her up. "I can't remember. We go back and back, don't we?"

That was the party where Russ drank too much too fast and had to take a cab home. I'll be fine, I told him. Never mind about me. It was one of those half and half parties, half Brits and half the rest of us, a stir-fry of Germans and Aussies, South Africans and Yanks. Expat nation. With enough booze and enough time, national rivalries always broke down. "We are the world, we are the people..." At some blurry point a bunch of us ended up on the sand, ankle deep in it, the Gulf glittering just beyond, arms around strangers' shoulders, singing and swaying.

"God, I love this place," Steve said. He'd taken me to a hidden spot on the beach. The others had gone back inside. We made love crouching against the outside wall of the neighbouring villa. It was so good, I cried.

OASIS, 1972

And so we've become a country. The United Arab Emirates, a long name for a small place. With the British pulling out of the Trucial States at the end of '71, Sheikh Zayed rallied the tribes of the seven regions, a monumental task considering the old grudges, blood lines, feuds over land and resources. What a strain on Baba Zayed as he brokered a deal that would have broken any other man. He has been less among us this year, as he travelled from emirate to emirate, negotiating, listening, compromising.

With his mother, Sheikha Salama, gone since a year, he also comes less frequently to Oasis Hospital. He used to visit her nearly every day; his brother, Sheikh Shakhbut, less often. But one evening they were here together. The Sheikha was failing, but she was so happy to have her sons with her that she sat up straight as a young girl against the pillows of the low sofa. The *majlis* was flickering with candlelight, the incense especially pungent. It was from the Sheikha that I learned about Arabian perfumes—*oud, ambar, zafran*, musk, sandalwood. I absorbed so much sitting with her during her stays in the hospital. She would sometimes laugh at my Arabic and correct my mistakes, though after ten years, I've become fluent enough to teach newcomers at the hospital. When I use some of her phrases now, Arab companions will ask, "Where did you learn to say *that*?"

Sheikha Salama would be so proud to see what her country has become. If she had lived just a year and a bit longer she might have stood by her son's side as he raised the new flag—stripes of red, green, white and black—on December 2, 1971. But even more, I think she would have been overjoyed that her sons were able to negotiate the change in leadership without bloodshed, so unlike the violence when her husband took the throne from *his* brother. The Sheikha even made her sons take an oath of fidelity that they would never resort to fratricide. If Zayed is now seen as the father of the country, it is in no small part due to their mother.

Shakhbut is a good man, but so tied to the old ways that he was nearly paralyzed when oil and fortune gushed from the sea beds. I've been told he even blocked the first attempts to build a hospital in Abu Dhabi back in '56. The year I arrived, crates and crates of medical equipment and construction material sent by the British were left unpacked on the beaches of Abu Dhabi. Meanwhile, Shakhbut and his family were treated abroad, doctors even flown in from Britain when Sheikha Salama fell ill. God love her, but God bless her people too. They also deserve the best care.

In the end, Zayed, the family agreed, would be the stronger, more fearless leader. The Brits, too, were happy to leave their once-protectorate in such capable hands.

But that last evening, all that history was like water flowing through a *falaj*. It was just a mother and her sons, laughing, talking, drinking coffee. The men began to sing *qaseedas*, old Bedu ballads. I'd heard Sheikh Zayed sing before — he sings even when driving — but that night his voice was especially rich, deep as a well at day's end. No one enjoyed it more than their mother. Her sons were singing for her.

It's almost impossible to recognize the hospital now. The original palm branch and mud-brick buildings, plus the twenty cement-block rooms built in my second year, are still used, but we've added a labour and delivery suite, an X-ray building, and a cold-storage basement for medicines. Later this year, another ten patient rooms — with private baths and air conditioning, such luxury — will be built. And, despite my preference for sleeping outside, we will soon be getting new staff housing.

The town of Al Ain is growing too, with super-markets, banks and travel agents springing up. Still, the centre of social life is here in the hospital, with some folks coming in every day just to chat. They actively seek our help now. There is less TB, less malnutrition, less ignorance. And healthier babies. We're also seeing the kinds of emergencies one finds at home: car accidents, injuries from machinery. One night last week, a Volvo roared down a sand dune, injuring two members of a Bedu family sleeping below, the dune their shelter from blowing sand. When I arrived in Al Ain, you could count the number of cars on one hand. Now there are 8,000 cars in Abu Dhabi emirate alone.

The country is being swept into the modern world at last. But who could have dreamed it would happen so fast? No man sauntering along on camel from Al Ain to Abu Dhabi in 1960 could have imagined that in a decade he'd be driving a Mercedes on a highway and arriving in less than two hours. Or that he would no longer be living with extended family in a little *areesh* hut, but in a spacious villa with every convenience.

When I worry about what might get lost in the name of progress, I look at my friends, my patients, even at Sheikh Zayed himself. I look around me—at the palms and the dunes, at the Bedu men who greet each other by touching noses. I feel the biblical rhythm of life. The desert is still home, will always be home, despite asphalt and airplanes, oil rigs and steel girders. No amount of money will erase who these people are. The sky, the heat, the emptiness will keep us rooted.

19TH & KHALEEJ AL ARABI

They'd been heading out that Friday morning, the humidity a damp haze at 5:00 a.m., Victor in front of him, pedalling in his frenzied, unorthodox form, Talbot yelling back to them both, into the dimness: Switch! Mathieu surging forward, Victor slowing enough to be passed.

Mathieu had seen it so many times, though once had been enough: their shifting line as they drafted into Talbot's slipstream, their controlled zig-zag down Khaleej al Arabi, the July sky lightening over mosques and tall cranes. It was a drill he'd known since the lycée in Lyon, since crazy coach Gervais took a riding switch to their sweaty legs. He'd been amazed that his calves could sweat like that, amazed that pumping his legs up and down a million trillion times could carry him so far. And not just down the road, Gervais would tell the panting, doubled-over boys. He'd been a philosopher, that Gervais.

Sandrine and the girls were in France when it happened. These were their summers now: his wife and twin daughters walking into the Languedoc village for croissants each morning, Mathieu grabbing a black coffee at Starbucks on his way into the Khalifa Street office. They talked every night by webcam, Mathieu leaning back in the office chair, watching the fuchsia faces of his family. The technology still hadn't been perfected. Sometimes the girls were just voices out of the darkness. "*Qu'avez-vous fait aujourd'hui?*" he asked every night. There were markets in Pézenas and Sète and old friends and day trips to *la plage*. It was hard not to be envious. He had his all-consuming job, Victor and the bikers, sometimes a flirtation in a bar on a Thursday night that slid into Friday morning. *C'est tout.*

He hadn't wanted to go out that morning. A big meeting with the Al Nafs people was scheduled for Sunday morning and he didn't have all the numbers he needed. Even if he worked all weekend, there still might not be enough time to fill in the holes. Two years of dealing with Abu Dhabi's investment body had shown him how fatal this could prove. Weeks of work down the toilet. He didn't like riding when he was this edgy, although Talbot was always saying this was the best time to get out there and pump your ass off. "Who isn't on edge in this place?" he asked. "Name me one person you know who isn't totally stressed out, especially in our world."

Talbot was a corporate lawyer for Amaal, the real-estate Godzilla in town. He and his wife had just split, Molly going back to Scotland with the girls. "For the best," he kept saying, but Mathieu had seen the terror behind the brave drinking and pedalling. Victor, mad Victor, was a cheery Aussie with a gorgeous wife and two boys he couldn't stop talking about. Even with the market slump he was upbeat. "Yeah, investment banking's in the sewer," he'd said to Mathieu the week before, as if he'd said, yeah, it's hot. The three usually went to Forty Fruity on the Corniche after biking. Victor always ordered the tallest triple-layer drink, noisily slurping the avocado purée at the bottom: "Put back the calories, mates."

But Victor was a demon on a bike, competitive as hell. Even with his irregular form—pitched slightly more forward than Talbot advised—he was the fastest among them. He'd confided to Mathieu that he wanted to tackle a triathlon next year. "I'd like that just once." And it was looking good, Victor surpassing his times each week, Talbot, even Talbot, looking impressed.

The week before he was hit, Victor told Mathieu he was thinking of going to Amman in April. "Heard it's one of the best triathlons in the region. You know… organized!" And they'd laughed, both of them having lived in the UAE long enough to appreciate that.

The place had you by the balls. So much money you could barely believe it. Kids happy as clams, carefree in their private schools, golf and piano lessons, wives relieved to have someone else take over the laundry, the cooking, the toilets, the daily nit and grit. Sandrine had slipped into the life as if she'd been born to it. And if it got too hot or too boring, if the nanny quit and you had to go through the maze of finding another, if the clogged streets and wacko drivers made you scream with helplessness, there were summers in France to set you right.

They'd stopped running, were walking now. Whatever Gillian did, he did. "My friends at the school tell me this is normal, that if I wasn't crying every second they'd be worried. 'She is,' as the papers said, 'inconsolable.' She is — thank God! — completely out of her mind." He thought she might laugh — she had a great, surprising laugh — but her voice caught. "What kills me as much as the stupid tank that cut him down and kept going is that I wasn't even here. Dad had a second small stroke and Mum thought it'd be a good idea to come home a week earlier than planned for summer hols. 'Were you afraid Dad might die, was that what you were thinking?' I asked her that on the phone last night. She calls every night, more worried about me now than she is about Dad. It was harsh of me, I guess. Like if she hadn't been her overly concerned self, always dramatizing Dad's health, I would have been here, instead of shopping with her that afternoon in Brisbane. I would have made it not happen." Gillian reached for the bottle of water Mathieu had extended to her and let out a shaky breath. "Don't tell anyone I said that last thing, okay?"

He'd called the day after the accident, left a message with her sister, who'd flown back with her and the boys. "Hello, this is a message for Gillian. It's Mathieu. I rode with Victor. I cannot tell you how terribly sorry I am. For you and for…" *Merde*, he couldn't remember the kids' names. Aaron? Cedric? He didn't know them, didn't know her. She'd been Victor's backstory, probably the reason he seemed so happy all the time. They'd only met Victor's family twice, running into the four of them at the Carrefour check-out one Friday evening, chatting longer than they might have because the lines snaked back into the aisles of chips and chocolates. An Emirati woman, hugely, modestly pregnant under her *abaya*, stood between the two families. Her eyes, bright, curious

even, watched them above the *shayla* that covered the
rest of her face. Amazing, the eyes of some of the women
here.

Unloading the bags into the back of the Volvo later,
Sandrine had commented on how beautiful Victor's wife
was. She wouldn't say that now. Gillian looked like a
woman who hadn't stood in front of a mirror for a while,
had lost track of herself. She was tall, nearly as tall as
Mathieu, and as she bent over to retie the laces of her
trainer, foot high on the Corniche railing, he could see
the outline of her back ribs against the jersey.

"You're not eating," he said.

"Nah," she said. And he saw the tears falling again.
Earlier, he'd been uncomfortable with how freely she
wept. He was getting used to it.

"Tell me again how he rode," she said.

It was what she'd wanted to know the first time
they talked. She'd phoned back that same day, surprising
him. She didn't know him. He wasn't family. He wasn't
Australian, not part of their circle. And there were all
the arrangements to make, so much legal crap to work
through as an expat. In this city where everything had
to be redone two, three, four times under the best of
circumstances, organizing a funeral would have to be a
nightmare. Yet she'd called him and he found himself
describing the way Victor hunched his shoulders over
the handlebars, the way he rotated his neck three times
to the right, three times to the left before heading off.
She listened as if she had nothing else to do.

"Thank you," she said, when he'd told her everything
he could remember, described as much as he could
without sounding like he was burnishing it too much.

He could never tell her that when they rode back to the corner of Khaleej and 19th to see why Victor was no longer with them, they found him lying on the side of the road, still on his bike, as if he'd just tipped over in the start of the curve. There wasn't a scratch on him, except that the back of his head was pouring blood, his helmet caved into his skull.

"May I call you again?" she'd asked.

Gillian was suddenly jogging again. Not used to the starting and stopping, Mathieu's hamstrings twinged, but he jogged too and caught up.

"I only saw him do two races," she said. "Vic was always up early, cycling or running while I was trying to get the kids sorted." Gillian's streaked hair, unbrushed, not quite clean, pulled into a high ponytail, swung a little as she ran. She was thirty-two? Thirty-four?

"How old are they now, the boys?" he asked, aware again of how little he knew.

"Cedric's fourteen going on twenty-five. Jake turned thirteen while we were in Brisbane that week." She turned to look at him whenever she spoke, not the way people usually talked to each other while running—heads straight ahead, eyes on the horizon. He worried she would crash into a cyclist or Rollerblader.

"Wow," he said. "Teenagers."

"Started young. Vic couldn't wait," she said, and Mathieu, running alongside her, was hit with such swift and sudden sorrow he nearly doubled over.

He didn't make too much of it with Sandrine, knowing she'd take it wrong. The night after his first run with

Gillian, he didn't mention it at all. "*Ça va, mon amour?*" Sandrine asked when the girls got bored and drifted away from the laptop. His wife's hair was wet; even in the purple light he could see that. He was sad, he told her, just very sad. *Pauvre p'tit*, she said. What was Gillian going to do now? she wanted to know. *Aucune idée*, he said. And really, he had no idea what she would do next. It hadn't come up.

They'd had a memorial at St. Edmund's the Wednesday after, the place only half full, mostly Victor's male colleagues from the bank, just a few wives. Many, like Sandrine, had gone home for the summer. Two of the women were dressed in black, but sexy black. Even in church, Mathieu couldn't help but appreciate the skimpy straps and open backs of their dresses. They were on home turf in the church, a little less careful. A few men in *khandouras*, probably seniors at the bank, stood at the back.

"Victor was such a galvanizer," one of the Australian wives told Mathieu as they stood in the rectory garden later, balancing tea cups and tea biscuits. It was all he could do not to make a swift, polite bolt.

"Yes," he said. "Yes, he was."

"Gill's going to need all the support she can get," she said. She and her husband, on home leave, had flown back from Melbourne for the service.

"Yes," he said. "Yes, she will."

"She'll want to be getting home," the woman said. "Nothing left to keep her here, is there?"

"No," he said. "No, I expect not."

He'd spoken to Gillian two more times after the first call. She'd wondered if either he or Talbot would like to give a eulogy at the service, but in the end Talbot had to fly back to Glasgow for the week — Molly wanted to finalize things with signatures and seals, not leave them vague — and Gillian's brother had been able to make the trip from Tasmania. "I hope you don't mind," she told Mathieu in the second call. "He and Victor were very close. He's going to try to speak." Of course, he didn't mind. It would have been an honour and sure, he had stories no one else could tell. He might have even been able to lighten things up with tales of Victor, gonzo biker, but he wouldn't have felt completely right speaking in front of people who'd known Victor far better and longer.

He wasn't sleeping well, was forgetting to eat. He found himself staring into space, even at work, even as the Al Nafs thing was steaming along. He'd wanted to cancel the Sunday meeting, didn't think he could stomach the usual dithering and double-talk. Yes, we go with the plan. Next week: what plan? But he'd shown up with his PowerPoint and his best Italian suit and somehow the parking project he and six planners had been working on for the past ten months got approved.

"We understand there is a problem," Sheikh Ali bin Rashid, head of the municipality's transport board, had said. No kidding, Mathieu had thought. It had taken him twenty minutes to find a spot for one of the two space-and-gas guzzlers Sandrine had insisted they buy when they moved here.

The Friday before had been spent at the hospital and then the police station, Talbot sitting next to him, saying almost nothing, though they'd both had to answer question after question, some from people whose accents made their answers just guesses. Talbot, though, was the one who'd called Gillian from the hospital. "I'm the coach," was all he said as he slipped into a stairwell with his mobile. The face of the surgeon had just told them what they already knew.

The who, the how? A mystery. Talbot and Mathieu, three years into this life, knew it might stay that way. Ugly facts were neatly tucked into a head scarf. And if it had been an Emirati who'd hit Victor, then that was truly the end of it.

"Do you think it was a local?" They were jog-walking again. A week deeper into July, it was so hot they'd met at a quarter to seven, promising each other a half-hour tops. Gillian seemed thinner even than the Friday before, her shoulder bones little knobs under tan, smooth skin. Still, her eyes were less bloodshot, her blonde hair washed. "I just keep picturing a guy in full Emirati regalia driving a Hummer at 160 klicks an hour, you know?"

He'd run over the possibilities so many times. Maybe it had been a taxi speeding to the airport or an expat pulling a runner, fleeing debts and bad memories. Maybe it had been one of those badly balanced beige buses, full of men on their way back to the Musaffah labour camps, Indians and Pakistanis who'd worked all night on cranes at the port or the towers in front of Emirates Palace. The city was a riot of construction and swarming crews in blue coveralls and orange vests. At night all the major streets were lined with dusty, spent men, sitting on curbs or cross-legged on patches of dry grass. Sometimes he saw them waiting at dusk on Hamdan Street, the most perfect, still, straight lines he'd ever seen. Perhaps that morning a driver had closed his eyes for a moment, letting the bus drift to the shoulder, then startled back to wakefulness by the wheels catching on sand. Perhaps the driver sensed movement, something brushing against the side of the bus, but then it was gone and he'd sped on because the men needed to be back in time for early-morning prayers and a few hours' sleep.

Mathieu hadn't heard a car approach that Friday. No cars had passed their tight, short line for at least five minutes, as closely as he could remember. But he hadn't hit his cycling rhythm yet, was still warming up, which took more concentration than it would ten minutes later when his heart would begin pumping in time with his legs. He was still groggy, still stiff, still fighting his body, preoccupied with the Sunday meeting and wondering what he was going to do about the Russian girl who'd texted her mobile number to his the night before at the Captain's Arms. These things didn't usually work out too well, though a month without sex was beginning to wear on him. Not that sex was a given when Sandrine was around. She was only sometimes in the mood the past few years. She'd been so pliant in their early days; now it was a constant negotiation. That was how he'd explained the thing with Angie a year ago. Not to Sandrine—why inflict unnecessary hurt?—but to himself. Still, the girl in the bar seemed like the undemanding type. He remembered the way her breasts tested the tiny buttons on her filmy blouse, wondered if her nipples were pale or dark, if she liked them sucked or licked or nipped... If Talbot had been able to read his thoughts that morning, he wouldn't have been impressed. Scattered to here and beyond. So scattered that as he and Talbot turned off

Khaleej al Arabi, heading down 19th toward the water, he failed to look back, failed to check on Victor.

Gillian had stopped again, had turned to face him, was looking into his face. She wanted to know: Did he think it was a local?

"It could have been anyone, Gillie," he said, surprised by using the name Victor had called her and by putting his arm around her. She didn't pull away.

"I think it was a local," she said. Her voice was flat, but tears had begun to gather in her eyes again. "Motherfucker."

"Maybe we can get a coffee," he said, surprised again and rapidly checking motivations and repercussions. Meeting to run on the Corniche was one thing. Coffee… he needed to be really careful here. She was in shock, deep grief, her heart run over. The last thing he should be doing was encouraging emotional dependence. Once, in university in the UK, Mathieu had comforted his flatmate's girlfriend after the flatmate dumped her. The girl had been near-suicidal and one thing led to another. The guy had a change of heart and everyone ended up feeling shitty.

Gillian looked at him, studied his eyes. "Okay," she said.

At Dome, she ordered a flat white. "What's that?" he asked.

"They don't have these in France?"

"No," he said. "What is it? Some kind of weird Aussie drink?" For a moment they were other people in another situation.

"Victor could drink four a day," said Gillian and they were back to normal.

"What are you going to do?" he asked.

"Cry for the rest of my life," she said and smiled at him. She was young and lovely and all she deserved she could never have again. "You mean, what am I going to do next?"

"Can you keep your teaching job? Do you feel like going home?"

"I don't feel like doing anything," she said. "I don't even want to be drinking this stupid coffee. For all I know the guy who killed my husband is the owner of this place." She waved a hand at the counter where two Filipina waitresses stood giggling. The café was empty except for them; the mall crowd would drift in after the noon prayers. "You know, not the real, working, do-something owner, but the local guy who does nothing but make money off this place and drive around in his SUV, running people down if they get in his way." She put her cup down. She was right. She was barely drinking it. "The doctor wouldn't even do a frigging autopsy. Can you believe that? 'It's God's will,' he said. Can you believe that?"

Anger was a part of grief, he remembered reading, a necessary part. Well, he would be her punching bag and the friend-for-now she needed. He would protect her, even from himself. And sitting in the echoing plastic sameness of Al Wahda Mall at 8:00 a.m., the call to prayer beginning on the loudspeakers, he felt for the first time in a long while almost good about himself.

VICARAGE

He'd told her gently when they first met, then more firmly several times after: Call me Dave. She stood before him now, tan and perfect in a white linen sundress, no moisture on her taut face though it was nearly 40 degrees. She blazed him a smile.

"Father," she said.

"Please," he said. "Dave."

"Dave," she said and he knew by the humouring way she said his name that they would be having this exchange again. Tina would never give in.

"We need to talk," she said, shutting the smile off.

"Let's talk," he said.

"Not here," she said, looking around the empty church compound.

It was late; the sun had already moved from its blistering noon position. There'd been tea and cookies in the vicarage garden. Dave could hear the tea boys speaking loudly to each other in Hindi as they cleaned up. Even the Ethiopian women, who gathered every Friday in the courtyard to sing and pray, their gauze shawls the holiest shade of white he'd ever seen, had gone.

He led her, with what he hoped looked like ministerial willingness, through the compound to the apartment, seven awkwardly arranged rooms filled with sagging, beige furniture. Even Suzette and the kids called it The Vicarage, a public place where they happened to live. They were used to it. Six years in Kuwait, four in Oman, two in Bahrain and now, Abu Dhabi. "Where are you from?" one of the ancient thrift shop ladies had bent to ask eight-year-old Erik the week before and he'd answered, "The world, I guess."

Arjun met them in the entryway. He was always there, discreetly there, never underfoot or hovering. Thirty years and seven ministers, a St. Edmund's fixture. How had he done it? His daughters in Cochin were grown now, his wife dead. Dave watched the man's lean back as he bent over yet another tea service, the thin cotton of his shirt damp at the base of his spine. After so many years in the Gulf, Dave was fine-tuned to the nuances of servitude. Secretly he worried he'd become too used to it: I tell. You do.

"Tea please, Arjun," he said, needing the ritual of cups and spoons and Arjun's steady presence padding in and out. Tina Souaidy was going to require more than he had this afternoon. Why did she want to talk on Friday after the main service, after he'd talked and talked? "Shot your wad," as Suzette delicately put it.

He gestured to the overstuffed Arabian loveseat rather than the larger sofa where he lowered himself, surprised by the heaviness in his body. He didn't want to sit side by side. "It's better like this," Tina said, moving to join him on the sofa. She smelled like sunscreen and something fruity. Peach.

"We have to do something," she said.

The Friday before, they'd visited the women's labour camp, a cluster of low buildings tucked inside the maze of the Musaffah camps. For several weeks, he'd announced the new outreach program from the pulpit, not encouraged by the looks on most of the faces: *Right, Dave, just how I want to spend a Friday afternoon.* It had been only the two of them meeting at the back of the chapel the previous week, plus a Scottish fellow who seemed to think they were going to Foodlands for the monthly post-service lunch. "Wrong group," he said and scurried off.

Dave had met Tina several times before, both relative newcomers to a parish that had been the pillar of British Anglican life in Abu Dhabi for fifty years and fully intended to remain so for the next fifty. At first, eager to connect, Dave looked for her after Friday service. Sometimes she came with a young man, probably her son. Mostly she came alone. Her husband, she'd told him as they stood in the vicarage garden during the weekly, obligatory meet-and-greet, travelled a great deal. "Mo works for the ruling family," she said. "He's Syrian Muslim, I'm Italian-American and Catholic. You can imagine how the folks back in Boston love that." And Tina had smiled so widely, so winningly that he almost missed the darkness in her eyes, the tightness of her jaw.

"You're wondering why I'm not over there, right?" she'd said, waving behind her in the vicinity of St. Mary's Cathedral, where throngs of Indians and Filipinos gathered for sixty masses a week. It gave a whole new meaning to the word *mass*, Dave thought when he first saw the beige, curtained buses unloading and reloading every Friday morning, the drivers yelling out return destinations in shrill voices. If he had even one-tenth those numbers he'd be named Primate of All England. Dave had made a point of meeting the Catholic bishop his first week in Abu Dhabi. His Excellency George Mueller: German, elderly, prim, cold as a Munich winter.

"You're thinking maybe that I feel out of place in that sea of brown?" Tina had fixed him with another smile, harder at the edges. "No, I welcome diversity. I just can't abide the bishop. One of Ratzinger's guys probably. Perfect fourth-century mind." She must have seen some recognition in his face, though Dave quickly tried to register only non-committal amusement. "Good line," he said.

Meet and greet. It had been the thing to do in those early weeks. There was the St. Edmund's old guard—ushers, readers, the thrift shop ladies—to have in for lunch at the Vicarage. They'd welcomed him with mild interest, talking among themselves through the cucumber sandwiches; even in this transient city-state they would probably outlast him. There were the religious leaders of the other churches in the block-square compound—the Bible Belt, Suzette called it—from the Syrian Orthodox priest to the Oklahoma-folksy minister at the evangelical church. Ed Woods had the hungry look of a proselytizer and wanted to get together every week. "Make it a regular thing, Dave. Talk about matters close to both our hearts."

There was someone he did want to meet. Sheikh Maktoum bin Zayed, a half-brother of the crown prince, was officially the deputy minister of cultural affairs, but he had a special interest in Christianity, having studied comparative religion at Oxford. "How did they ever allow him to do that?" Suzette had asked. The "Him" had changed with their postings, from Emir to Sultan to simply, Supreme Ruler. There was always a Him in these countries, as well as a They, the surrounding ruling circle, and you were wise never to forget that.

It was Bishop Mueller who finessed an audience with Sheikh Maktoum in Dave's third month. What those two had in common, Dave couldn't begin to fathom after the first minutes of conversation. The bishop sat stiff as a crosier on the least cushy of the couches in Maktoum's *majlis*, one of many such rooms, no doubt. Dave had expected to be dazzled—not that the elegant space, with its Italian marble floors and air of supreme privilege, was a disappointment. But it was a modest dazzle, as if Maktoum had wanted to minimize the space between them.

"How is your family?" murmured the bishop after three gracious maids had passed before them with trays large as sundials piled with chocolates, dates, chocolate-covered dates, date-filled chocolates. Dave felt full by the second round, but watched his host as to when he could gracefully decline, grateful for all those socially trying years in the Gulf. He was not an innocent. "Thank you," he said on round three, hand on heart, head bowed, after Maktoum waved off the women. The sheikh was older than he'd expected, a trim man in his early fifties with an impeccable, greying goatee, amused, inquiring eyes and an ease in his body that slowed one's own breathing. Dave felt himself exhale for the first time in months.

"My mother is doing as well as can be expected. You are kind to inquire, Your Grace," he said.

"Alzheimer's," he said, turning to Dave. "Such a terrible way to go. And what makes it even more painful is that there's such an effort to pretend it's something else. We need to know about Alzheimer's, not shut our eyes to it." Maktoum sighed and adjusted his *ghutra* slightly. "My country..." and he was speaking now just to Dave..."needs to take the blinkers off, put pride aside and get on with the twenty-first century. Read, study; open ourselves to other ways of thinking and being."

Bishop Mueller cleared his throat. "Your Highness, I do hope you will excuse me. There is a family coming to baptize their new baby..."

"Of course! So many people depend on you, Your Grace. Duty calls. Of course," and Maktoum stood. Lifting himself from the low couch, the bishop shot Dave a look, which made him also get to his feet.

"But you're not going too, Father?" The sheikh sounded crushed. "There is much to talk about."

The bishop left, looking a bit miffed, but it didn't seem to have an effect on Maktoum, who ordered in more food. The afternoon opened around them. He wanted to know about Dave's religious training ("your blessed calling"), his family ("one son, two daughters... lucky man!"), listened intently to Dave's experiences as an Anglican pastor in Bahrain. "What a bloody mess. Just give the Shia some rights and be done with it," said the sheikh, tapping a cigarette on the gilt side table before lighting up. "But tell me what you think of our funny little country. Don't worry, I won't deport you if you start quoting the last Human Rights Watch report."

Dave told Maktoum about the warmth of people—"especially my parishioners from Kerala"—

about discovering the beauty of the Liwa desert, about the sense of being "part of the build," a line he'd used in other postings. "And when I hear the *muezzin* from the mosque next door it really does feel as if the call to prayer is for all of us." This wasn't a stretch. In Kuwait and Oman, it had sometimes bothered him when the call to prayer drowned out the Anglican hymns. Here the call felt almost paternal.

"Come now, Father," said Maktoum. "What do you really think?" And Dave, feeling both nervous and relieved, told him about visiting the labour camps where he'd entered squalid, humid rooms, twelve men to a bunk, about the Ethiopian nannies fleeing employers who starved, beat and refused to pay them (he didn't say most of their bosses were Emirati). Some of these women now slept on the grounds of St. Edmund's, their slender legs curled inside the holy-white of their shawls.

There was no Ethiopian embassy in Abu Dhabi, Dave explained, and the consulate in Dubai had no money to help in any way. "I've tried." It had been his first mission at St. Edmund's, one he literally tripped over some mornings. But no one on the church council had wanted to commit the 18,000 dirhams a month to rent the empty villa across the street for the women. And even if they had consented, there would be no embassy on site to protect the runaways physically or legally. Any of their employers could come and drag them away in the night.

"I am ashamed," said Maktoum. He said nothing more for a long moment, eyes closed, before opening them and smiling. "We will do something. I promise you we will do something." And then just as Dave was beginning to feel the discomfort he'd often felt when speaking to Gulf Arabs about the places they called home, Maktoum wanted to know Dave's thoughts about the ideological tug of war within the Church of England, what he *really* thought of Rowan Williams. "I'm just fascinated," said Maktoum, settling back among the *majlis* pillows. "Your archbishop is quite the maverick."

It was wonderful, rare and wonderful, Dave thought later, as he followed a palace driver to a waiting Mercedes, to talk ideas with a deeply intelligent person. It was rare enough back home, but here in the oil lands, where consumption and piety had replaced ideas, where intellectual life was as hard to come by as a temperate day, it almost never happened. It was even rarer, if that was possible, to be listened to with such unwavering attention, as if every word, every inflection, was being taken in. It was only later still, going over their conversation as he tried to gather points for the coming week's sermon, that he heard that word: *some*. Give them some rights and be done with it.

Tina Souaidy hadn't touched her tea. She talked, referring to typed notes, looking up over her reading glasses to hammer in a point. She'd written a thesis. He should have seen this coming after last week.

It had been sweltering when they'd driven out to the Musaffah camps. Tina, who always looked like she'd just stepped from an air-conditioned shop, had even fashioned a fan out of the church bulletin. "Lord," she said, when they got out of the van. She'd brought two LuLu bags packed with board games, Bingo chips, playing cards. "The girls need some amusement, don't

they, poor things?" After several visits to the camps,
wandering through the neglected buildings of bunk beds,
communal kitchens and too many bodies, Dave wasn't
sure what was needed. Tickets home? Then what?

As a man, he'd been able to go only as far as the
front courtyard of the women's compound. Most people
didn't even know there was a camp for women out here.
Surrounded on all sides by the crumbling sprawl of the
men's buildings, it housed up to 100 women, Filipinas
and Bangladeshis employed by the city's large industrial
cleaning companies, women who mopped floors and
scrubbed toilets at Adnoc or HSBC headquarters at 3:00
a.m. You worked like a slave and then you came home to
this. Dave had to steel himself to come here every week,
to enter the shantytown that most expats sped by on
their way somewhere else, to Tarif or Liwa. The camps
were so *here*, but so invisible.

While Tina visited with the female residents, he
planned to drop into some of the men's rooms in the
camp down the road. The week before he'd played chess
with a red-bearded Pakistani fellow, a labourer on the
ten-year engineering joke known as the Sheikh Zayed
Bridge. The man had beaten him soundly at the game,
grinning all the while. When Dave pressed him as to
what he needed (sheets, food, pen and paper?), the man
shook his head. "Good," he said.

Dave had dropped Tina quickly at the entrance,
trying not to look at her face, which had frozen into
a mask of anxious good will. "Just be yourself," he
said, patting her arm before getting back into the van,
knowing this advice sounded as lame as the buck-up
he'd given Rachel, his oldest daughter, on the first

day in her new high school. She'd looked at him with adolescent pity.

The Pakistani man had not been there this time, and Dave had roamed around the large room, then two smaller ones, looking for someone to talk with. Some of the men looked up, some nodded, some smiled. But none gave a signal that they wanted more than this. Eventually he'd walked to the end of the road and then back, drenched by the time he climbed into the van. He'd had to wait nearly fifteen minutes for Tina. When she appeared, her hands were empty, her face full.

The women were "incredible, absolutely incredible." They were "the bravest people I've ever met." They put her "to shame." What did she have to complain about? "They enjoy life so much, even in that horrible place." She wondered, though, about Lola, their matron, who'd taken all the games Tina had brought as soon as she arrived and locked them in her own room. She worried too about the kitchen with its dozen open gas burners and no real walls to keep out the wind and heat. The week before, a woman's blouse had caught fire. And she worried about Shirin, a Bangladeshi girl, who'd been laid off by a cleaning company and was now being paid $50 a month for living expenses. "She can't afford to transfer her visa to another employer and she isn't making money to buy a ticket home. She's completely stuck. Did you ever hear anything more insane?"

"It's insane," he agreed, but she was already talking about another girl who'd been raped by her foreman.

"Forgive me for going on and on, Father," she'd said when he dropped her off in St. Edmund's parking lot. "I'm just so moved by what I witnessed."

Tina set down her teacup now and looked at him. She hadn't required any solutions the week before. Now she did. What were they going to do? This country supported modern forms of slavery. This country condoned institutionalized cruelty. "If we just sit here and beat our breasts, we're complicit," she said.

"We need to get more people involved," he said, the first thing he could think of. She'd thrown him with the sudden pressure.

"From the church, you mean? I don't think so, Dave," she said, and he realized it was the first time she'd used his name without prompting and that it was in a kind of rebuke. "You see the response you've gotten so far." And she pulled a blank face and shrugged, in an imitation, he guessed, of his sorry parishioners who called themselves good Anglicans.

"Perhaps we could form an ad hoc committee with the other churches," he offered. "Ed Woods is a good man."

Tina looked at him over her reading glasses. She hadn't smiled once. When she'd turned it off outside, it had stayed off. "I think we're going to have to rely on just ourselves here."

His body was already refusing, muscles tightening. It wasn't just the fact of being paired up with Tina, who was beginning to worry him. Their conversation was taking him back to things he didn't care to remember. In his early Kuwait days, he'd written an editorial about the plight of migrant workers. The piece had made it through the lines of amateurish command at *Al Watan,* an oversight, not a vote of confidence, as he'd first foolishly assumed. He'd been talked to by the bishop at Middle East headquarters in Cyprus, a knuckle-rapping, really, and a dozen families left his Kuwait City parish, afraid for their jobs and what came with them. Some he'd thought were friends.

"We do need to be careful," he said.

"Oh, I know," said Tina. But the way she said it made him think that even if she did know, she didn't care. What was a job, a livelihood, a future compared to the suffering of others?

"Let's talk midweek, shall we?" he finally offered. "See who else I can get on board." She'd continued to look skeptical as he stood and put out his hand, her expression not even softening when he helped her to her feet. And then Arjun was there, making everything polite again as he swept up cups and cutlery. Dave thanked him as he always did, but he saw the way Tina narrowed her eyes as she watched.

"Where in India is he from?" she asked as Dave showed her out. He could hear Erik playing upstairs on the Wii—what else was there to do in this heat?—and felt a twinge of regret. Most of Friday was gone now.

"From the south," he said, explaining how long Arjun had been at St. Edmund's, how valued he was. He felt he had to reassure her somehow and this irritated him.

"Poor man," said Tina.

It was later, after he'd had a nap and supper with the family, then gone out for a bit of air and to look for Erik's missing football, that he found the woman. He wasn't sure what it was at first. The white mound against the wall near the mosque looked like one of the Ethiopian women had left her shawl behind. Perhaps the wind had kicked up and blown it off her shoulders and she hadn't noticed. But when he got closer, he realized that inside the shawl was a woman, asleep—he prayed it was sleep—her bare feet sticking out one end.

"Excuse me," he said, bending as close as he dared. He knew not to touch her, not even her feet or the shawl that covered them.

She sat up instantly, drawing the shawl across her shoulders. "No!" she said. Then more forcefully, "No!" She was not more than twenty, he guessed, a girl with a dusky, troubled beauty. Her eyes were golden brown, suspicious. He hastily made the sign of the cross, and her face relaxed a little.

"Come inside," he said.

"Yes," she said.

This, he realized, after settling her on the loveseat with tea—Arjun showing nothing on his face as he glided in and out—was the extent of her English. No. Yes. And her name: Eden. Even the Arabic he tried on her was a miss.

"She can't have been here very long then," said Suzette, who'd acted only mildly surprised to see a beautiful young woman having tea with her husband. His wife, practical and plain-speaking to a fault—and sometimes it did feel like a fault—had seen just about everything there was to see in twenty-two years as a pastor's wife. He sometimes wished he could shock her, rock her steady little boat. He also needed that boat.

"Look at her legs, Dave," and he was embarrassed he hadn't noticed something so obvious. Fuchsia bruises and black scabs covered her thin shins. "She can stay, you know. Tonight, a few nights. Until you figure out where she's from, what to do. I'll have Lauren bunk in with Rachel." And before he could say, wait, I'm not sure about this, Suzette had gone to get the room ready.

Eden drank her tea dutifully, but declined the cookies when Arjun held out the plate to her. "No," she said.

"You can stay," Dave told her. "Okay?" But she looked confused now and after a few more stabs at communicating, Dave called one of the elders in the Ethiopian congregation. The man was reluctant to come at first, even with Dave offering to pay for his cab. When he finally arrived an hour later, he wouldn't sit down, but stood close to the door and when he spoke to the woman in their language, he kept his eyes on Dave's face. The girl seemed to have a lot to say, growing animated, then tearful, then angry, the man stopping only once every few minutes to turn to Dave and explain in short, vague sentences what she was saying.

The gist of it was that Eden, the girl, had been made to work twenty hours a day. Her employers wouldn't let her go to church on Fridays, locked her in her room, which had no window and no air conditioning, when they went out. Sometimes they visited family in Fujairah and she was locked in for two, three, four days with no food. She never knew when they were coming back. They had not paid her in months. Her family in Ethiopia was upset, hungry and uncomprehending.

"Who are her employers?" asked Dave. "Are they local?" And the man shook his head so absolutely that Dave had to assume they were. And then he was gone, refusing tea, cookies and further entanglement.

After the man left, the woman sat without moving, her head in its white wrap dropped slightly. Of course, she could stay; she could stay as long as she needed to. But it always came back to: then what? The woman was so still he began to think she was sleeping again. Arjun paused at the doorway and Dave put a finger to his lips. Let her sleep. These women were so tired they would sleep for days when they finally found shelter. Then he realized she was praying, whispers of words lifting the gauze slightly with her breath.

"Eden." He went to sit next to her, but didn't put out a reassuring hand. A strange man's touch in these countries, even if you weren't Muslim, was always a mistake and nearly always misinterpreted. It had taken him years to unlearn the impulse. When someone was in pain, you sat, you listened. You did not do the most human thing of all.

She was an easy guest, a "silent little thing," Suzette reported, and the kids took it in their stride. There had often been strange faces at the family table. "Doing God's work, right, Dad?" said Erik, when Dave tucked him into bed that night, and he wondered again about the new, intense devotion of his youngest child. A crazy thing for a pastor to be worrying about, but he'd known zealots and they scared him more than non-believers. Those folks, at least, knew to be quiet.

He put in a call to Sheikh Maktoum's office first thing the next morning. But it wasn't until late in the afternoon that he learned Maktoum was on a falconry hunt in Kazakhstan and wouldn't be returning for another week. Was this "an urgent," as the assistant called it, or could he wait for His Highness's return?

"It's urgent, yes, but I'll wait," he said, knowing it was likely only Maktoum had the pull to do something:

Repatriate the girl, talk with the abusing family, perhaps even employ her in his palace. Being sent home was rarely the outcome the girls' families had in mind. Dave had often imagined these homecomings, the women half-broken, while parents, husbands, siblings demanded to know just how bad *bad* was. Things were bad at home. Now what?

Eden would not be staying a second night in the Vicarage. "No," she'd told Suzette. "No, no, no."

"Maybe it was the doctor," Suzette said at dinner. She'd asked their family physician, a stately, serene Indian woman who'd been practising in Abu Dhabi for years, to come have a look at Eden's legs. Dr. Nadira didn't often make house calls, but when Suzanne explained the circumstances, she'd agreed. "I thought it would be okay, you know, because Dr. Nadira's so gentle, plus she's a woman. And it was private. I knew she'd never go to a clinic. But I could see Eden wasn't happy. She wouldn't let Dr. Nadira touch her. Next thing I know, she's saying no and she's gone."

Lauren and Rachel reworked their sleeping arrangements, barely registering the change. "The girl?" asked Arjun when serving late-evening tea. "No," Dave told him. And Arjun had simply nodded, all things being equal.

Dave found her the next morning, asleep by the wall facing the Orthodox cathedral. Her shawl was spread under her so that her long legs were exposed. She must have kicked the shawl off in the heat of the night, exposing more skin than she would have wanted. Dave looked around; then carefully, slowly, tried to rearrange the fabric before calling her name.

The girl didn't wake easily this time, curled away from him, leaving one lean thigh exposed again, allowing him to see what he couldn't have seen before: a wound on her inner thigh that made the bruises on her shins look like cat scratches. It was huge, gaping, like someone had tried to carve a piece out of her, and crusted with pus. He ran back to the vicarage, hoping to find Suzette, but she'd already left for Dubai. Some of the thrift shop ladies had invited her on a shopping trip to Dragon Mart. "Not exactly my cup of tea, sifting through a bunch of junk from China," Suzette had sighed the night before. "But what else are you going to do in this place?"

He tried calling the Ethiopian elder again, but his mobile was switched off. Maktoum's office was going to be no help with him still away. Ed Woods? He was in a prayer meeting but would call back later. Dave walked back to find the girl. He would need to be more persuasive. He made the full tour of the compound twice, but she was gone.

When Ed Woods called back an hour later he was jovial, full of the spirit, until Dave told him what he was calling about. "Ethiopian nannies? We've got them here too, Dave. Terrible situation, but what can you do? Their government's hopeless." He wanted to know the young woman's name. "Eden? Kind of ironic. But sure, I'll send up a prayer for little Eden. I'll ask my afternoon prayer group to pray for her too, how's that? And speaking of prayer, my friend, when are you and I getting together?"

That week Dave began getting up early, pre-dawn some mornings, to walk around the compound, sometimes rising even before Arjun, always the first up.

On Wednesday morning he found two young women huddled inside the thrift shop entrance, but they took off, startled birds, into the street. Back at the vicarage, Tina was waiting on the front steps. "Couldn't sleep," she said. "I figured you'd be up." She looked — for Tina — terrible. Even in the forgiving dawn light, he saw now that she was closer to sixty than fifty, that the roots of her hair were grey, not brown. She wore a pink track suit and matching sweat band. "Even running at 4:00 a.m. didn't help. I can't stop thinking about those women," she told him as he let her in. Arjun, there already, nodded and disappeared into the kitchen when he saw her.

Dave braced himself to hear another litany of labour camp abuses as he settled her — without resistance this time — on the loveseat. But Tina didn't say anything right away, sat looking at her hands while Arjun brought in the tea things. "I went back to the camps this week," she said when he left them. "I know, I know. I should have told you first." On the way back from their first visit to the camps, hearing the intensity of her reaction, he'd told her about the couple who'd been deported recently for operating their own outreach ministry. As a registered charity — whatever that meant in this country — St. Edmund's was their sponsor and protector. "The church has been in the UAE forever. The royal family trusts us," he told her. Probably because the church had done so little to change anything, he wanted to add, but didn't, realizing in the omission how little he must trust her. At any rate, he'd hoped the story about the couple would be warning enough, a gentle, but clear message to tread lightly.

"I got into a fight with Lola," said Tina. She wasn't staring him down today, kept studying her hands, twisting her rings.

He tried to imagine Lola—short and plump in jeans and T-shirt—and Tina, Pilates-lean and coiffed in a white suit, going at it. Lola with a frying pan perhaps. Tina with a shopping bag from Paris Gallery. He tried not to smile.

"It wasn't funny, Dave," said Tina, regaining something of herself. "She's a thief and she's not helping those girls one bit. We have to do something."

"Look, Tina," Dave began, and as soon as he said this it felt like such a relief, he wondered why he hadn't set down the boundaries with her earlier. "We're guests in this country."

"We serve at the pleasure of the sheikhs and if we don't like it we should just go back to wherever we came from?" said Tina, raising her face. There was some colour in it now, making her look younger again.

"Pretty much," said Dave, knowing he didn't completely buy this. How could he do his job if he did?

"That's what my husband says, that we're here to build their bridges and blow their noses, 'and if you don't like it, *habibti*, you know where the airport is.'"

"What does your husband think about your visits to the camps?" Dave asked, surprised this hadn't occurred to him before. Her husband was a big shot working for the ruling family. He would have a whole lot to protect. Dave half-guessed the truth before Tina shook her head. Her husband didn't have any thoughts about the visits because he didn't know about the visits.

Thankfully, Arjun knew, as he always did, the precise moment to make his slippered entry. Once again things were smoothed over, or at least stalled, as tea bags were dunked in steaming water and spoons swirled in cups.

"How are your children adjusting?" she asked.

"They're troupers," he said. "Fourth country in twelve years. They've got it down." But as he said this he thought of Rachel's flat answer to nearly everything these days: "Fine." And Erik's bedtime prayers: "Dearest, beloved, most-on-high, almighty, heavenly Father…"

"What about your children?" he asked, a little ashamed he hadn't asked before.

Tina laughed. "My children are so old, *they* have children. The two eldest are back in the States, both lawyers, both with two kids. No, it's only Paul, my baby, who's here with us."

"He's at the British school?" he asked and Tina laughed again. She could be quite…pleasant once steered away from her usual topic of conversation. "What is it about you Brits and that school?" she asked. "It's not the only high school in town, you know. No, he's a senior at the American Community School," and he watched her smile fail. "Only now he's hanging out with some Emirati boys, sons of my husband's employers. They dropped out this fall, so he's threatening to do the same thing or at least do so poorly he'll be expelled. My husband's ready to put him on a plane for home, let his older brothers straighten him out." And then, as if this subject was even more difficult than clandestine trips to the camps, she fixed him with a look he was coming to anticipate.

"So?" she said.

"I'll talk to Lola," he said. "We'll get things sorted."

She looked unconvinced, but before she could push for more, he cut her off. "And, Tina, you can't go to the camps on your own any more. You're going to get us both in trouble. Do you want to put our little program, such as it is, in jeopardy?"

No, of course, she didn't. "Righto, Dave."

He thought he saw Eden in the loose circle of Ethiopian women that Friday. Their circle of swaying, singing devotion, white muslin on brown skin, never failed to move him, to rejoice even. This was why he was here, far from home. This. But the circle broke apart quickly and in the blur of shawls and skirts, he lost sight of the one who might have been her. Still, he felt sure she would come back. Unless — and this was the thought that kept him circling the compound in the early mornings — something worse yet had happened.

The Tuesday after, he tried Maktoum's office again. Yes, His Highness was back, yes, they'd given him Dave's message. Dave called twice more that week, told each time the message had been passed on. The following Sunday, after the nine o'clock service, Maktoum called. "It's been a crazy week, absolutely mad. I sincerely apologize. What can I do for you? My office said it was a matter of some urgency." He was different on the phone, less expansive, as if they'd only exchanged pleasantries at their first meeting, not pondered matters of the soul.

"There's a young woman, Ethiopian, who's been sleeping in our compound," Dave said. "Someone took a knife to her, carved a chunk out of her." He didn't mean to say it quite so baldly, but the image of her leg had come back. What would that have *felt* like? Bloody butcher.

There was a gap long enough for Dave to hear phones ringing in the background, other conversations. "Where did you say she was from?" Maktoum asked.

"Ethiopia. I told you when we last met about the nannies and housemaids who seek refuge, temporary refuge at best, at St. Edmund's. They've nowhere else to go."

"Have you tried their embassy? I would think that would be the best route to go, don't you? Those girls are the responsibility of their own country."

"But as I told you, there is no embassy in the UAE, just some skeleton operation in Dubai."

"Then you'd better take her to the hospital yourself, if she's that hurt. Sheikh Khalifa Medical City would be my recommendation. They're discreet in matters like this."

And then he was getting another call and suggesting they get together sometime in the future and Dave was left with a phone in his hand.

"The girl she is back," Arjun told Dave when he let himself into the vicarage that evening. Eden was lying on their bed, eyes closed, a comforter over her, Suzette on a chair pulled up close. "She's burning up," said Suzette. "I was just about to call an ambulance, and then I realized I had no idea where to take her or who to call or anything." And his wife, stable, unflappable, North England Suzette, sometimes better in a crisis than day-to-day life, began to weep. "I saw her leg. Who would do that to someone?"

It took two hours of phone calls and misunder-standings—one ambulance driver even refusing to take her—but they finally got Eden, delirious now, to Maktoum's hospital of choice. "We're run by the Cleveland Clinic. She'll be okay here," the intake clerk reassured them. "Some of those other places? You don't want to know."

They were still in the emergency waiting area when Bishop Mueller called to confirm a meeting for later in the week. "It sounds like you are at the bus station," he said, and Dave explained—briefly—where they were and why. The bishop didn't say anything right away and Dave wondered if he should have kept him out of it. "It is beyond shameful, isn't it?" the bishop said finally, clearing his throat. He hoped Eden would be all right. He would pray for her. "We have some rooms here at St. Mary's. Under the radar, of course, and nothing fancy. The girls help out when they are able and we finesse their visas, calm the angry employers, etcetera. When she is better, you send her to us."

"Who was that?" asked Suzette, closing the Arabic fashion magazine she'd been flipping through. In the green light of the hospital corridor Dave saw the effect of the years, the moves, the effort.

"I think it was an angel," he said.

"'For they are like the angels.' Good old Luke," she said.

The infection was serious, according to the young Lebanese-American doctor who came to speak to them an hour later. Eden seemed to be responding to the drip of aggressive antibiotics; her fever at least was coming down a little. Still, if the infection had penetrated to the bone… The doctor shrugged. "Different scenario."

"Do you want to report this to the police?" he asked.

"Yes," said Suzette.

"No," said Dave.

The doctor looked at them for a long moment and they looked back at him. "Well, no sense in staying. We have your mobile, right?" he said.

She was sitting on the steps again, but in shadow, so Dave didn't recognize her right away, and she didn't speak, even after Suzette had settled her inside on the sofa, sent for Arjun and slipped out of the room. As a pastor, Dave had been witness to such moments before, such stories, but they were always and forever new in the terrible way of terrible news. Tina's son Paul had gone out to Liwa, to Mehreb Dune, with his Emirati pals for a day of dune-bashing. "I didn't even know he was going," she said.

The boys had roared up and down the massive mountain of sand—Dave could hear the sound, the ugly, polluting roar of the bikes—and then they'd gone for one last ascending attack and the bike had flipped out from under one of Paul's friends and he'd fallen backward, tumbling over himself and the bike, down and down the sand until he landed near the bottom.

"The boy?" he asked, afraid.

"He might be paralyzed." Tina, who'd been staring at the wall behind him, lowered her eyes.

"But Paul, he's okay?" said Dave, willing him whole and upright, as he'd been the last time he'd seen the young man, awkwardly balancing cup and saucer in the vicarage garden.

She didn't cry as she told him about the police, about the cocaine they found in Paul's shirt pocket, when they came out to investigate the accident. The other three boys had quickly dumped and buried their stashes in the dune. "Who could find cocaine in all that sand?" Paul had not been quick enough. And despite all the good, shared, wild and crazy times, Paul's friends had not come to his defence. They looked him as if he were a stranger. He was an outsider, after all, not a member of the clan.

"The police didn't even check the other boys," said Tina. They were sent home with a reprimand about safe driving and Paul was now in a prison in Al Ain.

One of her son's friends did try to call, but her mobile had been switched off. "You know why?" Her face when she turned to him was stricken, but also defiant. "I was at the camp. The girls had a karaoke machine and they put on Abba and we were singing to 'Dancing Queen.' They were so happy I was there and they were feeding me rice and beans and we were dancing on the beds. They kept giving me the mic and I kept saying, no, no, I have a terrible voice. 'Sing anyway!' they said."

And now she was doubled over, crying, "Father, Father," and he was doing what a father would do, holding her through the next hour and into the next.

VELVET

Something snapped in Holly that Thanksgiving night, snapped like the breastbone of the eighteen-pound Butterball she'd spent an hour stuffing with homemade cornbread, chestnuts and morels. First, it was the Pakistanis — lovely people, really — who served themselves mere tablespoons of food. It was a tribute to their adventurous palates that they'd even tried her candied sweet potatoes and cranberry sauce. (Holly had scooped out a dozen satsumas and refilled them with homemade sauce, something she'd seen Martha Stewart do on TV.) But there was trepidation in their eyes as they lifted fork to mouth; Tamur, the husband, had looked alarmed when Holly ladled gravy onto his stuffing. Her brothers would have made history of that gravy, pouring it over everything, including the satsumas.

It was Jersey's idea to invite friends and colleagues who weren't American that year. "It would be so Abu Dhabi, Mom," she'd said the week before, laying her head on Holly's shoulder.

Where they would all be next Thanksgiving was anyone's guess. Jersey wanted to go to Penn State, where Justin, a year older, was studying engineering. Her husband Mark's two-year tour of duty in Abu Dhabi was up in August. Every two years — three, if they were lucky enough to get an extension — it was someplace new. Or someplace old, if they were going back to Washington for home stay. Of course — she thought immediately of Turkmenistan — some countries made you wish those two years were two weeks. The pulling up and putting down. She was tired. Every bit of her was tired. *Women Who Move Too Much.* Could be the title of her life.

But Thanksgiving! Thanksgiving could always revive her. It had all gone fairly smoothly this year, despite the long shopping lists that required visits to Lulu, Choitram and Carrefour, despite the sad-looking cranberries at Spinney's, the near-flop with the pumpkin mousse. Mostly fine, until Ryan and Linda's six-year-old Jeremy piped up with: "Who were the Pilgrims anyway?" It was the first actual reference to the holiday they were celebrating and Holly responded with the energy she was known for: "I am *so* glad you asked, sweetie. Well, the First Thanksgiving's a little bit of a story…" But she never got to tell any of it because Mark was being asked to pass the mashed potatoes and Tamur's wife, Aisha, dropped her fork and by the time it was all handled — seconds really — it was over. She tried to break in for the first little bit, tried to draw people back into the tale of that first feast and why it meant so much to Americans. She might even have told Jeremy about how her brothers dressed up every Thanksgiving when they were kids — Vince as a Pilgrim in a tall, black paper hat he'd made in Kindergarten and which they hauled out every year, Pete with a headdress from Indian Guides. Too late: Mark and Ryan were back into complaining about Etisalat's Internet service; Tamur and Aisha were explaining Eid al Adha to Linda, who'd recently arrived from the UK; and Jersey, who might have been able to corral the conversation, was in the kitchen repairing the broken crust on the apple pie.

And there she was, alone at her end of the table. The one who'd brought everyone together, lined up the damask napkins, buffed the holiday crystal, the one who'd stuffed the stupid satsumas. Who were these people and what were they doing at her Thanksgiving table?

She tried to explain it to Mark in bed later, after the guests had gone, after they'd texted Justin, who was spending the holiday weekend with a friend's family in Philadelphia. Post-parties were usually good for a little romp, a couple glasses of wine loosening Mark's mostly buttoned-down libido. "You know what I mean, don't you?" she asked, slipping her nightie back over her head. "I'm not explaining it well."

"I think so," he murmured, and then he was asleep.

It wasn't until the next morning, after a patchy night of sleep—all those courses not settling well—that Holly could wonder at what had left her feeling so bereft. Maybe she was being overly dramatic—the downside, Mark sometimes implied, of all that "energy." But really: Was this *it*? One Thanksgiving following another? One more turkey to be trussed? Countries passing, kids leaving, families changing. And always, always missing people.

Get off the pity pot, she could hear her mother say. What the hell were you expecting, Hollyhock? She'd loved and hated when her mother had talked like this: the thrill of her *hell*s and *shit*s beside the accurate, often painful, aim of her observations.

The spectre of time passing pretty much sobered anyone over the age of forty, didn't it? It had to be something more specific than this. And then, watering the bougainvillea on the balcony, its coral petals flying off in the wind, she saw what had been amiss the day before, what had thudded in her soul. It was the gravy.

Gravy was Holly's one gift as a cook. She was competent enough in the kitchen. Mark would say she was exceptional, but then Mark thought Old El Paso tacos were something else. There was no gravy recipe per se, just years of practice. What she lacked in culinary talent elsewhere, she more than made up for when it came to scraping drippings from a pan and transforming them into what her brothers used to call Velvet.

"Hey, Sugar, pass me some more of that Velvet," Vince would say and Pete would put out his plate too, though his white meat would be swimming in sauce. They were already man-size in their early teens, cute, hardy boys in big sweatshirts. "Hey, Hol, ever think about bottling this stuff?" Even at sixteen, the year their mother packed up and moved out, Holly knew this was something that would define her: loyal friend, head for numbers, klutz at sports, makes really good gravy.

Black Friday, a shopping bacchanal at home, was dead quiet in the UAE. But then so were most Fridays, at least in the morning, before noon prayers, before families packed up food trunks — they were trunks here, not mere baskets — and installed themselves in parks around the city. It wasn't about chasing a ball or a Frisbee. It was about parking yourself on something that might be grass, unloading the food, cooking the food — cubes of lamb or chicken on a grill—serving the food, then sitting and talking deep into the evening, kids darting back and forth, though they were rarely the centre of attention. Picnics were for parents and grandparents, a sedentary pleasure.

Holly was sorry they hadn't gone out more on Friday afternoons during the lovely winter months. Mark was hopeless with a hibachi, and the kids, older teenagers by the time they'd arrived in Abu Dhabi, grew impatient after an hour of sitting. ("Mom, I've got to study.") Now driving past clusters of women in headscarves and men smoking *shisha* on a Friday afternoon, everyone sitting around nothing more eventful than a metal grill, could bring tears to her eyes. They made it look so easy to belong exactly there on that spot.

The parking lot at Spinney's wasn't empty—it was never empty—but she found a space at the back near where the recycling bins had once been. "Too ugly," the store manager, a gracious Indian man, had tried to explain six months before. "The municipality take away." "But why?" she'd asked, knowing this was a question for which there would be no logical answer. "Maybe they bring back, madam." The manager had bobbled his head politely. They both knew those bins—the only recycling deposit in the entire city—would not be coming back. True, they weren't pretty, but they weren't the eyesore of the rusting dumpsters parked on every street, filled with garbage, busted Ikea furniture and crawling with feral cats.

The store was out of fresh cranberries now, the display having been ravaged two days before. More tomorrow, *insha'allah*, a clerk told her. So they could do without the cranberries. Holly bagged more potatoes

(Idahos grown in Saudi Arabia), a few bulbs of garlic, a fresh baguette, picked up a can of pumpkin and another pint of whipping cream. But the Butterballs were gone, every single one. Holly asked a man at the meat counter if they might be getting more. "Before Christmas." The smiling, shrugging Filipino butcher couldn't tell her more than that. "But I need one today. I have to have one today," and in the way her voice rose and stayed there, Holly realized how much hinged on this Thanksgiving redux.

Every couple of years—okay, more than that—she would come to a juncture where things stood out in too-bold, too-sad relief. Usually there was a trigger. Justin's departure for university had set off mornings of tears. He's gone, she'd think as soon as the alarm went off. Some of their departures—Paris was one of those—felt so premature they broke her heart too. "But we just become *les amis*," cried wonderful Juliette, someone she'd met only a month before decamping. It was often like this—the very loveliest people surfaced after two years of loneliness, as if now that it no longer mattered, Holly could loosen her grip and let things happen. "Where have you *been*?" she would say to some smart, sympathetic, interesting woman in a café, as somewhere across town the apartment was being packed up. There's email, there's Skype, they would reassure each other. But how do you stay in intimate touch with fifty people? A hundred? She'd shared the wonders and weirdness of life abroad with so many good souls. But when you left, you left.

These junctures were mostly internal, though after twenty-five years together—he was not an insensitive man—Mark could see a dip coming. He would take her out to an expensive dinner, call from work more often, try to be more attentive in bed. But there was something dutiful in his efforts as he stroked her breasts a bit too roughly. Holly could practically hear him curse her mother: Why couldn't you have just *loved* her?

Abela, a store she didn't often shop in because it was expensive, had turkeys. Well, two turkeys. Someone had ordered them for Thanksgiving, but failed to pick them up. Holly imagined a woman, some oil-and-gas wife from Pittsburgh or Santa Barbara originally, waking up on Thanksgiving morning, the sun pouring through the giant windows of her villa, thinking: Fuck the turkey. Who needs it when the InterContinental caters a top-to-bottom Thanksgiving dinner for 2,000 dirhams? They were small turkeys—she'd need both—probably the runts of the lot, but they smelled okay and the butcher gave her 20 percent off.

Back home, the Gulf a glory of turquoise beyond the tenth-floor kitchen windows, the fixings for another Thanksgiving close at hand, Holly began to run low. Not a loss of confidence exactly. Conviction maybe. She'd just *done* this, all the effort, the concentrated focus. And Mark might worry. She was glad in that moment that he had gone into the office as he did on so many Fridays. She was not even sorry that Jersey, such good company as she'd gotten older, had gone to Dubai with friends for a day of shopping. "Got an American tradition to uphold, Mom," she'd said, tossing a pashmina over her shoulder on the way out.

Holly put on music—*Glee* was good for a boost—poured herself a glass of last night's wine. Rinsing the turkeys in the sink, she suddenly thought: This isn't the First Thanksgiving, it's the Second. And laughing—this really was quite insane—she started in on the stuffing.

Vince and Pete hadn't meant to drive their truck off the Sakonnet River Bridge. They'd called it Suck On It Bridge when they were kids, then Suck My Dick Bridge when they hit their early teens, now that they knew what was what, causing their mother to rear up in indignant fury. She even grounded Vince for a month when he called the dog a "dumb shit." "Where the hell does she think we get it from?" Pete, older than Vince by a mere eleven months, said later. They were a trio. Hey, Sis, got your back. Hey, Vince, got yours.

They were in Beijing that year, Mark having been promoted into immigration services, not the top spot, two notches down. Jersey and Justin were still young, six and seven, going to the American school, where Holly taught remedial math three days a week. It was still dazzling, the travel, all things new, feeling opened so wide. There was less to say to old friends back home in Rhode Island. Even with her brothers, there was more air to fill, though Pete and Vince loyally watched their slide shows every summer. "Wow, you been there, Hollyhock?" Pete was especially impressed by Angkor Wat. "Always did want to see the Taj Mahal," Vince said.

"Any time," Holly told them every summer. "You know we've got the room."

But there was always something. Vince had a bad fall off a ladder, was laid up for nearly a year, pins, surgeries, therapy. Pete's longtime girlfriend died of a misdiagnosed appendicitis. There was constant work on the house their father had left them. "Gee, thanks, Dad!" the three would joke when the furnace exploded or half the roof blew off in a storm. Holly contributed to the repairs. Mark was making more money than her brothers' salaries combined, and technically, though she couldn't imagine living there ever again, she was part-owner.

They'd just been home for Thanksgiving, Mark having finagled a meeting in Washington for early December. It was brief, eight days, not enough time to get over the jet lag, but enough time to gather in the family bungalow. They celebrated Thanksgiving on the day itself—a treat after living abroad where Thursdays weren't a day off and gathering people for a feast meant postponing it a day or two. The turkey that year had been on the dry side, Mark managed to mangle his trademark mashed potatoes, little Jersey dropped the pumpkin pie as she shakily carried it to the table and Justin couldn't think of anything to be grateful for when they went around the table giving thanks. But the gravy? "Haven't lost your touch, Sis," said Pete, and Vince gave her a thumbs up, misting unexpectedly.

The gravy *was* exceptional, though Holly had done nothing radically different that year: roasted the turkey over a bed of onions, carrots, celery and fresh thyme, later caramelizing the vegetables as she added wine, plus broth made from the giblets and neck. The gravy even looked gorgeous that year: rich mahogany with a nearly iridescent glaze and molasses-thick. She didn't make too much of the flavour, which was subtle, deep and complex, knowing her brothers would throw her scornful looks before teasing her to death. "Hey, Hol, we know it's good!

We're having thirds, okay?" They were seven at the table that year; Vince had thought to invite an elderly aunt who would have otherwise been eating institutionalized turkey at her seniors' residence. Vince and Pete pulled her chair out, pushed it back in, fluttered around her like big turkeys over a nest. It was low-key, a nothing-to-get-fussed-about Thanksgiving, and Holly left for China thankful for what they'd shared and for the life she now had. What the hell did you expect, Hollyhock? Well, Mom, everything, I guess.

It hadn't been a particularly white Christmas that year, light flurries on Christmas Eve, Pete said over the phone when he called Christmas night: "Deck the halls with boughs of Holly." He'd been singing this to her since they were kids, cracking up when he got to her name. But at the start of the new year, temperatures all along the East Coast shot up, an accidental spring. Vince emailed Holly a picture of Pete floating on a spare tire in the backyard thaw. And then the temperature dropped: a sudden minus 30 on the night of January 20, the night Vince and Pete were coming back from a party in Tiverton. Those signs on the side of the road as you approach a bridge, the ones that say BRIDGE ICES BEFORE ROAD? They're true.

"You see, what happens is the cold air surrounds the upper and lower surface of the bridge." The police officer who'd found the truck in the frozen river the next morning must have thought knowing the details would be, if not a comfort, then a way to understand the tragedy. "This double exposure causes the water on the bridge to freeze faster than that on the road." He'd remembered to say how sorry he was and that he hoped her family had some "closure" soon. Vince and Pete would have snorted at that word.

She'd been overly ambitious, Holly realized after baking the cornbread for the stuffing. It was now one o'clock. If the turkeys went into the oven within the hour, they'd be lucky to eat by eight. Eat. She hadn't actually thought beyond the shopping, cooking, baking part. Who was going to eat all this food? Parting the birds' legs to push in the stuffing, she saw again how small they were, how puny compared to last night's Butterball. And again it struck her as completely nuts—a piled-high platter of leftover turkey sat in the fridge—to be doing this. "Can't make lemonade without lemons. Can't make gravy without a turkey," she said out loud and heard herself laugh again.

But she could do without the non-essentials. She'd bake the potatoes instead of mashing them, ditto for the sweet potatoes (who needed all that butter and brown sugar again?) And for dessert there was plenty of leftover apple pie and pumpkin mousse. The night before, Holly had tried to pack up leftovers for her dinner guests, but after the Pakistanis threw each other startled looks, she'd stopped. She would never, ever, completely understand another culture. After twenty years abroad she knew this for a fact. It was time perhaps to stop trying. It was time perhaps to go home.

Their mother hadn't been a vain woman, not one to get manicures or spend a lot on clothes. But she was bold and bright, a tall redhead with a wide mouth, olive-green eyes accented with a sweep of pearly shadow, a small waist—what men used to call "a looker"—and the mouth of a truck driver. You couldn't miss her. You didn't want to miss her if you were one of her chosen.

Carolina chose people, pulled them in from the crowd. She didn't necessarily go for the obvious power-brokers, like bank presidents or school principals. But she wooed their teachers, their coaches, anyone who might be able to open doors and eliminate the rest of the competition. "You can't say Mom isn't ambitious for us," Vince once said after Holly and her mother had finished each other off in a shouting match, begun when Holly refused to give chocolates to her teachers before exams. "Ungrateful bitch!" Carolina had growled. That mouth, that tongue. Even after her mother left them to pursue another life, Holly could still hear the names: Slob. Brat. Pain in the freaking neck. Bitch.

Finding Carolina wouldn't have been that difficult. There had been various addresses and phone numbers over the years, mostly from aunts or cousins who'd heard from her. But she never contacted them, the family of four she'd let fall away, even after their father died at fifty. And so she didn't hear what had happened to her boys—thirty-six- and thirty-seven-year-old bachelors, managers at the Safeway in town, best friends. "Why should she know?" Holly asked Mark, who knew better than to offer anything but a soft-eyed nod. She must have known, of course. Word would have reached her somehow.

Holly slipped the turkeys, propped on a mound of sliced onions, celery stalks and unpeeled carrots, into the oven just at two. And then, even though she knew it was not a sign of mental stability, she went back out in search of cranberries. She'd already checked in the obvious places, but something kept whispering at her, and finally, at the other Choitram's, the one in Khalidiyah, a store you couldn't even get near with a car, she found one sad bag. It was thirty dirhams, an absolute crime, but she bought it anyway. Back home, the kitchen was warm with the smell of roasting birds. She tipped the cranberries into a pot, stirred in sugar and orange juice and felt the knot that had been there since yesterday loosen. Cranberries were part of what made Thanksgiving dinner a feast, not just another big dinner, and she had found them.

"Have you recovered from *le grand bouffe*?" Mark always called at 4:30 unless he was in a meeting. Lately he'd been involved in a U.S. Embassy program on human trafficking. It was a hard sell, he said. "You know this part of the world. They want to look good, they want our respect and regard, but they don't want to change." He sounded tired, like he was the one who needed recovering.

"Everything's pretty much back to normal," Holly said and surveyed her counters, grateful again that she'd never employed a maid here. Who needed that scrutiny? A household was complicated enough. Bags of flour and corn meal, parts of vegetables, knives and cutting boards, plastic wrap from the turkeys covered the granite counters for the second time in twenty-four hours. She'd never been a neat cook. Well, it was. This was normal.

She started on the roux while the turkeys roasted, working her magic on the birds' innards. And when the turkeys came out at six she was ready, broth and flour in hand. This was the part she loved best: placing the roasting pan over two burners, turning up the flame and stirring like a dervish as the drippings turned dark as burnt caramel. Then came the wine, scraping the browned bits, pressing the remaining moisture from the spent vegetables, stirring, reducing, straining. And then…velvet.

Mark looked stunned, anxious, then simply blank as he stood in the kitchen door, shaking his head finally, surrendered, as he came to hug her.

"You are something," he said.

"It was the gravy," she said. "It wasn't right."

Mark nodded. "Do I have to keep my suit on for this?"

Jersey looked delighted when she came home. "Why didn't you tell me we were doing Thanksgiving all over again?"

"It was the gravy," Holly said, her only explanation.

The turkeys were surprisingly tender for such little guys, the baked potatoes better than last night's mashed potatoes with roasted garlic and crème fraîche, the stuffing crunchy and soft in the right places, the cranberries sweet and puckery. They broke the garlic bread—"Like croutons!" cried Jersey—in chunks over the salad of spinach and butter lettuce. And the gravy, while not her best-best, not quite to the level of that Thanksgiving in a Rhode Island bungalow a dozen years before, was splendid. Good gravy is no mere condiment, Holly read once in a cookbook. It's the tie that binds.

"Hey, guys, remember that time in Jakarta? We'd invited some under-secretary from the Laotian Embassy for Thanksgiving?" Jersey's face was bright with wine.

"Cambodian," said Mark.

"Yeah, whatever, and the guy thought that the cranberries looked like some poisonous berry and he got really scared?"

"What about Turkmenistan?" said Mark, and they both groaned. Their two Turkmen Thanksgivings had required improvisation. The first year, Justin had been so disappointed at the sight of flatbread pieces and chickpeas in the stuffing he'd cried.

"Or the Thanksgiving where we just decided to keep it the four of us…where was that?" Holly asked.

"Paris," said Mark. And she saw their apartment again. It had faced Les Tuileries and the two bedrooms had been flooded with light and there was a wonderful *boulangerie* right downstairs.

"What about that one when we went home and Uncle Vince and Uncle Pete and that crazy old aunt of yours danced around the kitchen?" said Jersey. "I think I dropped the pumpkin pie or something."

"You remember that?" said Holly and had to look down at her plate because the room was suddenly swimming.

"Sorry, Mom," said Jersey.

"I'm a tough old bird and don't either of you forget it." Then realizing what they were eating, Holly laughed, a laugh she could feel in her chest. And they were laughing too.

"This was quite…unexpected," said Mark, when he laid down his napkin finally, regarding his wife with a look of long, complicated love before she sent him off to the den.

Alone in the kitchen later — so much to wash and put away, so many containers to rearrange in the fridge — she caught sight of an Emirati family, they seemed like a family, taking a late walk on the Corniche: one *khandoura* followed by five *abayas*. Wives? Daughters? One was never sure. Families came in so many shapes and sizes. She watched them walk the full length of her window and disappear into the frame. Perhaps they were all going out for ice cream, *baba* treating his girls.

NATIONAL DAY

You know how parents tell kids as their marriage is busting up: Honey this has nothing to do with you it's between me and Dad (or me and Mum) it's not your fault we hope you understand sometimes grownups just can't live together anymore we still love you honey this has nothing to do with you?

My parents couldn't say that.

They worked — she still does — at the New Medical Centre. She's an internist; he's an ob/gyn. Babies, private parts. I never got why he would pick that specialty, but Dad says he just loves pregnant women. "He loves women in general," Mum says, but not meanly or jealously. Other women weren't the problem.

We have an agreement going, now it's just the two of us. We will not badmouth Dad. We will not be negative. We will not be dramatic. That one's for me. My mother could star in an ad for Xanax, she's so fucking calm. She could open a yoga studio, start an ashram. Dr. Nadira, doctor of serenity and bullshit. But I'm not supposed to crap all over her either. Them's the rules.

Dad's take is that I don't have enough rules. "That's what this place does to kids," he says. "This place" happens to be my home sweet home and I'm never leaving it. Another issue, I guess you could say, between me and the rents. I love my Abu. I love it to pieces. The heat's ridiculous and sometimes it gets to me how other Indians are treated. Like there are these guys who wash the windows of our apartment tower. Twice a year they're out there on this creaky, stupid little box with their squeegees and they look so tired and sweaty and like they *really* don't know what they're doing and I know they're probably getting about a dirham an hour and living out in the labour camps. So what do I do? Pull the blinds. Rude and basically useless, that's me, but I can't watch.

The British School Al Khubairat, where I'm cruising Grade 10, is for precocious, entitled kids with ambitious, guilty parents. "We're so sorry, sweetie, for taking you away from your friends in Flitwick (or Henley-on-Thames or Glossop...take your pick of any British backwater). But we shall make it up to you, my darling diddums. Promise!" The joke, of course, is that kids love it here. They love it after five minutes. What's not to love? The city's buzzing. The beach, the sun, the shopping, the travelling. Golf lessons, billionaire buddies, gold dust on the chocolate mousse at Emirates Palace. Freedom.

My cousins back in the UK don't believe that last thing. "Really, free as a bird," I tell them when we visit in summers. "But, Raakhi, it's, you know, *Muslim*." It's standard that Brits — even Hindu Indians, who should be more tolerant — get vexed when it comes to Muslims. That's why so many Brits are moving to France and Spain. Most won't actually come out and say so. They just roll their eyes and say something about lax immigration, blah, blah. It's dred.

I have a theory why kids feel so free here. The dads are flat roofin' it at some job with insane hours and random bosses. The mums are bored out of their skulls, so they roll with a bunch of other expat ladies. Their world's busy, too busy for kids. Besides, there's always the nanny or the maid or both. If your folks are working, and doctors to boot, you basically write your own ticket. I had a nanny when I was younger, but she ran away when I was ten and Mum hasn't trusted anyone since. "We manage," she says, which means she calls every hour to check on me and leaves samosas from Lulu in the fridge for after school. Oh, the life of an only child.

But that's not what's bugging me now. Not even missing Dad with all my hard little heart—his words—comes to the level of being grounded for National Day. National Day is brill. National Day is jokes. National Day is wicked fun.

First off, it's December 2, so it's blue skies, no clouds and not a drop of humidity. At school, the day before, we come in national dress. Somewhere in our closets we all have an *abaya* or *khandoura*. Just for this one day I glide along in my long black dress, jeans underneath, slut-heels on my size 6s, like a real Emirati lady. I love the way the material—light as nothing—swivels around my legs when I walk, the way the *shayla* slides off my hair onto my shoulders. So buff.

Mum says she might let me go for the school thing if I don't pull any drama between now and next week. But National Day, the real holiday, she's taking me to work with her. No parade on the Corniche. No watching the fireworks on the beach in front of Emirates Palace. No meeting up with friends. First she said she might take me up to the roof of the hospital to watch the fireworks. Then she thought about it. "Better yet, I'll order in from India Palace. It'll be fun."

Last National Day, me, Miles, Rahim, Becka — mates from Al Khubairat — walked all the way down Khaleej al Arabi to the Corniche, Becka and me complaining all the way about our feet. At 7th Street, we got spun around in the crowd and lost each other in seconds. Miles miraculously found me on the corner, looking madly in all directions.

"Hey, isn't this the way we wanted it?" he said. He was lush, with these burning blue eyes and artist hands. We'd been texting each other like crazy for a week. We've been classmates since Grade 6, but it was like we'd just noticed each other, like we'd just woken up.

Of course, we couldn't hold hands, but we walked as close together as we could, passing the long lines of honking, grid-locked SUVs, sports cars, Hummers. Each was like a work of art, covered in red, white, green and black decals, crêpe paper, balloons and every gaudy, out-there decoration you could imagine. Some people had even got their cars painted green or red for the day. Happy Birthday, UAE! Thirty-nine years old, a baby of a country, if you think of Merry Olde. The car windows were open, Arabic music blasting out, people inside waving and yelling and squirting out green and red foam from giant canisters. Some green landed at my feet and I nearly slid into the people in front of us.

Two little kids were perched on the sunroof of a red van plastered with photos of Sheikh Khalifa and Sheikh Mohammed. "Look!" Miles was pointing at the kids, but I didn't want to. A couple of years ago a three-year-old boy slipped off the roof of his family's car onto the hood and got caught under their front wheels. They took him to hospital, where my parents were working. "These people," Mum said, shaking her head. She doesn't think much of Emiratis. "If you saw what comes through our ER, you'd lose all respect," she says.

When Miles and I finally waded through the traffic and reached the Corniche, it got crazier — ten lanes filled with cars inching along, mobs of Indian and Pakistani men in pastel *shalwar kameez*, women in saris, girls in *abayas*, cops trying and failing to keep order, kids dashing in and out of the street. A boy in a *khandoura* stuck his arm out of his Porsche and shot a long stream of red foam at the Pakistanis. It landed in their hair mostly, but one man, near me, doubled over, clutching his eyes. The boy took aim again, laughing and shouting in Arabic, and sprayed the men, aiming at their shoes.

"This is nuts," yelled Miles, and took my hand since no one could see. In this party mood, nobody probably cared either. His hand was electric.

It was hardly my first National Day, but it was the first time my parents had let me come down here without them. "Only if you're with friends, understand?" Mum had insisted. "And it probably wouldn't hurt if there were some boys in the group." Dad had looked at her doubtfully.

Back in our flat, Miles asked me to touch him and I did and then he touched me and then the thing just happened, though I was scared the whole time and hearing things. Miles kept saying it was just the cars on the Corniche. "They'll be out there all night burning rubber with their Lamborghinis. Idiots."

Afterward, I changed into my trainers and we walked all the way to the Marina for the fireworks. My folks wouldn't have been happy about any of it—splitting off from the gang, going to the beach. And the other thing, a big thing I could never tell them. Miles and I didn't talk about it; instead we joked about our stupid UAE social studies class in Grade 8 and how Miss Khadija had made us memorize the names of the leaders of all seven Emirates. "I bet you can't remember them," said Miles, turning to grin at me. His hair was messed up and adorable and for one scary moment I thought maybe I'd fallen in love back there.

I named the only one still in my brain. "Fujairah… Sheikh Hamad Bin Mohammed al-Sharqui. Remember old Sharqui?"

"The colours of the UAE flag are highly symbolic," trilled Miles in Miss Khadija's high voice. "Red for sacrifice, white for peace, black for oil and green for…" he hesitated. "Not the environment?"

"Money," I said.

"Right," said Miles, and then about 100 years later: "Let's not make a big deal about…you know."

The beach was so packed with bodies and blankets and camping chairs and hibachis and coolers that we stood on the sidewalk for ten minutes, scanning for one square foot of unoccupied sand. Miles finally dragged me to a place in the dark, somewhere to the left. We sat, the sand surprisingly cool. I pulled my knees to my chest. My body was sore and I now had oozy blisters on the back of both heels. Miles passed me a lit cigarette. It was just a cigarette, though, not the interesting stuff, which we would have been crazy to smoke out here, even if it was National Day and the whole place had gone postal.

It was a happening crowd—people dancing and playing music, laughing and eating, mostly eating. All nationalities, all ages: a baby crawled in front of us. "I think we may be the only Westerners here," Miles said. Interesting, I thought, to be included as his "people," considering my ethnic origins. Though if you've never actually lived in India, are born in the UK and raised in Abu Dhabi, who's to say what you are?

I did go to India two years ago, the folks deciding I needed to discover my roots. Even my grandparents back in Brixton have only ever *visited* their parents' village. They're essentially British, but Brits who wear saris to weddings and argue about their curry.

I had been pissed about going at first. "Why are you taking me somewhere I'm going to get sick?" But Dad got me all the right shots, Mum loaded up our carry-on with antibiotics and it turned out, I absolutely loved the place. The poverty makes you want to cry every minute, but there's so much life and beauty, and my relatives—Dad's family, who live in Delhi—are like the sweetest people. I was spoilt rotten. "You come back," they said.

"Get a look at those Pakistani guys over there. Where the bloody hell do they think they are?" Miles was pointing to a group of men to our left. They were dancing in a circle, holding hands—one guy seemed to be in the middle—and everyone around them was clapping in rhythm.

"They're having a good time," I said and then there was a sound so loud and close, so skull-splitting that I lunged to the side, rolling over in the sand, as an

SUV — green and red and white crêpe-paper streamers flying behind, horn blasting — roared down the sand toward the water, men and women and kids spilling out on all sides, as it ran over blankets and barbeques. The car slowed only when it came close to the water. People were screaming and running in all directions and Miles grabbed my arm, pushing me against and through the crowd running toward us, toward the accident. I was hit in the face by a shoe flying, someone stomped on my foot, but by now Miles was behind me, shoving me hard toward the sidewalk. One cab only was on the street and we ran toward it, Miles jamming me inside, before sliding over on the seat.

"Get us out of here," he yelled to the driver, who was watching the horror through his open window. He didn't move, didn't speak.

"I mean it. GO!" Miles thumped the back of the front seat, and the man, as if in a dream, still watching, turned the key in the ignition.

"Fucking Paki, go!" Miles yelled and kicked the seat so hard, the driver lost his footing on the brake and the cab lurched.

I looked over at the boy with the cute hair and wished with all my heart I could live my life over. I got out of the car, ran back across the street, joining the tumbling mob. I saw bodies carried out by wailing men, women running with food hampers on their heads, blood coming down their arms, little kids turning round and round in place before getting trampled. I wanted so badly to help. But what could I do? I was a useless sixteen-year-old girl. When I couldn't stand there and watch any more, I limped back to the Corniche. No empty cabs still, just slow-moving cars. They looked sad now, inching along with their garlands hanging half off and dragging in the filthy street. It took me an hour to get home, but I managed, even with bleeding feet, to beat Mum and Dad.

The next week I couldn't eat. Gastro, I told them. "What did you have that night? Was it from one of those new restaurants on the Corniche?" My folks were ready to have the health department check every single one of them. "It's just a bug," I kept saying. I lost a stone in a month.

The people who got hit were taken to Sheikh Khalifa Medical City and others to my folks' hospital, so they knew some of what had happened. As far as I could figure out, they were the Pakistani men I'd seen dancing. It was hard to put it together because *The National* only mentioned it on page six two days later and didn't actually say if anyone had died. They made it look like one crazy kid was responsible when the SUV had been loaded with locals. There was nothing in *Gulf News*.

I heard nothing from Miles either, not even a text. When we went back to school after National Day break, he put up his hand from across the classroom. I read it more as bye than hi and he didn't try to make me think he meant it any other way. Mum and Dad worried that I was becoming anorexic and because telling the truth was worse, I said, Yeah, I want to be thin, really thin. Food is my enemy. Stuff like that.

Then the dreams kicked in. Not dreams of that night, but dreams of people wanting to hurt me, coming to get me. I started locking my door at night, which freaked the folks. "What are you hiding in there?" Dad said. "You'd better not be doing drugs." Dad, God love him, is as stick-up-your-ass as Gordon Brown. Straight as a golf club. No to drugs, sex before marriage, shit marks, disrespect to the elders. Yes to stellar grades, virginity, Oxbridge, suitable marriage, big bucks as doctor/lawyer/prof. He's a traditional Indian man with no fucking clue how to handle an acting-out, messed-up teenage daughter. Mum murmured a lot of stuff about third-culture kids, hormones, history of depression on Dad's side (news to me), a New-Agey mumbo-jumbo of theories that totally let *them* off the hook and had piss-all to do with me.

But it wasn't until I started cutting myself—tiny little scratches with a nail scissors on my upper arms—that they got it. The nicks didn't hurt too much. They even looked sort of cool in the bathroom light, like the lines of an etching. Late at night, the folks asleep at the other end of the flat, I would draw out designs on graph paper from my maths notebook, then copy them onto my arms. I was a skin artist. Sometimes, though, it hurt so much I couldn't sleep after and then I'd be a total wreck at school next day. I was already losing it at school. A couple of teachers took me aside: "Raakhi, is everything okay? You've failed the last two quizzes."

Who was there to tell that everything was so not okay? Mum? Dad? Becka, who did everything *but* with Rahim? And what would I tell them? I have pictures in my head that won't go away? I am so fucking disappointed in myself? I'm a screwed-up third-culture kid? I already knew what I'd hear from a counsellor type: Everyone makes mistakes, luv. My bet is you'll feel a whole lot better if you tell your parents what's troubling you.

The really crazy thing is that life in Abu trundled on, like nothing had happened. I googled "National Day," but all I could find were YouTube videos of some big, Emiratis-only celebration at Zayed Stadium. Even the one story that had run in *The National* wasn't posted online any more.

Miles and I weren't even making eye contact by then, but one lunch I went over to his table in the school canteen.

"Yes?" he said, looking up.

"Did you ever read anything about what we saw on the beach that night?"

"What night?"

"National Day, Miles."

"You mean the partying? Those labourers dancing?"

"The SUV that drove through the sand and ran over people."

Miles looked at me like I was nothing. Not the girl he'd wanted so much, the girl he'd touched as cars squealed down the Corniche, the girl he'd known since Grade 6. "No idea what you're on about." He picked up his tray and walked off.

That night I went onto our balcony. It's one of the coolest things in our flat, wraps around the kitchen and living room, with a slice of the Corniche showing between buildings. Mum tries to grow things out there each winter, but has basically given up on anything but cacti. Summers it's impossible, of course, even at night. But by then it was mid-January, a bit cool. I don't like heights so I never look down when I'm out there, just concentrate on the Corniche or a book or my iPod. But that night I made myself look down. I stood at the edge of the balcony, leaning on the railing, and looked straight down. It was so far to the street, to the shawarma place where Dad sometimes stopped on his way home from the hospital, the hole-in-the-wall bakery where they bake flatbread in a tandoor, the mobile store where Mum got my first phone. If I leaned a little further out, I could see kids playing cricket in front of the mosque. So. Far. Down. My legs began to shake so I went back inside.

Mum came home looking grim a couple days later. "Show me your arms," she said. I pulled up my sleeves to the elbows. "Whole arm," she said. Someone had caught sight of my artwork in PE and told the coach. Snowball effect naturally, since I was already on the Watch That Girl list. Mum cried, Dad lectured, I told them everything. What happened on the beach, what happened in my room.

"She's depressed," said Mum.

"She's lost," said Dad.

I suppose they were both right, but four months of Paxil and Ambien, hours of yakkety-yak with an Indian child psychologist who threw the word "should" around a lot, plus "more honest dialogue" between me and the rents (shrink's idea) produced one tangible result: Dad left for a job in Delhi. He wouldn't come out and say it was because of me, but he's a very black-and-white, good/bad kind of guy. When you fail, you fail. There's no making up. I had too many "issues." I was damaged goods. I was a supreme disappointment. Mum and Dad made sounds about the Delhi gig being a "great opportunity," but come on, I knew.

A few weeks after our last shrink session, I met him at the door, a big, fake, Dad-pleasing smile on my face.

He looked finished. Too many babies being born that day, I guess. But I couldn't wait. This was urgent. Lady Gaga, singer for all time, was playing this year's Formula One. I had to go.

"No," said Dad.

"The tickets are only 295 dirhams, Dad. It won't break you."

"No," said Dad.

"But, Dad, everybody's going. They're going to fucking sell out!"

"This is not an argument you want to pursue, Raakhi."

But I did. In the spirit of more honesty, I begged, I raged, I called him names. I ran out onto the balcony and threatened to jump.

And as I stood there, leaning hard against the railing, it was like I was seeing my city for the first time, like I was a baby again or a new immigrant. I was like one of those Indian window washers taking it all in from this high point—the water all shimmery under the moon, the green lights from the minaret of the mosque a call away, the cars streaming along the Corniche.

BRILLIANT

And now they were leaving. After years of life abroad, they were packing a few pots and pillows, the decorated chest from Pinky's that had required driving hopelessly through the hinterlands of Sharjah and which had probably — Edwina never really wanted to know — been painted by Indian slum children earning a pound a month. It was back to Liverpool.

The movers drove down from Dubai, three guys from Kerala in a wreck of an open-back truck that said Paradise Movers on the side. They arrived at 9:00 p.m. — "right on time," sighed Gerald — and packed quietly through the night. When Edwina looked out the front window of the villa the next morning, the men were tying the mess of boxes down with what looked like lengths of yellow plastic.

"Don't look," said Gerald.

"Wait, did you print out the plane tickets before they packed the computer?" she asked.

He looked at her. "What do *you* think?"

She'd been crying for weeks, even through rounds of golf with Georgie and Harriet, part of the original quartet.

"But you can't leave us here! We won't let you!" Georgie had been saying since the news of Gerald's situation hit their circle. Harriet couldn't talk about it without her small, blue eyes spilling over. They'd been through so much already—just surviving the back-and-forth of boarding schools with their broods was a forever-bonding experience. But nothing had prepared them for this, not even Kat's departure for Cyprus three years before. Kat still came back a couple of times a year—both sons worked here in Abu Dhabi—but Edwina knew she wouldn't be coming back. How could she? Airfares were up. Gerald didn't have a job as such—he was close to retirement age—and her skills as a school nurse were rusty from years of disuse. She'd be lucky, at her age, to find something part-time in a Heyworth Street shop.

The girls were sad, sorry and besotted with sympathy, but that didn't stop them from talking endlessly about the send-off party.

"Of course we'll have it at The Club," said Georgie. "Remember how they pulled out the stops for Kat? Fireworks on the beach, dancing till dawn. I had so much sand in my shoes, I couldn't walk."

"All those good times," said Harriet, eyes misting on cue.

"All that juicy gossip," said Edwina, struggling to keep it light.

"Like how Annie March has the gall to wear a bikini, let alone a swimsuit of any cut or style, in public," said Georgie, looking around, just in case. They weren't at The Club, but their second-favourite cafe, Vivel, downstairs from Harriet's Corniche-view flat. "Whatever happened to the sort that went to the knee?"

"She could always wear an *abaya*," said Harriet.

"What do you think, Edwina? Shall I speak to the chef at The Club?" said Georgie. "Roast beef? Chicken? Maybe both?"

But then Georgie and Harriet converged again on the guest list—should they invite the Abbotts under the circumstances?—and Edwina didn't have to commit to either. "After all," said Georgie, pushing down her reading glasses, "Kevin Abbott is the one who wrote Gerald that awful letter."

"I might give that man the finger," said Harriet.

"I might bite him in the leg," said Georgie and the two collapsed on each other's shoulders in giggles.

"We could hire a yacht," said Edwina.

"We could," said Georgie slowly, looking at Harriet whose face had fallen. "We'll work it out, darling, no worries," and she patted Edwina's hand.

Gerald had always wanted a yacht. Edwina discovered this on their south-of-France honeymoon, one of those out-of-nowhere facts one discovers after the vows have been exchanged. He hadn't come out and said, "This is what I want, by Jove!" (Gerald didn't speak that way, in any case.) But the way he'd looked at the yachts docked at Sète, dream boats with polished wood prows and bronzed blondes on deck sipping vodka collins in the fading French light, she knew. She'd have liked him to look at her that way (the boats, not the women), as if she was what he'd always imagined for himself. Not that she was complaining. All the parts worked, his and hers, no problems there. And they were setting off on an adventure come honeymoon's end: Muscat,

Oman, where Gerald would manage a desalination project.

"They're beautiful, aren't they?" she'd murmured, as they walked slowly along the quay. "That one there, look at the name: *The African Queen*. Oh, I loved that movie. Brilliant, wasn't it?" And Gerald had nodded and squeezed her hand, but his eyes, alive with wanting, were on the yachts.

The Oman job lasted four years, long enough for Gerald to make friends in the right places and get invited on a cruise. "Sorry, cherub, no ladies allowed," he told Edwina. The yacht belonged to the sultan's son, the crown prince, but along the way they would be joined by the crown prince of Kuwait and *his* entourage on *his* yacht, then sail to an island off the coast of Yemen in the Gulf of Aden to a private hunting reserve. Both were super yachts; the sultan's measured seventy-five metres, Gerald said. Edwina had no point of reference for the length of yachts, but it sounded big. Gerald named everyone on the guest list—of the thirty invited, he was one of the few civilians—but it was lost on Edwina, who still got the *al*s and *bin*s mixed up, something Gerald had memorized early on. He'd even picked up a workable Arabic. "Greases the way," he said. "You should take a class, Edwina. They do offer them to the wives."

But the parts had worked so well that by the end of the third year they had two babies. And even with help—a Filipina named Nellie for baby Sara and a Sri Lankan who called herself Lu ("real name too hard," she said) for baby Alec—there wasn't time for anything except lunch with friends and a little shopping at the Mutrah souq. Then, too, friends were forever flying down from the UK for a cheap, Arabian getaway. Edwina was always tired, always busy. By the end of the Oman years—another baby on the way—she'd lost track of Gerald somewhat, his wants and needs, his yacht dreams. And then they moved to Abu Dhabi.

"We have to settle this," said Georgie the next time they met. "Are we inviting the Abbotts or not? Totally your call, Edwina."

Edwina had liked the Abbotts well enough—Merry was a hoot at a party, especially with a few drinks in her, though the rest of the time she could be remote. And Kevin was solid, if colourless. Solid pretty much amounted to a full-out endorsement in this part of the world. She'd met so many flakes, so many stray dogs here, and not the four-legged kind. But Kevin had seriously let them down, had shimmied out of his responsibilities to his longtime, mostly loyal staff, of which Gerald was the most longtime and, to Edwina's mind, most loyal. The year before, Kevin had been under fire from the Emirati CEO to tighten the ranks—in other words, lose some—and Gerald had handled it all, down to delivering the news himself, even escorting families to the airport for 2:00 a.m. flights back home. Now the news had been delivered to him. And in a letter; no stalwart Gerald to break the news gently. Cold, so cold.

But the effort to not invite the Abbotts seemed too big to Edwina, sitting between her two closest friends at The One, their third-favourite café in the city. What would she do without *them*? After so many years away, no one else really knew or understood her. They couldn't. Not even the kids, who once had been part of this life. But that was another story for a braver day.

"Oh, just invite the Abbotts," Edwina said. Her tea was cold. The staff here wasn't as attentive as they were at The Club. "Who needs the bad blood, right?"

"You are so strong," said Harriet.

The first boat Gerald bought didn't qualify as a yacht per se. Technically, it was a cruiser. Still, it did the job, he said. They called her *Mad Summer*. And they did have some mad times on the boat, docking her at Al Bateen marina, where she sat idle only through the very hottest months. The rest of the year they were out on her every Friday and Saturday, often leaving the (now) four kids behind with nannies and maids. Edwina did have twinges as they set out at seven in the morning, knowing she wouldn't see the little darlings until at least eight that night, but Gerald needed his recreation. He was working long days with terrible deadlines, unreasonable bosses and fabulous money. He'd earned it with his now-fluent Arabic—a rarity among expats—and his genius with water conservation projects. Even more winning was his handling of labour matters. Gerald was no soft touch with the unskilled workers and that earned him stars with his Emirati bosses. "Those Indian fellows are lucky to have a job," he often said. Edwina had also seen how the male halves of some of their friends behaved when left to their solo selves on these sailing jaunts. Gerald was a good-looking man and those blondes and vodka collinses were everywhere, despite this being the UAE.

Mad Summer took them through four breezy, glorious seasons. And then Gerald met *Blind Date*. She was the real thing: a yacht, admittedly a small yacht compared with the ones Gerald was sometimes invited on. But the kids—now old enough to come along—adored her. The two boys were even learning to skipper. Edwina enjoyed her too, though her attachment paled next to Gerald's. "I don't think I've ever loved anything so much," he admitted one night as they sat on the deck working their way through a bottle of merlot Gerald now ordered by the case from African & Eastern. Work was still mad—deadlines changing weekly, bosses monthly, hours expanding, plans made and shredded. But the money. They'd never had so much money. Like many of their friends, they bought a villa in the south of Spain, vacationed in Cape Town, Hong Kong, Paris, Sydney, New York, sent the children to boarding schools in Switzerland and the UK. *Blind Date* was part of that life, the stage for gatherings where everything just flowed and flowed. They earned a reputation for throwing the best parties in town. "World's our oyster," Gerald said after one where a few royals had made an appearance. And then he pulled down the bottoms of Edwina's silk pajamas. "Come here, my pearl."

The boats had to keep pace. *Blind Date* (fifteen metres) became *The Wave*—at thirty-two metres moving them officially into the league of mega-yachts—became *Soulmate*. For the first time, Edwina understood Gerald's consuming passion. She also understood for the first time why boats were referred to as "she." *Soulmate* was a beauty from bow to stern: forty-seven metres of luxury and grace, a lady. Edwina loved nothing more than to sit on her deck at dusk, the lights of the city spread across the water. Sometimes Georgie, Harriet and Kat would join her. Sometimes she had a whole gang over for afternoon tea, the tea turning to cocktails as the sun went down.

It was all worth it then. The years away from home, the children scattered, a husband married to his mobile.

But Gerald never seemed to fully appreciate *Soulmate*. His jubilation at her purchase lasted mere months. He wasn't entirely happy with the way she steered, he tried to explain. And the panelling needed replacing. And... he had a whole list of improvements that would need to be made before she was truly seaworthy. "She's perfectly seaworthy," Edwina told Georgie and Harriet. "I have no idea what he's on about."

But she'd begun to dislike the expression he wore when they took *Soulmate* out. As if it was a trial. Sailing a lovely big boat wasn't supposed to be a trial. It was supposed to be a lark. Whatever was the matter with him? Yes, things at work were strained and insane. What else was new?

The fall of 2008 brought something new. "Downturn, crisis, crunch, whatever you call it, it's not touching us here, is it?" And Kevin Abbott had chuckled into his rum and Coke. They'd been standing by the pool at their new villa in Marina Village. It had taken Gerald a year of string-pulling to get them in. Everyone wanted one of these places. Beyond the tile-lined pool, the dark waters of the Gulf stretched to the Arabian wedding cake of the Emirates Palace Hotel. "Lucky to be alive, aren't we?" Kevin said and clinked her glass.

Edwina had seen Judith before, her pinched little face sometimes appearing in the mirror as Edwina lifted herself in a neck-killing cobra. (Yoga was one Club activity she would not miss.) She'd never thought about Judith, really. Lacklustre, if she'd had to put a word to the woman. And here she was sitting between Georgie and Harriet at their usual table at The Club.

"Of course, you know Judith," said Georgie.

"Of course," said Edwina, sliding onto the end of the banquette. She was used to sitting in the middle. She felt like she might slip off. "How are you, Judith?"

"Smashing," said Judith. "Absolutely smashing."

"Judith's just come back from a month in, where was it exactly, Judith?" said Harriet.

"South of France. A little port town called Sète. Brilliant. Neville loves it."

"Sète," said Edwina, and found she couldn't say anything else.

"You know it? You've been?" asked Judith, smiling, which made her look not exactly pretty, but pert. She was, up close, obviously younger than they were. Late forties perhaps.

"Yes," said Edwina. "A long time ago."

"It's changed a lot," said Judith, unfolding her napkin.

"Judith has offered to help us with the party," said Harriet, blue eyes anxious. "Georgie and I realized we were a bit out of our depth. Jude's a pro."

"Wedding planner back in the UK," said Judith. "Pity you're leaving. Your friends," and she looked from Georgie to Harriet, "are going to miss you."

"Don't get me started," said Harriet.

"Chin up," said Judith. "Everybody's on Skype. Now for the hors d'oeuvres, I'd suggest miniature spring rolls."

By the end of an hour—Harriet taking down every word Judith said on a pad of flowery stationery—they'd got the buffet sorted. Chicken, it would be ("More economical," pronounced Judith, making Edwina wonder how much she knew), a sideboard featuring roast beef, eight side dishes (three Indian, five Lebanese), a salad bar, some sort of stuffed pasta dish for the vegetarians ("more of those these days") and for dessert a tiered cake to be executed by the Club's pastry chef, who, Judith said, had trained in France. "Now for the table decorations, I'd suggest vases of white roses for every table. Tied up with white tulle, maybe? Simple, elegant, and again, not outrageously expensive this time of year."

"I'm not getting married," said Edwina, and the three women looked at her, as if they'd forgotten she was there.

"Would you prefer red then?" said Judith. "With sprigs of baby's breath perhaps? Again, low in cost."

"Oh, Judith, what would we do without you?" sighed Harriet. "Isn't that so, Edwina?"

But Edwina was thinking something she couldn't say, at least not in front of Judith: Couldn't we just hire a yacht?

They sold *Soulmate* after a year. It wasn't her decision, but then it wasn't her money. Gerald was the one working seventy hours a week, taking calls at midnight, hopping on planes with an hour's notice, the one bobbing and scraping. If only they'd kept that money. But Gerald was already in love. This time it was serious. Three million pounds serious. "She's worth at least four, you know," said Gerald. Her name was *Cheeky Tiger*. She roared, she clawed. Sixty-six metres long, the boat placed them finally in the realm of super-yacht owners. Spanking new, *Cheeky Tiger* had been built for an American banker sucked down in the financial undertow. The new yacht had an expansive foyer ("A foyer?" blinked Harriet), three interior decks with spiral staircases connecting them, six bedrooms and a pool.

"It's too much, Dad," Alec, their oldest son, said when he came with his fiancée for Christmas. "The world's going to hell in a hand basket. I'd be a little more prudent, if I were you."

What did he know? Gerald asked Edwina after Alec had gone back to London. "Always was a conservative kid. Scared of risk. Good thing he's gone into academia." Edwina hadn't told any of the kids they'd sold the villa in Spain and that the family home in Liverpool—without tenants for a year—had just been bought for quite a lot less than it was worth. But that was the market these days, wasn't it? The kids were grown now, married or engaged, with lives and homes of their own. Sara had two young children; Jewel was expecting her first. None of them had used the Spanish villa in recent years, Gerald pointed out. "We're downsizing, divesting, consolidating." Every time he said this, Edwina felt a small flutter in the region of her stomach. The downsizing measured sixty-six metres long and three-million quid wide. Something the downsizing did not include was the BMW, the Mercedes and the villa in Marina Village. "We can't let it *all* go, can we?" Edwina said. "And I still need Pansy for the tidying up and laundry and cooking." There were appearances to keep up, even though Gerald's company was no longer covering their rent. Times were tough. The $18,000 US monthly rent was now theirs to pay.

And now for some reason, the parts weren't working so well. Gerald apologized, Edwina reassured.

"It's the job, dear, is all." But the fact was that Gerald couldn't seem to do it anymore. The glue had unstuck. What had usually put things right was now part of what was wrong. "There are drugs," Edwina murmured. But Gerald didn't want drugs or help or sympathy. He didn't want to talk about it either. He now stayed up half the night — pottering around the villa — lest they turn back the bedcovers at the same moment. Weekends, he sailed *Cheeky Tiger*.

Why did they have to keep meeting about the party? It had all been settled days ago. "Judith wants to review the final details," said Harriet. "She's so thorough."

They were now at a new place, Judith's pick this time: Café Arabia. "I'd recommend the *fatteh*," Judith told the three friends, sunk deep and a bit too snuggly in a brocade couch. Georgie and Harriet ordered as directed, but Edwina, feeling rebellion rise as the sweet-faced Filipina waitress turned to her, said, "Toast with butter, please."

"You won't try the *fatteh*?" Judith pressed. "It's quite yummy."

"I don't eat Arabic food for breakfast," said Edwina.

They seemed to be talking around and above her. Georgie was going on about some future concert on the Corniche and Harriet started talking about their summer plans. They wanted to go somewhere cool this July. "Jack's thinking about Vancouver. Have you been to Canada, Judith?"

She hadn't and Harriet and Georgie seemed to forget that Jewel, Edwina's youngest, lived in Calgary now. But no one asked her.

"So what do you think about what's happening in Egypt?" asked Judith, pushing away her half-eaten bowl of *fatteh*. "Alarming, isn't it?"

"Scary," said Georgie.

"Really, really scary," said Harriet.

"And Syria and Yemen are rumoured to be next," nodded Judith. "Jordan too. It's all gone pear-shaped. And here we were planning on doing that trip down the Nile in April. You know, from Cairo to Luxor."

"Up," said Edwina, the first thing she'd said since ordering toast.

"Excuse me?" Judith said.

"If you're going from Cairo to Luxor, you're going upriver."

"Well, it doesn't matter. Now we may have to rethink our plans."

"Those people have lived in poverty for a long, long time," said Edwina. "They've been oppressed, you know. How would you like to live like that?"

Georgie and Harriet turned to look at her with matching expressions: *Do we know you?*

"But, Edwina, is any amount of oppression, as you call it, ever an excuse for looting and lawlessness?" asked Judith. "My dear, it's absolute chaos."

Truth was, Edwina had only been vaguely following the news, reading the headlines mostly, catching sound bytes on the Beeb, while she packed crates, cancelled utilities and manoeuvred around Gerald's worrying mood.

"I suppose not," she said, suddenly winded, and insisted on paying the entire bill, despite the worried looks between her two friends. "Well, it looks like all systems are go for Friday night," she said as they hugged goodbye on the sidewalk outside. "Thank you," she said to Judith, who actually smiled. "I love you guys," she said to Georgie and Harriet, and then she was hurrying to her car.

Kevin Abbott's letter came by courier five months after mooring their lives to *Cheeky Tiger*. Gerald looked for something else, even got the usual thirty-day grace period for unemployment extended to three months. But he was fifty-eight now, close to sixty, when he would be required to leave anyway. Besides, hydraulic engineering wasn't what it had been. The world wasn't what it had been. Without a job, they couldn't stay. They sold *Cheeky Tiger* to the first buyer, losing almost a million pounds, the market favouring sellers even less than it had just a few months earlier. Remaining stock got divested — even the account offshore in Jersey. The last bit of Edwina's gold jewellery was sold off, as was the piece of land outside Manchester left to Gerald by his grandfather. Anything with any value was exchanged for not nearly enough. Gone.

"Did you call Sara? Give her the flight details?" asked Edwina. The movers had driven off an hour before — the chest from Pinky's propped precariously on its side — but Gerald was still standing at the window.

"I think I did," said Gerald. "Yes, of course, I did."

Edwina made a note to call their daughter that afternoon from Doha, where they were laying over. Just in case. She dreaded the conversation, the frosty disapproval in Sara's voice. When they'd first asked, their oldest daughter had been disbelieving. "But what happened to all that money? Where did it all go? What were you guys doing all those years?" And when Edwina had tried to explain—bad investments, no talent for saving, a love of beautiful things—Sara had responded, "That's just fucking brilliant." Of course, Sara felt put upon, especially with two little ones. But where else were they supposed to go?

"I've got no maid, you know," she'd said. "Don't expect me to pick up after you two."

"Of course not," said Edwina. It had hurt to tell Pansy she'd need to find a new sponsor.

They would put the remainder of their belongings—the things they hadn't been able to sell—in storage, keep just what they needed. Sara's guest room wouldn't hold much. Edwina hoped the Indian chest, reminder of an exotic life, would fit.

And she hoped Georgie and Harriet would forgive her. She'd been trying to persuade Gerald for weeks now. "I don't want to go. I can't, don't you understand?" he said, his voice sometimes breaking. But in the end it was she who changed her mind. She didn't want to go to the party either. Friends, roses, speeches. No. She booked their flight for the day before.

THE GIFT OF THE MAGI

Twenty-three dirhams and twenty-five fils. That is all. And eighteen dirhams of it is in change. Coins saved one and two at a time by sacrificing a coffee on a late-night shift, mending pantyhose with nail polish instead of buying a new pair, texting Jimmy rather than calling. Her salary—900 dirhams a month—doesn't go far. Three times Adella counts it. Twenty-three dirhams and twenty-five fils. And the next day will be Christmas.

There's nothing to do but lock herself in the shared bathroom, bury her face in a towel and cry. But she's due downstairs in the lobby washrooms in five minutes. Floors to mop, toilets to scrub. Adella pats cool water on her eyes, slips back into the darkened hotel room. When she first came to work in Abu Dhabi a year ago, returning to this room each night had made her heart sink. It doesn't much resemble the other guest rooms in the Yas Island hotel. With no tourists or businessmen to impress, it's just three single beds, a suitcase tucked under each. Adella has tried to make her corner personal: a framed picture of Jimmy and little Eddie on her nightstand taken the summer before, a nosegay of roses—petals crisp and yellow—left behind by guests at a wedding, a small cross carved from olive wood. "Remember who you are and where you come from," Mom said when she gave it to her. Adella tries hard to do this, but this place is so far from the Philippines, so far from the family home with its breezy porch, the kitchen with its uneven floor and heavenly smell of frying plantains, the abundant garden always in need of pruning. A work in progress, Jimmy laughingly calls it. But home.

Adella moves to the window, careful not to brush against Haydee's bed. Her roommate has just come off a sixteen-hour shift, hasn't bothered to take off the beige blouse that's part of their uniform. She stirs as Adella tiptoes by, murmuring something in her sleep. It's not quite 5:00 p.m., but already the light is going. At least there is something to look at now: Ferrari World stretches like a scarlet amoeba across the road. Before it had been just sand and scruff, a no-man's-land that made her feel even further from Jimmy than the twenty kilometres that separate them. A housekeeping job in Jimmy's hotel had been promised by the agency back home, but like so many other promises… She can't think about this now. It's Christmas. From six storeys above, Adella watches a couple push a pram around the fountain. Wind lifts the edge of the woman's white headscarf and the man catches it in his hand.

> <

Everything depends on tonight's tips. Jimmy plunges his hand again into the front pocket of his uniform trousers, fingering the coins, willing them to be more. He'd always thought the holidays made people more generous. Of course, business is down even in Abu Dhabi this year, especially in the Tourist Club area, where construction on Al Salaam Street has limited access to the hotel. For a Christmas Eve, the lobby is echoingly quiet—only a few private parties in the restaurants tonight and one banquet. "Please," he'd begged Aziz, his boss, a week ago. "Please let me work the large party." Tips from a banquet, especially one expertly, graciously served, could more than triple what he'd managed to save so far. Aziz said he'd think about it, but this morning assigned five other waiters to the event. "Lobby café, noon to ten," he told Jimmy and walked away before Jimmy could ask him to reconsider. The lobby café is a cluster of low ebony tables and bright-orange banquettes set back from the hotel's front doors. The menu is minimal: coffee, sandwiches, biscotti. Ladies talking too long over lattes, kids parked with nannies. Low tippers, non-tippers.

He's been plotting their Christmas Day for weeks. It takes plotting to even arrange the same day off. Although he's been working at the hotel for nearly four years, it barely amounts to seniority. Some of the older waiters, like Raj and Manuel, have been here twelve or fifteen. It was Raj who traded his day off with Jimmy. "You have wife here," he said. Raj has two daughters in college back home in Bangalore. The last time he could afford to go home was three years ago. "What to do?" he says.

The last time Jimmy and Adella saw each other was in September, the humidity making their joined hands moist as they walked around the yard at St. Mary's Cathedral. Adella had been almost shy at first. "Your hair," she finally said. "Too short?" he asked, an old bit of married business. Adella adores Jimmy's thick hair, the way it falls into his eyes, moves when he walks.

Years ago, she cried when he came home with a buzz cut. "No," she said, looking up at him. "It's perfect." They walked around the church compound many times that afternoon, talking about Eddie and his school, about Jimmy's mother, who hadn't been well, about his job and her job and how much it would cost to put a new roof on the house back in Cebu. Over dinner at Chow King later, he felt his chest rise and fall. He was breathing, really breathing, as if he'd been holding his breath, waiting to exhale, since the last time he'd seen her.

Tomorrow morning, Christmas morning, they will meet at church for the Tagalog mass. It will be crowded and they will probably have to stand, but they will not mind. They will see friends, maybe some cousins from home. But they will not linger long in how's-it-going conversation. Jimmy will bring sandwiches from the hotel, Adella some fruit and they'll make their way by bus to the Corniche. Once settled on the sand — *bring blanket*, Jimmy makes a mental note — he'll pull a small packet from his pocket and place it in her lap.

It's the perfect gift for Adella — small, beautiful, yet practical. He's been eyeing it since forever in one of the ground-floor shops at Hamdan Centre: a pink suede mobile-phone case studded with heart-shaped rhinestones. Adella's mobile is her prized possession — not because it boasts any special features, but because it connects her to home and to him. "My lifeline," she said the last time they were together and kissed it, laughing. He'd checked last week; two pink cases were still left. But it wasn't the availability of the case that worried him tonight. The case costs one hundred dirhams. He has forty-seven. Two weeks ago it had looked promising, his tips surely accumulating in the days leading up to the holiday. But customers seem distracted this year, oblivious even. Last week a party of eight in the hotel's steakhouse ate and drank up a bill of 4,000 dirhams, then drifted out three hours later, leaving nothing at all. "Maybe forget," said Raj.

And now this: an empty café, "Joy to the World" playing discreetly through the lobby's speakers, untended boys circling the massive, gold-flecked Christmas tree on roller shoes. *Adella*. What to do?

> <

She knew the moment she saw the case that it was made for Jimmy. Certain things just belong to certain people. She imagines Jimmy pulling his mobile from his back pocket, people turning, stopping to admire the sleek black leather. His phone is a few years old, the face scratched, but Jimmy sees no point in buying a new one. "Each thing we buy slows us down," he tells her. Jimmy has a plan: three more years for Adella, six for him. Then, God willing, they will have enough to buy a taxi service back home and send Eddie to a better school. He's a smart boy.

But every time Adella vacuums the hotel gift shop, she admires the mobile case displayed in the window. Doesn't Jimmy deserve this? The shop manager, another Filipina, has promised Adella a 20-percent discount. She could offer 75 percent; it would still be more than Adella can cobble together by tomorrow.

And then as she's emptying the trash in the ladies' washroom, something comes. On a five-minute break she takes the elevator up to the room. Haydee is awake now, watching TV, still in her uniform. Fatigue weighs on her pretty face.

"Del." She pats the bed for Adella to join her. "You still on?"

"Till three," says Adella.

"We must be crazy," says Haydee.

"Haydee," says Adella, sitting down. "You know my mobile…?"

And it is decided. Haydee's phone has been acting up for weeks. Adella returns downstairs, eighty dirhams richer.

> <

Jimmy is grateful the stores downtown stay open so late. At home on Christmas Eve, everything closes by six, everyone rushing home to cook, eat and dress for midnight mass. Here it is and it isn't Christmas. He remembers—hurrying himself now to Hamdan Centre—his confusion that first December, seeing the red, green, white and black decorations at Lulu for National Day and mistakenly thinking they were for Christmas. It seems pretty funny to him now. Still, he's grateful for the tolerance here. St. Mary's is testament to that.

Though it's nearly eleven, the shop is still open. The deal is struck, the little package slipped into his trousers' pocket.

> <

Christmas morning comes, balmy and glorious. But Jimmy has to work after all—Aziz shrugs, can't be helped—and when Adella tries to call him from St. Mary's, borrowing a mobile from a friend, there is no answer. She's waited through two masses, scanning the crowds for her husband, walking countless times past the giant Christmas tree decorated with white paper petals. But Jimmy's mobile sits in a Hamdan Centre shop, battery and SIM card removed, for resale. Sixty dirhams. Cheap.

Jimmy calls Adella many times that day, borrowing Raj's mobile. If only he could reach her. The message says the same thing over and over: *The mobile you are trying to reach has been switched off.* Haydee is sleeping before her next shift.

That night, Christmas night, Adella finds herself at the window again. The gift for Jimmy now sits on the nightstand with her cross and photo. She looks across the island to the lights of the city and she feels him there.

The magi, as you know, were wise men—wonderfully wise men from Arabia, Persia and India—who brought gifts to the babe in the manger. They invented the art of giving Christmas presents. Being wise, their gifts were, no doubt, wise ones. Wiser perhaps than those of a couple in Abu Dhabi who most unwisely sacrificed for each other their greatest treasures, their lifelines to one another. But perhaps of all who give gifts, these two were the wisest. O, all who give and receive gifts, such as they are the wisest. Everywhere they are the wisest. They are the magi.

The last lines of this Abu Dhabi retelling of "The Gift of the Magi" belong to William Sydney Porter, otherwise known as O. Henry. They cannot be improved upon.

PLEASE DRIVE TO HIGHLIGHTED ROUTE

"You're taking me the wrong way, Fiona." Deborah turned her left signal on and swung into someone's driveway, winter tires shimmying. The snow that looked fairyland pretty the night before, their first snowfall in five years, had turned that morning to slush. Snow, ice, rain, weather. She didn't know how to do any of it anymore.

"Recalculating," said Fiona.

"Oh, shut up, Fiona."

It was the first thing she'd said all day, other than a groggy "bye" to Harris as he left for work at seven. She'd planned to get up and make breakfast, had planned to do this every morning that week. But sleep seemed to be holding her down lately, a deep pit of a place neither guilt nor duty could dislodge her from. "I'm sorry," she'd told Harris the day before when she called him at work. "I just can't seem to get going these mornings."

"Regime change is never easy, dear." Harris had sounded work-distracted, but even distracted he could think of something clever to say. The night before they'd howled over a *New Yorker* cartoon: An elderly couple sit primly on adjacent sofas, the woman reading a book, the man looking out the window as helmeted soldiers with tanks and guns swarm the house. Regime change is never easy, dear, the woman says to the man.

"Well, that might be a bit extreme," Harris had laughed. An office phone was ringing in the background. "More like regimen change, right? Go easy on yourself, Deb. We've only been back in Canada a couple of months. See you at six, traffic depending."

"Please drive to highlighted route," said Fiona. Deborah turned the car around and yanked the plug.

Having a GPS in Abu Dhabi would have been an exercise in insanity, though that didn't stop people from buying them. "How do you program it?" Harris had asked the Indian sales clerk at Carrefour Hypermarket. They were still new to the city then, which meant they were lost every time they got in the car. The clerk had placed the box on the counter as tenderly as if it had contained a Rolex. It had been the usual mad Friday in the store, shopping carts piled with kids and twenty-kilo bags of rice, the electronics counter teeming with testosterone. The store—large as a football field—hummed with consumption. "You plug it in," said the young man; Safik, his name tag read.

"But there are no street numbers here." Deborah had had to shout over the din of Arabic and Hindi, English and Urdu.

"Numbers, yes," said Safik, nodding knowledgeably. "We have numbers."

"I mean street addresses," Deborah had tried to explain. "You know, like 96 Elmwood." Their old address in Ottawa had popped up, unbidden. She could almost smell the lilacs in the backyard. She had almost cried.

The man looked confused. "Wood?" he said.

"Come on, Deb," Harris had said, taking her arm, and smiling brightly at the clerk. "Thank you so much for your time."

"You're always so unfailingly polite," Deborah said when they had escaped the roar of the store. "Don't you ever feel like shaking these guys and saying: 'Just tell me you really don't know what you're talking about'?"

Harris had put his arm around her, then let it drop quickly. "Nearly forgot where I was. Come on, let's go to Forty Fruity. You need a Honey Bunny."

Driving down route something or other now, the frosty, layered promise of that drink, the cloud of ice cream on top, the pulpy mango, the chunks of pineapple, the honey's drippy sweetness, came back with the force of first desire. She wanted a Honey Bunny and she wanted it now. Instead, there was this: Grey fields disappearing into grey sky; folks saying, "I'll give you a shout"; Home Depots and Tim Horton's and maple everything. A civil society. Yes, indeed.

"Maybe you need a hobby," Harris said that night as they were washing up after dinner. Now that it was just the two of them again, they rarely used the dishwasher. It sat empty as the extra bedroom upstairs.

"That's rather patronizing, don't you think?" she said. "I'm supposed to take up quilting or something? Hang out at Michael's in the mall with all the other unemployed, crafty empty-nesters?"

"Oh, Deb," said Harris. Until they'd gone to Abu Dhabi, Deborah had been a lobbyist for the rights of the disabled. She had the three boys, each a project in

himself. She'd had her early-music choir, her book club.
She had *him*, a full-time job, Harris himself would say.
What would she want with a hobby? "I was thinking
of something along the lines of, I don't know, scrap-
booking? We have all those photos you keep saying you
want to organize."

"Oh, Harris," she said.

She hadn't wanted the expat life. "I like my home! I
like my life!" she'd protested when Harris accepted
an administrative post at Al Nahyan University after
eighteen years of marriage, after a dozen years teaching
journalism at Carleton. A much-younger colleague, one
of the New Media guys (*his* caps, not Harris's), had just
edged Harris out of what would likely be his last shot at
tenure. "I mean I like to travel. I *love* to travel. But this
is different."

The heat, the chaos, the sand, the traffic, the malls,
the snotty Brits, the impossible distance from home.
What had they done? "I'm not sure how long I'm going to
last," she warned after the first month, after the flurry of
furnishing their flat in Late Ikea—no point in shipping
the contents of their Ottawa home—and after the
boys had gotten settled. They were in different schools
that first year; the eldest, Thom, in the French high
school; the twins, Jon and Terry, at the British school.
Teenagers already, they'd been seriously unhappy about
leaving Ottawa. But within a month they had chums and
rugby practices, trips to the desert and Dubai, beautiful
classmates with posh accents and rich fathers. Harris's
days at the university were long, with uncertain end
times, and packed with meetings, plans and promises.

"They want it all—master's programs, accreditation, visiting Nobel scholars. And they think we can give it to them," he said, shrugging. "Emiratis are so proud of their desert roots, but also kind of ashamed, have you noticed?" She appreciated that Harris seemed to be keeping his weight on both feet, hadn't lost his critical faculties, his old irreverence. Other expats they met had had a conversion experience.

"Been out to Sadiyaat?" A silver-haired man in an expensive dress shirt had cornered her at a hotel *iftar* that first Ramadan. He was balancing two plates, both piled with rice, samosas, pita, *fattoush*. "If you want to understand this place, really get into the Abu Dhabi head space, you owe it to yourself to go out there and see the Sadiyaat Story. These people are so ambitious they're planning to build both a Louvre *and* a Guggenheim. The 2030 plan? Brilliant." He glanced over at Harris and the boys, slowly making their way down the twenty-foot buffet. Jon, the taller twin, was bouncing on his heels. All that food, even if they hadn't fasted all day. "Great place for kids," the man said. She was trying to place the accent, a new habit. Not British, maybe South African.

"We've just arrived," she said.

He gestured to a window—the restaurant was on the twentieth floor with eye-popping views of water, sand and sky. "Can't be immune to that."

"It's beautiful," she said.

"Spectacular," said the man. Deborah strained to see her gang. Perhaps they were sitting down, chowing down, already. "Be sure to attend an *iftar* during Ramadan," Harris's Egyptian secretary had told her. "Being invited to someone's home is nicest, but some of the hotels do a lovely spread." This was a spread all right, but the celebrants looked to be expats like herself, strangers far from home, simply having dinner out.

The man seemed to be waiting for something more. He smiled encouragingly. *Heaven on earth. Go ahead, say it.*

"Jury's still out," she said, knowing she already had an opinion.

"Hey," he said. "Relax. Have fun. Enjoy yourself."

"I think I just got advice from a sex therapist," she said to Harris when she found their table.

"Huh?" The boys had actually looked up from their plates.

She was miserable. Not just the first year, but deep into the second. She'd thought the second year would be easier. It wasn't. She'd initially hoped to make at least one Emirati friend, gain one opening into life behind the *shayla.* Who were those women gliding through the malls, the sequined hems of their *abayas* skimming the marble? Were they repressed? Fulfilled? She envied Harris's female colleagues who taught English and computer courses to rooms of Emirati young women. What a window they must have.

But they didn't have locals as neighbours and if Harris's Emirati colleagues extended a social invitation it was just for him, men only. As the months went by, Deborah began to see how naïve it was to have expected anything else. The worlds didn't intersect. There were the landowners and those who worked the land. Meanwhile, the boys continued to be admirably, annoyingly adaptable. Thom began seeing—discreetly—the daughter of the Tunisian vice-consul. Terry and Jon lived the life of British prep boys.

Deborah tried to keep their lives normal, i.e., Canadian: no live-in maid, two smallish cars, Friday lunch at home instead of champagne-blurred brunches at the Sheraton or InterContinental. But Saturdays the boys were now mostly off with friends at yacht clubs and private beaches.

Harris was more absent than he'd been the first year, travelling to Morocco and Jordan to recruit students. Emirati enrollment wasn't as high as had been hoped. It will take time, Harris tried to explain to his bosses. "We're building a reputation, growing our profile." But they didn't like hearing this. And he couldn't say part of the problem was that Emirati families continued to send their brightest sons abroad for university. He'd already seen that anything other than extreme diplomacy could be job-threatening. One of his colleagues had practically been escorted to the airport after (loudly) questioning the university's academic standards. "I'm just not sure they're willing to put forth what's necessary," Harris told Deborah after another contentious meeting. "Money and pronouncements, sure. Openness and transparency, not likely. Rigour? What's that?"

Saturdays, with the boys out and about, he began taking long naps. At home in Ottawa, she would have welcomed the quiet, the chance to read, email friends, putter. But here she found herself staring into space for unquantifiable amounts of time. "Maybe," she ventured to Harris during one of those still afternoons, "maybe I go back to Ottawa next year, take the boys, get a job and you stay here and work for another year or two…" But the boys were happy and Harris was more gainfully employed than he'd ever been during a long career in academia. She was the minority vote.

There *were* outlets—the Abu Dhabi Ladies Club, Women in Abu Dhabi and Canadian Women's Connection—that offered organized activities, like shopping hauls to Dubai and bus tours to Yas Island to admire the new Formula One arena, plus endless coffee mornings at various hotels. "One of the great things about being an expat is that you can reinvent yourself each year," a woman from Edmonton told Deborah at one. The coffee had been lukewarm and she'd had to put twenty dirhams into a silver bowl to pay for it. "Each year you can be and do something different. Who's to know?" the woman chirped. Who are you this year? Deborah wanted to ask. The American wife of one of Harris's colleagues, a mousy little thing, had started a conspicuous affair with their tennis coach. You could call that reinvention.

"Sweetie, why don't you get a job?" Deborah's sister in Vancouver asked more than once. "They must have special education programs or advocacy groups for the disabled. Something, no? You seem so adrift." How to explain this place to anyone who didn't live here? There was a high-profile fundraising program called Donate a Brick to guilt the city's über-rich into supporting a special-care centre for Emirati children. With the high rate of intermarriage, the local gene pool had shrunk disastrously. Down syndrome, chromosomal disorders, rare birth defects, even rarer cancers.

"Never seen anything like it," a Canadian pathologist told her at a party. "We've been telling them for the last fifteen years: 'Don't marry your cousins!' But that wouldn't keep the money in the family, would it? The government turns a blind eye, then sends these poor kids off to a sanitarium in Switzerland." They'd received a flyer under the doormat seeking donations for the centre: "Planted on Earth…Fruited in Heaven to revive the Endowment Route, help the poor and the needy to elevate life burdens off their shoulders through our endowment expenditures as well as strengthen social & family armpits and parents benevolence through our projects." They'd laughed themselves silly over the translation. "Oh, yes," said Harris. "Give me your tired, your poor, your family armpits."

The only other possibility was the Horizon School for disabled kids. Deborah had visited once and had no plans to return. The staff was well meaning, even compassionate, but severely under-equipped in training and numbers, even philosophy. It was too painful to return to a time best forgotten in her own country when the disabled were pitied more than helped. With so few doors open professionally, she cooked more, parented harder. Under "occupation" on her UAE visa it read "housewife." She'd enjoyed the absurdity of that title at first. Then it rankled. Then it began to feel true.

In the fall of their third year—she'd cried at Pearson on the way out once again—Deborah dragged herself to another coffee morning. There were a few vaguely familiar faces; mostly it was newcomers, smiling hard. It was a relief to not be new anymore, to know the drill, to not expect too much. You did come to know yourself here, she thought as coffee was poured and introductions made, to see who you were and who you weren't, like when the garrulous French woman next to her complained that they were all paying their nannies way, way too much, *mon dieu*.

"Let's ditch this joint," a busty blonde stage-whispered from across the banquet table and Deborah found herself following the woman's large frame out of the Hilton. "All those stupid teacups and fakey smiles. Believe me, when you turn your back they'll be bad-mouthing your bloody handbag or whatever else they can feel superior about." Davina was on her second cigarette by this time, the two having narrowly dodged speeding SUVs to cross the Corniche. It was mid-November, the temperature almost human again, the benches facing the water crowded.

"How did you know I was dying to get out of there?" Deborah asked.

"Your face, luv," said Davina. "Everything about you, luv."

"I tell myself every morning: Get out. Meet people."

Davina nodded. "You miss Canada?" she asked.

"Not right this minute. I'd be getting out the snow tires."

"Tell me about it," said Davina. "Well, not snow. This time of year Glasgow's like a pig trough. Ruddy, muddy mess."

They'd laughed so hard, Deborah had to wipe her eyes. Not that either of them had said anything that funny. But at last, someone real. "Shawarma Hut, Khalifa & Airport. C U @ 11?" Davina texted the next morning. And so it went.

Davy, as she preferred to be called ("Davina is pit on the gentry"), was essentially childless in Abu Dhabi. Her son, Robbie, had learning problems the city's Canadian and American schools had dusted their hands of, and was now at a boarding school in the north of England. "Brits got hold of him. What are you going to do?" she sighed. And their husbands, they agreed, would have little in common, so it was just them, members only, shopping for Iranian pottery at Mina Zayed, trying *shisha* in a café, meeting up at Emirates Palace for an exhibition of Islamic embroidery or mediocre Emirati art. They spent hours in Magrudy's shopping for books — Davina scoping out the latest chick-lit titles, Deborah the cookbooks and historical fiction — once even successfully petitioning the removal of a stack of *Mein Kampf*, displayed prominently as if it was new on the bestseller list. "What is the matter with this country?" Davy fumed.

They did the touristy things too, like taking photos with the tired, dusty camel at Heritage Village, cracking up over the creative translations on plaques posted throughout the grounds: "The dominant desert start to disappear its place is in the utmost rear." "Well, it rhymes," said Davy. Mostly they laughed over what Harris now called Abu-surdities: Plumbing that was never quite fixed despite crews of solemn-faced workers tromping through your kitchen or bathroom, phones inexplicably disconnected for weeks, buildings with no addresses so that landing in the right place felt like an accident. The things that had made Deborah scream with frustration before were now, if not a hoot, material.

"You know those glasses of mine, the ones I keep taking back to the optometrist in Al Wahda, the ones with the loose screw they can never seem to fix?" Deborah told Davy over coffee one morning. "This time I insisted on taking them to their lab myself. You want to know what the adorable Filipino optometrist wrote on my referral? 'Needs good screw.'" Davina's laugh — she had a raucous, head-turning one — made the stupid, sweaty three-hour errand almost worth it.

"Poor man, he'd be mortified if he knew what it meant," said Deborah.

"So did they fix them?"

"Come on, Davy. Where do we live?"

"Hey," said Davy another morning in another café, "how many Emiratis does it take to change a light bulb?"

"Wait a minute," said Deborah, already laughing. "Three. One to call an Indian labourer to do the work, and two to brag that it was the brightest light bulb in the world."

"Way too few," said Davy. "How about one to heckle the Indian manager, who's supervising four unskilled labourers from Bangladesh; one to call the newspaper and report another milestone for Emirati ingenuity; one to shoot photos on his iPhone. How many does that make?"

Each version — it got so bad they were texting each other several times a day — bested the last: "Twelve. Six Indians and Pakistanis speaking different dialects: one to ring the doorbell, one to explain in a mix of Hindi and English why it took two weeks to come out; a third to carry the six-foot ladder to reach the bulb in the twelve-foot ceiling; three to watch and scratch their heads; two Western journalists to rhapsodize on how the changing of the light bulb reflected the vision of Sheikh Zayed; one editor to kill the anecdote about Sheikh Zayed's fifth wife; and one Emirati to explain how the changing of the light bulb fit in with Abu Dhabi's 2030 Plan."

"I think that's only ten," Deborah texted back.

Actually, they decided one afternoon after too many coffees, the correct answer was zero. Emiratis didn't do manual labour and they didn't make house calls. "And in my building, which, as you know, is brand new, once a light bulb burns out, that's it. Never changed," Davy added. "This joke doesn't really work here."

"They can build the world's tallest building, but they can't change a light bulb," said Deborah. "Ironic, eh?"

"Irony doesn't work here either," Davy reminded her.

By now Deborah had grown skeptical about the country's dreams of meteoric, painless success, painless to locals because it was built on the backs of migrant workers, paid abysmally and treated worse. She'd grown weary of We Are the Biggest, We Are the Best. The 2030 Plan—she longed to tell that silver-haired man of long ago—was going to sink like The World, Dubai's man-made islands, which were rapidly going under. Dust to dust, water to water. Even in more fiscally solvent Abu Dhabi, construction projects were being scuttled as global markets tightened and choked. We Are the World had never been truer or more unfortunate.

Sometimes they still hit one of their old coffee mornings. They were good for gossip, good for a laugh. Davy was a terrific mimic—could duplicate the Texas purr of oil wives so well she might have been from the Big D herself, though she could also nail the disdainful, disappointed tones of a Brahmin Brit. "I think we're turning into bigots," Deborah said over falafels one morning. Davy had just impersonated a Japanese woman who'd come to speak to "the laddies" about feng shui. "Well, it was almost English," said Davy. "Didn't stop her from going on like a peppermill. Racist? This place does it to you."

In late March, Davina's husband, Jack, got laid off by the construction company that had brought them there. A huge project—two towers of 100 offices each—got the thumbs down four days before building was to start. "Postponed, they're saying," shrugged Davy. "Meantime, they've cancelled everyone's visas. We've got thirty days to find something else, but other companies are laying off too. Even the Guggenheim and the Louvre are being stalled. Just like that, in a crack." She'd teared up, something Deborah would do for months afterward when she drove past Davina's building. "There's nothing back home, nothing."

They'd stayed in loose touch in the two years since, Deborah writing missives every few months, Davina replying with funny, cryptic notes. Letter-writing wasn't her thing, she admitted. And she was working two jobs in a suburb of Glasgow—secretary in one school, nurse in another, so time was tight. Robbie, too, was back home and in a regular school, and Jack's employment was hit and miss since their return. "Wanna meet somewhere for a shawarma?" Davy wrote every now and then.

Crazy the things she was craving, Deborah thought as she plugged in the GPS. She was venturing out again, though sky and air threatened snow, though the sight of a disembowelled raccoon on Walker's Line, outside Burlington, had nearly made her turn back. She'd almost forgotten the sensations—bitter wind penetrating everything not padded, nose hairs tingling. But shawarma! In the morning-cold of the car, she could almost smell the meat, see it falling onto a platter as it was sliced from the spit. She'd had her pick of three shawarma places within walking distance of their first Abu Dhabi flat: Al Sultan Good Foods, Just Falafel and her favourite at the end of the block, Lebanese Flower, where the slick-haired

Palestinian waiters greeted you formally, respectfully, but like family, especially if you threw in a few Arabic phrases.

Deborah unplugged the GPS, cutting off Fiona mid-"recalculating," pulled over and took the stick-it from the dash. Harris's get-a-hobby comment of the night before had done some damage, but it was galvanizing too. She had to find a job, volunteer work, something. She plugged the GPS back in, programmed the address — somewhere in Brantford, wherever that was from there. People assumed that if you came from Ontario, everything from Ajax to Windsor must feel familiar. But Burlington was nothing like Ottawa, nothing like home. The condo compounds and cookie-cutter developments separated by farmland and green spaces was a foreign landscape peopled by no one she knew. It wasn't Abu Dhabi either.

"Please drive to highlighted route," said Fiona.

When they'd bought the GPS their first week back in Canada, they found it amusing that they could choose between an American voice or a British one. "You'd think we've heard enough of both," said Harris. In the end, out of something close to affection, they went for the plummy Oxford accent. "We'll just have to call her Fiona," Harris said. Half the time they argued with her; the other half, they ignored her. She was their guide and as lost as they were.

"They're pretending, you know," Harris said at the end of their third Abu Dhabi year. "They don't really care about teaching or learning." He'd been a lecturer in the English department the first semester, downgraded by the Irish provost, new that year, the third in as many. McGuinness had refused to call it a demotion, more a strategic move to capitalize on Harris's real strengths. "We're moving from strength to strength here at Al Nahyan University, meeting the challenges of a dynamic twenty-first-century world," he'd said every time he got the chance, and *The National* and *Gulf News* had dutifully quoted him each time.

He hadn't lasted. McGuinness's curriculum vitae was less résumé than blarney, apparently, and the administration sent him packing mid-year. The resulting cabinet shuffle saw Harris made dean of student services, though he was still expected to teach his full course load. Befitting his new status, they moved into a stunning, paid-for villa in Khalidayah: four bedrooms, huge kitchen, tiled pool just steps from their door. Even the maid's room — a space so minute in their first flat, they'd used it as a storage closet — was big enough to hold a single bed. The boys loved it, especially the pool. Even Deborah felt something shift. They were lucky to have what they had. Harris wasn't around enough to notice.

"Who knows what they're going to want next year," said Harris. "Full accreditation? Harvard profs begging to get hired?" They were having supper at India Palace, a last alone-meal before Deborah and the boys left again for the summer. This time Thom would be staying in Ottawa to start university. She loved the summers with old friends and old routines. And she dreaded them, the pain of reconnecting and disconnecting again, the packing and unpacking — their Ottawa house was rented — as they went from friends to relatives to friends: a week here, four days there, the missing of Harris, who would be enduring 50-degree days and an empty flat back in Abu Dhabi.

He would join them for the last two weeks of August, a marathon of family gatherings, lunch with one set of friends, dinner with another. Wonderful and insane.

And as the Ottawa summers went on, something neither of them cared to admit had begun to show. They didn't live there anymore. Their friends were interested in their travels and adventures, but to a point. "You really don't have to cover?" some still asked Deborah. "But you can't drive, right? I mean, it *is* a Muslim country." It didn't seem to matter how they answered—"Of course, I drive!"—the questions felt stuck in 9/11. Even the boys felt it: "Why does Uncle Ron keep asking me if I feel safe there?" "How come Gran doesn't believe there are real churches there?" And truth be told, it wasn't that thrilling to keep talking about Canadian politics, issues they weren't following so closely any more, events that paled next to those now closer to home. Would the new Indian president defend the rights of migrant workers in the UAE? Would the Saudi Al Gosaibi family come clean about its dealings with the Saad Group? What would happen to Nakheel and Dubai World now that the bottom had fallen out? Would the Federal National Council start holding real elections?

But if they no longer lived in Ottawa, where did they live? Abu Dhabi wasn't home; it could never be. "Listen," she'd had to say to Thom, who was now as sad to leave Abu Dhabi as he'd been about leaving Ottawa three years before. "I know you like your life here. It's a great little life. But we all have to leave at some point. Even if we were to stay here until Dad retires, we'd have to leave thirty days later. No job, no visa." Thom, not a crier, not a hugger, had cried and let himself be hugged.

She understood; of course, she understood. During those cooler, greener summers she found herself missing Lebanese Flower and Carrefour, the call to prayer filtering through windows, the Indian friends who brought over roti and kebabs, the whoosh of relief when you stepped from impossible heat into air conditioning, the Sudanese guard in their building who put his hand over his heart when she greeted him. Small things, really, in the face of what she often hated and railed against. But missed things.

Deborah had watched Harris as he'd reached for the last onion bhaji, an India Palace specialty. He hadn't seemed to notice she'd had only one. He'd bulked up in that third year: too much stress, too many meals out. "Did I tell you about the Emirati student I have this term who comes in and talks on his mobile the whole time? He sits there, right in front of me. Can I fail him? We both know the answer to that."

"Have you told him what you expect?" Deborah had asked, but she knew how it would go. He would talk and the student would listen attentively, nodding, letting him have his little teacher rant. The next day out would come the phone. Kids like him were untouchable. And, Harris said, unteachable.

"Should I pack my bags as if we're not coming back?" she'd asked. And he'd given her a look that made her feel small and stupid. There were no jobs at his level back home and even if there were, they wouldn't pay nearly as much. Then there was the matter of taxes, the reason so many expats stayed on and on. Income tax, who needed it?

"We're here for a while, aren't we?" she said.

She didn't have an interview, per se. The Grand Erie District School Board was looking for a special ed teacher, according to their website. She hadn't taught in a Canadian school for more than a dozen years, had moved into advocacy work in the years before Abu Dhabi. While she couldn't quite imagine facing a room of jaded faces again, there was always the resource room. With more kids being coded, she might be able to find something part time. She'd go to the school board, fill out an application, act as if she was moving in a constructive direction.

But the map didn't make sense when she looked at it on Fiona's screen. Upper Middle Road? Was there also a Middle Middle Road? They hadn't explored Burlington or the neighbouring area yet, not that there seemed much to explore. There was an Ikea and a Lee Valley, a store she used to dream about the first year in Abu Dhabi. And reno store after reno store, as if people here lived mostly for their granite counters and in-ground pools. It was enough to make her want to sleep till noon.

"Which, of course, is what I'm doing, isn't it, Fiona?"

"Recalculating," said Fiona, and Deborah realized that instead of getting on the 403, she'd taken a turn toward another generic strip of box stores and chain restaurants. She passed Kelsey's and Montana's, Jack Astor's. Ribs and more ribs. But there on the left was a shawarma place. Sana Grill was a hole in the wall and packed.

"Arriving at destination on left," said Fiona.

"Can you believe it? She took me there after I'd been thinking I'd kill to have a shawarma. I didn't tell her to do it, but she did it," she told Harris that night. He'd arrived home early, looking grey around the edges and not especially talkative, though she got a smile out of him about the shawarma. "Was the food any good?" he asked. "Should we go back?"

That wasn't the point, she wanted to argue. But she knew that grey look. "Why don't you watch a little TV, go to bed? I can clean up." He hadn't resisted, pushed off wearily from the kitchen counter. "What were you doing out there anyway?" he asked.

"Cruising," she said.

"Oh," he said. And she understood she could have said almost anything: I was looking at houses, I was meeting a man, I was going ape shit at Ikea, and he would have nodded and said good, sounds good. She didn't tell him about the job or that she'd stayed in the shawarma place for over an hour, eating, watching people, chatting with the owners, who were from Lebanon and had lived in Dubai in the '90s. She didn't tell him that after, she'd driven home, made a cup of tea, pleasured herself and napped.

The beginning of their fourth Abu Dhabi year was so different than the beginnings of the previous three that it felt as if they *had* been reinvented. After a summer of cottage stays and hotel rooms, the new villa felt vast, luxurious. The neighbours were dazzling, too, high-flying diplomats, lawyers, investment bankers. None went beyond "good-morning" friendly, though Talbot and Molly, the Scottish family next door, seemed down to earth. Not that they needed the neighbours for a social life. They were being invited everywhere now: cocktail parties at various embassies around town, openings at the new gallery space on Sadiyaat, eighties-music nights at the Sheraton.

"Get someone in to help with things," Harris suggested in November. "Free yourself up." Leena, tiny, smiley and fluent only in Bahasa Indonesia, had been the nanny of a family they'd known through the French school. Now after six years on a CAE flight-simulator project, they were headed back to Montreal. "I don't know how we'll manage without Leena," the wife told Deborah. "My kids will have to learn how to make their own beds again. *En tout cas…*"

Transferring Leena's visa went quicker than expected, though it had involved an excessive number of photocopies, staples, stamps and signatures. Leena had worked for one family; now she worked for them. She arrived on a Saturday with two suitcases and headed straight for the kitchen. "Indonesia okay?" she asked, scaling the *hamour* she'd found in the fridge, then expertly filleting it. An hour later, the twins were going for thirds. "Don't bother cooking any more, Mum," Terry said.

Even with years of every-other-week housekeepers, Deborah had often felt uncomfortable having someone clean her stove, her bathroom, her mess. But here it felt almost okay. They would pay her well by Abu Dhabi standards — 4,000 dirhams a month, the equivalent of $1,100, nearly $500 more than the Quebecers had paid. Leena would have the summers off to visit her three children back in Indonesia, plus every Friday and Saturday during the school year. The twins wouldn't demand much in the way of care and Harris would eat just about anything. What was there to apologize for? It helped that Leena was hardworking, grateful for a job

and overjoyed to have them as employers ("Canada good!"
she said often, her small teeth bared in a perpetual smile).
She was a breath of fresh air after the stories Deborah
had heard from other expats. "It's like having a fourth
child," one woman had complained at a coffee morning.
The bad-nanny stories were fodder for much griping,
sniping and nastiness on the Abu Dhabi Women's chat
board.

"Can you believe my nanny asked for a raise? As if
1,200 dirhams a month wasn't generous enough!"

"I caught my husband looking at our maid last night.
You all know what I mean: *looking*! I'm going to have to
forbid her to wear T-shirts."

"Think our nanny's screwing around. Should I do
like some of my friends and lock her in at night?"

Deborah had only gone on the board occasionally
in the first years. Now she checked the back-and-forth
messages several times a day, though she changed her
board name frequently: Canuck Gal, MOMx3, Desert
Deb. Some of the discussions made her nearly sick with
embarrassment and rage. Who were these people who
wrote so callously of the women who made their new
lives possible, the women who cared for their kids, washed
their cars, scrubbed their toilets — all for a fraction of
what they would have paid at home? Had these women
always harboured a sense of superiority, thwarted only
by political correctness back in Atlanta or Adelaide? Or
did this place do it to them? Maybe one of those bitchy
women lived in the villa across the way. Maybe one was a
colleague of Harris's.

"Why don't you stop reading that stuff?" Harris
would ask when she'd vent over dinner, using the excuse

that she wanted the twins to know what was *really* going on in this country.

"Do you like feeling mad all the time?" Jon asked.

"Yeah, why can't you just be happy here?" Terry said.

Harris might have been happy, should have been happy that fall, but if he was, it was lost on them. Mostly he seemed distracted. And frantic, over even small things. "Does Dad have ADD?" Terry asked one morning after Harris had torn up two rooms looking for his office keys. He seemed to barely register Thom's absence, even sometimes missed their Skype chats. "Where's Dad?" Thom would ask, looking pale on the laptop screen. "Tell him hi for me, eh?"

Thom was gone and Leena was now cooking, cleaning, laundering, shopping, even ironing, something Deborah hadn't done for decades. It left time, swaths of time. She was, as Harris put it, freed up. An affair? Harris was so absent these days he deserved it, she thought in her loneliest moments. But you had to have real desire, a knack with lies — not to mention an interested, willing man — to pull that off. Instead she signed up for an Arabic class.

"It's going to be really, really, really hard, Mum."

"Face it, Mum: You don't even speak French that well." The twins, in their fourth year of obligatory school Arabic, were not encouraging.

Arabic wasn't hard; it was impossible. For ten weeks she sat in an overly air-conditioned room at Mother Tongue Language School, moving further back each class in the hopes of not getting called on. Nabil, the instructor, was a lovely Egyptian guy, full of stories and teasing humour, used to hand-holding Arabic-challenged expats. And her classmates, half a dozen German businessmen and a handful of Indian doctors, were also lovely guys, helping her with homework, clapping when she answered a question almost correctly. If only she could just sit and listen to Nabil's stories about the revolution in his country, his lyrical riffs on Islam, the joking of her classmates as they faltered, though far more nimbly, in the new language. It was such an effort to utter even a throaty *kayf halek,* so difficult to keep up with the daily vocabulary. She didn't sign up for Arabic II.

At a school concert—the twins were now playing alto and tenor sax—she met a British woman in expensive, hip clothes who seemed to want to talk about something other than A levels versus O levels, Cambridge versus Oxford. ("My sons," Deborah had grown weary of explaining, "will be attending Canadian universities. We have some excellent schools back home.") "Ever think about volunteering at St. Edmonds' thrift shop?" Judith asked when Deborah mentioned her stab at Arabic, her search for something satisfying.

"I'm not Anglican," Deborah said. "I'm not really anything."

"No worries," said Judith. "Father Dave's one of those We're-All-One pastors. One of the shop ladies is even Jewish." And her blue eyes had widened, as if she'd just said something slightly shocking. "Of course, she doesn't tell that to too many people here."

Judith was pleasant enough—and decent enough not to give Deborah the usual eyes-up/eyes-down greeting of other British School mums—and seemingly eager to pursue some kind of friendship. She was also boring as hell, Deborah discovered after two lunches at

Café Arabia. Her sons, her husband's job, their summer house on the Costa del Sol, the thrift shop, her former career as a wedding planner back in the UK. Deborah learned all about it. There was barely time to nod and smile between the stories; at some point Deborah gave up trying to do either. As for the church thrift shop, after shuffling through old trainers and being bossed by two elderly British ladies for an afternoon—"No, no, it goes *here!*"—she knew there had to be something else that needed her time and attention.

"What about going back to the Horizon School, Deb?" Harris suggested one Saturday afternoon. "I hear they've gotten some new funding. Who knows?" The twins were out in the desert for their favourite annual event, the camel beauty contest. Having begged off going with the boys this year, they'd just had taken-by-surprise sex on the sofa. And because Harris was so with her in that moment, she'd said, "All right."

Had Novembers always been like this? Deborah remembered bright, if cold, days from her childhood in Gatineau. Novembers brought the promise of Christmas and hot chocolate and new skates, a glorious Canadian childhood that seemed now to belong to some other girl.

Fiona was unplugged again, Deborah having no particular destination in mind this morning. The walls of their rented condo had felt too close; even the prospect of more frozen fields would be better. But the sky! Had she never noticed the November sky before? So heavy, so dispiriting. Jobs, sons, friends, house—these had kept her eyes straight ahead for nearly two decades, no time to look up.

"I am not going to turn into one of those women whose kids have left, whose careers have petered out, who now spend their days driving from sale to sale," she'd told Harris again the night before. "I am not going to turn into a cliché." Harris had come home later than usual, the old cloud over him.

"It's just going to take time, Deb. Give it time." He'd looked so spent, she'd let it go: time would make it better. She would find her way again, make friends, find work, get her groove (what a stupid expression) back. He said so.

But time for what? She wasn't sure what she wanted to happen next. She'd spent four years waiting to come back, but here she was: still suspended.

"Where should we go today, Fiona?" she asked, plugging in the GPS again.

That morning there'd been a story in the *Hamilton Spectator* about a new mosque opening somewhere on Hamilton Mountain. It was a warm story, full of quotes from city councillors, local imams and worshippers—photos of men in skullcaps, men bent in prayer—and she'd felt a momentary swell of appreciation for this tolerant country, this Canada, where if you wanted to wear a hijab or a yarmulke, or Native headdress, for that matter, you could. So why wasn't she enjoying it more? Why was she finding all this tolerance smug, even showy? The place was still run by white guys with money. She'd spent four years scrutinizing Abu Dhabi's ills and contradictions, its secrets and abominations, but she'd never looked at her own country that critically. (Sure, Harper was a jerk, but that was an easy position.) What was valued here? How did people *really* live? Did it hold up so much better?

"I miss Abu Dhabi, Fiona. I hated it, but I loved it too, and I want to go back."

"Please drive to highlighted route," said Fiona, apropos of nothing, and Deborah saw on the screen that the Sana Grill was still listed as the destination.

"You're demented, Fiona, you really are," said Deborah, and pulled into traffic.

The Horizon School had either undergone massive changes or her standards had fallen after three-and-a-half years in Abu Dhabi. There were separate classes now, organized by grade level, instead of by age or disability, and teachers, actual teachers, not just well-intentioned aides. The principal was a friendly chap from Auckland who practically cheered when she told him about her background. Of course, they needed her. "Would next week be too soon?" he asked. "Our Grade 3 teacher just told us her husband is being transferred back to Melbourne at the end of the month. Way of life here, but it makes running a school a nightmare. Our kids need stability. But you know that."

The class was small—six boys, five girls—and higher functioning than she'd dared hope. Four of the eleven were Emirati (all but one had Down syndrome), two were from India, while the rest were from Russia, France and the UK. Several of the children had cerebral palsy, two had language delays and two were clearly on the autism spectrum. But everyone was reading (if slowly), everyone could add and subtract (if not always correctly), and, best of all, they loved one another.

"I've never had a class like this," she told her men over dinner. "Plus the principal's a dream, the staff's friendly, and the other teachers actually seem to know what they're doing. Who would have thought?"

"It's still the honeymoon, Deb," Harris said.

"Yeah, Mum," said Jon. "It's just the first week."

What did they want from her? Fine, she'd curb her enthusiasm in front of them, and quietly go about being productive and happy. She would be useful at long last, would make her small contribution. Not that the boys noticed much of anything that did not directly concern them. They were deep into university applications and girls that winter. And not that Harris was noticing much of anything that did not concern his job. The intrigue at Al Nahyan University had reached new heights of Abu-surdity that winter. The new *new* provost had gotten the boot, and the search was on for another; number twenty-three, was it? Truth was, she'd heard so many faculty stories over the years, the dirt, the skinny, the scoop — usually about people Harris was up against for tenure — that they'd begun to overlap. Sometimes when Harris would talk about a particularly obnoxious, lazy or scheming colleague, she'd have to remind herself that this wasn't so-and-so from Carleton.

Still, she had to admit, none were juicier than the stories out of Al Nahyan. Harris himself had been embroiled for most of the school year in a grievance involving an Emirati student caught stealing a classmate's iPad. The girl's family — connected to the ruling family in some way, though these ways were always mysterious — was now trying to get Harris fired. He had discredited their daughter. He had brought shame upon the family.

In the past, Deborah would have stood by her man, working herself into a froth defending him, only to watch the crisis fizzle before merging into the next. There was no shortage of crises in academic life and no pay-off for caring. In fact, it sometimes irritated Harris that she got emotionally involved. And in this case, the allegations were so clear — there was footage of the girl tucking the iPad into the folds of her *abaya* — that even in this logic-free zone, justice would have to prevail. Besides, she had her own stories now, her own life again. Somewhere she sensed this might not be an entirely good thing for them as a couple, but as she began telling herself: Tough.

Looking around the teachers' lounge that first day, she realized this was what she'd come for. It was so different than the faculty lunchrooms back home, where colleagues sometimes barely spoke — not because of bad blood, but because they were madly marking, photo-copying or calling parents. They were often windowless rooms, furnished with rejects from someone's cottage and smelling of damp boots. But the teachers' lounge here was like a family kitchen, filled with delicious smells and a dozen conversations. Someone would be stirring a curry on the stove or steaming rice, someone else slicing mangoes and watermelon. Large plastic containers were popped into and out of the microwave. "Try this, please." One of the Indian teachers shyly pushed a large bowl of dal toward Deborah her first day. "But what will you eat?" Deborah asked. And the woman had bobbled her head in the Indian gesture of pleasure, agreement, all good things. The Hindi equivalent of *prego*, Harris called it. "There is always enough," she said.

A striking young woman in a bright headscarf sat at the end of the lunch table that first day. Every time Deborah looked over at her, she smiled and waved a little welcome. When the room emptied, she came over. "Tomorrow I will bring some of *my* food for you." Hynda, Deborah learned over the next few lunch times, was Somalian, though she had never actually been to Somalia. "The troubles there, you know." Raised in Kenya, she'd come to Abu Dhabi as a bride of nineteen with her engineer husband. When he'd left her after six years with four young children, she'd gone back to school for a teaching degree. "I love kids. Well, of course, I'd have to love kids," she smiled. They had "a girl," Hynda explained, a nanny who lived with them and did most of the cooking. It helped that there was no man to take care of any more. "Who needs them?" Hynda said, laughing. "Big babies."

The school was like a village: Risa, the single, Grade 1 teacher, who sent nearly all her salary home to a family of seven in Sri Lanka; Suha, from Amman, who had a PhD in linguistics and could speak seven languages, including Bulgarian and Portuguese; Vera, who'd converted to Islam when she married her Sudanese husband and whose family in Hungary had disowned her; Hari, an Indian Brit who'd lived in eight countries in fifteen years, following her diplomat husband from post to outpost. ("Best?" she told Deborah. "Paris. Worst? I think here.")

At the end of the semester, her students gave Deborah a collage of the flags from their countries. One of the mothers had attached them to Bristol board and each child had signed his or her name next to their flag. "To Our Dear Miss," was rainbow-lettered at the top.

On the last day of school, Hynda invited her to dinner. "Please excuse the late notice, Deborah. I have wanted to ask you since the first day. But, you know, with the children and the teaching, so little time." There was an obligatory, end-of-year Al Nahyan faculty party at the British Club that night, the kind of event Deborah had come to dread, not knowing who to make nice with any more.

"The next night then," said Hynda. "You are my sister now."

The children—three girls, one boy—were as handsome as their mother, with bright eyes and velvet skin. "My husband was very tall," Hynda explained. "And, yes, handsome." She wasn't wearing a headscarf when she met Deborah at the door, no males, other than her young son, being present. "Oh, my hair, don't look," she said, laughing and smoothing the front of her short do. "There are all *kinds* of good reasons for wearing a headscarf, as you can see."

Hynda gave her a tour of the aging villa. "We've been here forever. The landlord is good to us." There was no clutter—hardly a book or a painting—though overstuffed brocade couches filled two of the five rooms to near capacity.

"Are you Muslim?" the oldest girl asked Deborah over dinner.

"No," said Deborah. "But I am very interested in your religion." This was actually beginning to be true. She'd had a vague notion in the first year to read Karen Armstrong's books on Islam, but only since meeting Hynda and some of the other women in the school had it become a desire. Next year, she told herself. Next year, it will be part of my reinvention. Not a conversion, of course not. But she would educate herself, read, ask more questions.

"What are you then? You're not Jewish, are you?"

"Amina, we respect everyone, remember?" Hynda said with a warning look.

"It's okay," said Deborah. "I like being asked questions. Well, let's see... I was raised in the United Church of Canada, but I can't say I'm really anything anymore. I don't go to church except on Christmas and Easter. I'm kind of bad about that. I do believe in God, though." She realized this might be too much contradictory information for an eight-year-old, and was aware of something lacking, of looking less in the girl's eyes than the woman she should be.

"Allah is great," piped up the boy. He was five, Hynda had said.

"Yes," said Deborah, not knowing what else to say. "Yes, he is."

"Mohammed too," said one of the other girls.

"Peace be upon him," said Hynda. It was clear she wanted this conversation to end.

Afterward, over coffee served in the sitting room by their Bangladeshi maid, Hynda apologized for the children's questions. "They're just curious," she said. "I want them to know about other religions, but it is delicate, you understand. They are still young and impressionable. It is enough to grasp our faith."

She said it so naturally: our faith. It was inside her, part of the identity of the family she was raising. Deborah couldn't refer to her own wavering path this way. As for her family, the boys had never seemed compelled to attach themselves to a formal belief. Her fault, probably. It might have been an anchor for them, perhaps even for her.

It was a different summer, the fourth one, the one that had just passed, less hectic than the earlier ones: fewer lunches, fewer doctors' appointments. She no longer spent hours shopping for things she couldn't find in Abu Dhabi. The first summer she'd stuffed their suitcases with boxes of maple sandwich cookies that grew stale next to the packages of *maamoul* in her Abu Dhabi kitchen. Some of their Ottawa friends she hadn't even alerted to this summer's return, not having the energy for all the back-and-forth emails: *Deb, we're at the cottage for the month of July, then in Vancouver for the last two weeks of August. When are you heading back to Abu Dubai? Let's try to squeeze in drinks. Hi, Deborah, we'll be in PEI all summer. Sorry to be missing you.* She and the twins rented a condo near the Byward Market. Not cheap, but at least there would be less reliance on friends and family, more meals in. She could even have people over, if anyone was around.

It was wonderful to see Thom, of course, by now an old university hand. He was full of advice for the twins, who would be going to the U of T in the fall, but also full of wistful questions. "Have they finished the construction on Al Salaam Street yet? Who played at WOMAD this spring? Is Felice still there?" Thom had not forgotten anything, including the daughter of the Tunisian ambassador. "You'll miss Abu Dhabi," he warned the twins. "You'll miss it like hell." He'd already announced that he planned to go back as soon as he finished engineering school. "Get a job. You know."

"We'll be right behind you," said Terry. "Better look for a flat for three, right, Jon?"

"You mean you're not going to live with us?" Deborah asked, pretending to be stricken.

"Face it, Mum, you and Dad are going to be long gone by then," said Terry.

"Dead, you mean," she said, laughing now.

"No, no, back here, living the boring, good life and dumping on Abu Dhabi every chance you can get," said Thom.

"But I like it," said Deborah.

Her sons turned to look at her.

"Since when?" said Thom.

"Since…I don't know. It creeps up on you. One day you realize, this is my life and I seem to be living it here. I mean, there."

"What about Dad?" Thom asked. "He seemed so on the moon this year."

"Hates it," said Jon.

"Your father's had a hard year," said Deborah, and as she said this she understood two things: She didn't really know *why* it had been so hard for him (the iPad caper was just that, a caper), and two, she could say this about most of his years. He was freighted with discontent. Discontent was his default. And here came a third thing: She was tired of it.

Still, it turned out to be one of their best summers. Thom was working at a Canadian Tire during the day, but free most evenings. He'd come for dinner, the four of them going through a bottle of wine, the twins teasing her that they missed Leena's cooking. Good company. It would be hard leaving again in August, saying goodbye to these young men, who by some miracle, had turned out pretty well. At least this year the boys would have each other — they were already talking about meeting up in Ottawa for Thanksgiving — plus they'd told Harris that all they wanted for Christmas this year was to spend it in Abu Dhabi. "Man, I cannot wait!" Thom kept saying.

"How're you going to live without us?" Jon asked one of those nights. They were sitting on the condo's small balcony, squeezed around the plastic patio table. It was wonderful to sit outside in the summer. That day, according to *The National*, which she still read online daily, it had been 46 degrees. Even now, 6:00 a.m. Abu Dhabi time, it would be in the mid-30s and dripping with humidity.

"It'll be tough," she'd answered, knowing her voice would give way if she tried to make a joke of it. "But I have a sort of life there now."

"Good on you, Mum," said Thom.

It must have been the middle of the night. She didn't remember the phone ringing or picking it up. "I'm on my way home. I'll explain when I see you."

"When?" she asked, trying to remember how deep into the summer they were. In the past, she'd counted the weeks until Harris's arrival; she hadn't kept such close track this time.

He was arriving the day after next, Etihad, direct to Toronto. "Thank God there was a seat," he said.

"But why?" she said, realizing this didn't sound especially receptive. "Did something happen? Harris?"

But their connection was gone, and when she tried to call back on their landline, there was only a recording in Arabic. His mobile didn't seem to be working either.

All the next day she walked around feeling light-headed. What could have happened to change their plans? Perhaps things had heated up with the Emirati student and the provost had advised him to get out of town for a few weeks, that they'd have it sorted by September. Or perhaps Harris had been given another promotion and needed to move up his vacation so as to get back earlier. It hadn't been a particularly close summer, warm with constant communication like their first summers apart. "Dad sure misses you," Thom would say after Harris Skyped twice in a day. "Tell him to buck up, would you?" This summer they'd spoken only every few days, Deborah secretly grateful to not be receiving daily updates from drama central.

He looked okay at the airport, though his breath smelled boozy. "God, what a long flight. And then I had to wait forever at Toronto Island for the Porter flight here. How're the boys?"

"Honey? What's going on?" And she knew when he turned to look at her, his face unable to contain anything but the truth, his face frighteningly sober, that they wouldn't be going back. The Emirati student's family had enough pull with the ruling family to engineer his dismissal, he told her. The security-camera tape had been "misplaced" and it was simply his word against hers. Hers was the one that counted.

"And now what?" Deborah asked as they pulled up in front of their flat. She had no memory of driving there. "We have an apartment full of stuff, a car. We have Leena. I have a job, remember?" She was afraid she might hit him. "And what about my friends? I can't even say goodbye to my friends!"

"I know it's a lot to wrap your mind around," Harris said. "Believe me, I'm still reeling. It's been a real blow. But we'll pull through this. We're coming back home. It's what you wanted."

"It's not what I want," she said.

"But you hated it there," he said.

"I didn't. I'd come to accept it. I was just getting started."

"I only heard how unhappy you were," he said, voice going cold, no more pleading.

"You weren't listening," she said and got out of the car, slamming the door so hard the car shook.

The boys were heartbroken. "It's not like any of you were going back to Abu Dhabi in September," Harris said. "I don't really get the big loss here."

"You wouldn't," said Jon.

"Christmas," said Thom. "I was living for Christmas."

There were missing parts of the story, the truer bits trickling out over the next few days. The newest provost, an economist from New Delhi, had already formed an opinion of Harris, not a favourable one. Harris was too hard on students, he said, not positive enough about the university's long-range goals. "We need idealists, Mr. Harris, not realists." They'd had a row, Harris saying things he shouldn't have. When Harris's case with the Emirati student came before the board, the provost said little in his defence. "Fed to the salukis," Harris said.

And there was something else. It had started in November. And, no, it had nothing to do with not loving her, not caring about her. He didn't want to leave her, not then, not now. And, yes, he finally said, after she pushed so hard that he cried: Yes, sometimes it felt like love, impossible and impossibly exciting. The woman was a student, Moroccan, from an influential Casablanca family. "It was getting crazy. I had to leave," Harris said. "I'm sorry for all of it." And then, as if this would be a comfort: "I got Leena another placement. She'll be fine. And I donated our furniture to Take my Junk. Remember the guy who fixes things and gives them to needy people, good causes?" His voice trailed off. "And there might be something else."

It took him a while to get at what that else was, circling, approaching, then skirting, as anxious to deny as to admit. "I might have hit someone on the way to the airport," he finally said quickly. "I'm not saying I did. I looked back and there was nothing. It was almost more like a sound than something I felt. It was really early in the morning, you know, with that veil of humidity that makes visibility just about impossible. Remember the haze along Khaleej in the early morning? I thought I felt something bump up against the rental car. Lightly, not like a body. I don't know. It could have been anything, right? I was so stressed out with what was happening at school and…with her, plus knowing I was going to have to come home and tell you everything and what it might do to us. Of course, it could've just been my imagination, my guilt, making me imagine things. Impossible to know for sure, right?" Once started, he couldn't shut up.

Was it all equal? Running someone over, putting himself inside another woman, getting fired, ruining their lives? In those terrible first days of his return, the word *impossible*, his favourite new word, rumbled round her head like a rock in a tumbler.

She ordered two shawarmas this time, taking the second to go, or takeaway, as they called it in Abu Dhabi. She must look out of place — an English-Canadian woman of a certain age, in an out-of-style-now quilted coat, eating a shawarma by herself. At some point she would have to get back in the car, drive to the rented condo, make supper for Harris, ask about his day — he'd been lucky to find a one-year contract with the Halton District School Board, an education reform project — wash the dishes, read a little, get ready for bed, try to sleep.

She remembered the location vaguely, a main road somewhere on Hamilton's East Mountain. Stone Church. A pretty name, right for someplace spiritual, even if it wasn't a church per se. Fiona guided her — "Please drive to highlighted route" — and Deborah travelled the long length of the two-lane road, past condo complexes, farmland, a landfill, hoping she would find it without having the exact address, kind of like Abu Dhabi. Surely there would be a minaret lit up in the green luminescence she used to search for on the highway between Dubai and Abu Dhabi. There would be a crescent moon atop a dome perhaps.

The mosques in the UAE were beautiful, though none more stunning than the Sheikh Zayed Grand Mosque. It was — like everything Abu Dhabi — the biggest and the best, though this time they actually got that right. The block-long expanses of hand-knotted Iranian carpet, the ton-heavy crystal chandelier, the gold, the mosaics, and the domes, which reflected the phases of the moon. Navy clouds played over the white marble when the moon was a slivered crescent. Soft clouds of lavender grey undulated over them as the days eased on. And finally at month's end, they glowed brilliant white. One could mark time by the domes. On every return trip from the airport, the mosque had been there to welcome her reluctant self.

"Arriving at destination on left," said Fiona. But it was a Leon's, the big-box furniture store which seemed to have outlets everywhere. They'd gone to the one in Burlington when they'd first arrived, outfitting their generic condo with a generic sectional. They had nothing any more, the house in Ottawa rented for another year, their Abu Dhabi furniture in a labour camp.

"Why didn't he drive back to look, Fiona? How could he not have done that?" But Fiona had nothing more to say. Deborah pulled into the closest driveway to turn around.

And there it was, stuck between Leon's and a bowling alley called Splitsville. It could have been a real estate office or a government building, sitting brown-brick ugly in an empty parking lot. A peeling sign read: Hamilton Mosque. Discover Islam. And as she sat there, looking at the sign, smelling the wrapped shawarma, all that she might have discovered hit her with the force of the wind outside.

On her last visit to the Grand Mosque she'd taken a tour with a female guide, a statuesque woman with an Australian accent and unnaturally bright-green eyes — coloured contacts? Deborah had wondered — her auburn hair just visible along the edge of her *shayla*. A Western woman! A female at the holiest of holy places! But most moving was the way the woman explained her adopted faith, the way her voice deepened into perfect Arabic when she said the words *Holy Quran* and *Allah*, the way her body bent to the carpet in surrender.

There was another sign, Deborah now noticed, at the exit of the parking lot: "In the name of God, the Compassionate, the Merciful. All praise be to God, Lord of the Universe, the Compassionate, the Merciful, Sovereign of the Day of Judgment. You alone we worship and to you alone we turn for help." She read the words silently, then aloud, then got out of the car, though it was now beginning to snow. No, it was freezing rain, the stinging wet pelting the top of her head.

"Help," she said.

OASIS, 1973

The sand is a sea. It touches the far shores of sky. The sand is a wasteland of craters and cliffs, a furnace burning under tender feet, a twister absorbing all in its path, a carpet, a blanket, a cradle. How can sand be only particles of dirt and rock, when it is, in fact, everything?

Our driver navigates the narrow crests of dunes, searching for the perfect plunge point, and then we are falling and falling, before surging up again to another height. Standing in the back of the open Land Rover, hair whipping my face, arms open, I feel every plummet and rise. I could be tossed out with the next jerk or drop, but this place is making me brave. "Here in the desert I had found all that I asked," wrote my hero, Wilfred Thesiger, the British explorer who criss-crossed these lands on camel in the late '40s, nearly twenty-five years ago. He had been leaving for the last time, heartbroken and despondent about what he saw coming. "I was averse to all oil companies, dreading the changes and disintegration of society which they inevitably caused." I will admit the sight of black-orange flames—gas flaring off at the oil wells as we came into Liwa this afternoon—looked strange among the curving dunes.

Still I pray I will never leave the way he did, or perhaps never leave at all.

Sheikh Shakhbut has requested the pleasure of a visit. Now that it's winter and cooler again, Pat, Marion, their children, Aslam, their houseboy, and I—plus five days' provisions and bedding—are making our way from Al Ain to the Liwa Oasis, the Al Nahyan ancestral home. On the way we lunched with Bedu, who waited on us hand and foot, the family insisting we rest from our travels and cool off in the shade of their tent, while they slaughtered the goat and cooked rice. A few hours later we reached the beach at Tarif, setting up camp right on the sand, an expanse of startling white.

And now the sands of Liwa. We stop at the bottom of Mehreb Dune, so tall that a forty-five-gallon oil drum at the top looks as small as a can of cola. How do you climb a dune? I don't think you do. I scramble on hands and knees, while the children push past me, laughing. The sand here is fiery red, so different than Tarif and different than the gold of the dunes that border the Empty Quarter. We are close to Saudi Arabia here and those epic first journeys of British explorers—Bertram Thomas, St. John Philby, Thesiger himself. The Bedu, of course, have been crossing this beautiful desolation, Rub al Khali, for centuries and will keep doing so.

At prayer time, as the dunes turn auburn in the setting sun, their shadows unfurling, our driver lays a small rug on the flattest spot he can find, drops to his knees and touches his forehead to the ground. Before him, sand without end. I feel him praying for us all.

AUTHOR'S NOTE

I am greatly indebted to Gertrude Dyck, the pioneering Canadian nurse who spent thirty-eight years in the United Arab Emirates. Her wonderful book, *The Oasis: Al Ain Memoirs of Doctora Latifa* (Motivate Publishing, 1995), gave me the foundation for the "Oasis" meditations and a sense of what had once been. *Diamond in the Desert: Behind the Scenes in the World's Richest City* (2009), an honest and startling book by British journalist Jo Tatchell, added greatly to my own Abu Dhabi experience. Thanks also to *The National*, the English-language newspaper of Abu Dhabi, and to radio station Abu Dhabi Classics, for publishing and broadcasting "The Gift of the Magi" on Christmas Eve 2010. The largest thanks go to my husband, Raymond Beauchemin, novelist, journalist, editor beyond compare and one-man cheering section. Someday, *insha'allah*, we'll go back.

Some of the names of companies and places have been changed, and events altered, to suit the needs of fiction.

GLOSSARY

Abaya — A loose, usually black, robe worn by Muslim women.

Agal — A thick, double, black cord fastened around the keffiyeh (see below) to hold it in place.

Alhamdulillah — "Thanks and praise be to God."

Areesh — A palm-frond house.

Baklawa — Middle Eastern sweet with a ground-nut filling between layers of phyllo.

Dirham — The UAE currency, pegged to the US dollar at 3.67 dirhams to one US dollar.

Falaj — An aqueduct or canal system that uses gravity to deliver water for irrigation.

Fatteh — Dried pieces of flatbread layered with yogurt, garbanzos, oil and pine nuts.

Fattoush — A Lebanese tossed salad, heavy on the lemon juice, sumac and featuring toasted pita chips.

Fils — UAE currency equal to one hundreth of a dirham.

Ghutra — Another term for keffiyeh.

Habibti — Term of endearment equivalent to "darling" used to address a female; the masculine form would be "habibi."

Hajj — Annual pilgrimage to Mecca that every Muslim is required to perform if financially and physically able.

Halal — Acceptable. Particularly used in reference to foods.

Halloumi—A salty, semi-hard, unripened white cheese.

Haram—Sinful. Any act forbidden by Allah.

Insha'allah—"God willing."

Iftar—The meal that breaks the daily fast during Ramadan.

Jelabiya—A loose-fitting cotton garment.

Kayf halek—"How are you?"

Keffiyeh—The traditional headdress of an Arab male, it is made of cotton and can be checked or solid white.

Khandoura—Ankle-length, loose-fitting garment worn by Gulf Arab males; usually white, always starched.

Khnafeh—Arabic cheese pastry soaked in sugar syrup.

Maamoul—Small shortbread cookies traditionally filled with dates, pistachios or walnuts.

Majlis—An outer room, used particularly to entertain guests.

Masha'allah—"As God has willed," used in praise and recognizing all good things come from God.

Muezzin—The man who calls Muslims to prayer.

Saluki—A tall, slender dog bred in the Arabian Peninsula.

Sfiha—An Arabic pizza-like dish, often topped with lamb.

Shayla—A thin black veil worn by Emirati women.

Shisha—Tobacco for smoking in a hookah, especially when mixed with flavourings such as mint and apple.

Shalwar kameez—Cotton pants and shirt worn by men and women of the subcontinent.

Yalla—All right! or Let's go!

ALSO BY DENISE ROIG

Butter Cream
A Year in a Montreal Pastry School

Wise, funny, and warm—Denise Roig's *Butter Cream* is a sumptuous read—both confection and feast. I loved every last bite."

—Diana Abu-Jaber

978-1897109-30-4
EBOOK: 978-1897109-67-0

Any Day Now

"It is rare to encounter a writer that works in a mode both realistic—even naturalistic—yet deeply imbued with ideas. Heartbreaking. Wincing. Beautiful."—David Manicom

978-0921833-98-7
EBOOK: 978-1897109-73-1

A Quiet Night and a Perfect End

These are delicate but solid, weight-bearing stories."—Grace Paley

978-0921833-40-6
EBOOK: 978-1897109-78-6

ABOUT THE AUTHOR

Denise Roig is the author of two critically received collections of short stories: *A Quiet Night and a Perfect End* (Nuage Editions), and *Any Day Now* (Signature Editions), and the memoir *Butter Cream: A Year in a Montreal Pastry School* (Signature Editions). Denise's first collection was translated in 2000 as *Le Vrai Secret du bonheur* (Éditions de la Pleine Lune) and her fiction has been heard on CBC's *Between the Covers*. As a journalist, Denise's work has appeared in *The Gazette* (Montreal) and *The National* (Abu Dhabi). Denise is the co-editor, with her husband Raymond Beauchemin, of two anthologies of Quebec English literature: *Future Tense* and *The Urban Wanderers Reader*.

Born in New York, raised in Los Angeles, and a longtime resident of Montreal, Denise moved to Abu Dhabi, capital of the United Arab Emirates, in 2008. She now lives in Hamilton, Ontario.